"I Don't See What We Have to Talk About."

"Oh, I can think of a lot of things. It's been ten years since I've seen you." Link was silent for a moment. Then he disconcerted her by asking abruptly, "How about your love life?"

Her cheeks burned. "That's a very personal and impertinent question!"

"Really? I didn't mean to insult you. I just wondered if there's been any special man in your life since we parted company."

"I don't think that's any of your business."

"I think a husband has a right to know who his wife has been running around with."

PATTI BECKMAN

is one of Silhouette's most prolific authors. She has won much acclaim for her interesting backgrounds. Patti thoroughly researched *Thunder at Dawn* by interviewing many of Hollywood's top stunt girls.

D0234260

Dear Reader,

We introduced Silhouette Special Edition last year for our readers who wanted a story with greater romantic detail. Since then many of you have written in, telling us how much you like Silhouette Special Edition.

Special Editions have all the elements you enjoy in Silhouette Romances and *more*. These stories concentrate on romance in a longer, more realistic and sophisticated way, and they feature greater sensual detail.

I hope you enjoy this book and all the wonderful romances from Silhouette.

We welcome any suggestions or comments, and invite you to write to me at this address:

Jane Nicholls
Silhouette Books
PO Box 177
Dunton Green
Sevenoaks
Kent
TN13 2YE

PATTI BECKMAN

Thunder at Dawn

Silhouette

Special Edition

Published by Silhouette Books

Copyright © 1983 by Patti Beckman

Map by Ray Lundgren

First printing 1984

British Library C.I.P.

Beckman, Patti
   Thunder at dawn.—(Silhouette special edition)
   I. Title
   813'.54[F]   PS3552.E28/

   ISBN 0 340 34975 1

Printed and bound in Great Britain for
Hodder and Stoughton Paperbacks, a
division of Hodder and Stoughton Ltd.,
Mill Road, Dunton Green, Sevenoaks,
Kent (Editorial Office: 47 Bedford
Square, London, WC1 3DP) by
Richard Clay (The Chaucer Press) Ltd.,
Bungay, Suffolk

Other Silhouette Books by Patti Beckman

Captive Heart
The Beachcomber
Louisiana Lady
Angry Lover
Love's Treacherous Journey
Spotlight to Fame
Bitter Victory
Daring Encounter
Mermaid's Touch
Tender Deception
Enchanted Surrender
Forbidden Affair

Thunder at Dawn

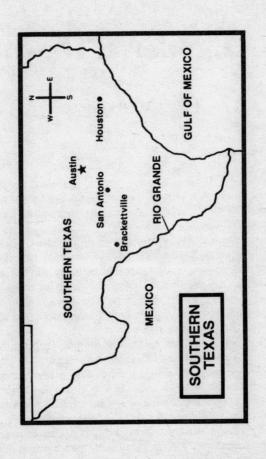

SOUTHERN TEXAS

Chapter One

*G*inger Lombard felt the rush of the wind tugging at her hair. Above her, the helicopter blades spun in a giant, flashing arc against the sun. Below, the earth was a moving blur.

But she was aware of only her target; the truck on the dusty road hundreds of feet beneath her. Her concentration was intense. Her body, lithe and nimble, conditioned by countless hours of training, was a coiled spring tensed for the precise moment when she would spring away from the helicopter and go hurtling through space.

She felt a vibrant awareness singing through her being, an exhilaration mingled with fright.

Was it being so close to death that made her feel more intensely alive than at any other time? Was that the seductive allure of a stunt career? Or was it the magic of the illusion she was creating . . . a hunger for a more satisfying kind of drama than real life offered . . . a way of entering and living a gripping story that made life mundane by comparison?

Days had gone into careful preparation for the tension-drenched moments now about to explode into action. Nothing should go wrong. The timing had been checked and rechecked and rechecked again. Nevertheless, at these crucial split seconds, just before driving a car over an embankment or falling from a burning building on a movie set, Ginger always experienced a dampness in her palms, a cold knot in her stomach.

Today's stunt was tricky—a fall from a helicopter to a moving truck. On the bed of the truck, hidden from the eyes of the cameras, was a huge, inflated nylon air bag that would cushion her fall. Her target, the center of the bag, was marked with a great red *X*. She must land on that exact spot or she would slam into the side of the truck with an impact that could break every bone in her body.

This kind of stunt was her specialty. She knew she was good at it; that's why she got so many jobs from the top movie producers. At age twenty-seven she was already one of Hollywood's top stunt women. Yet there was always that nagging anxiety. A shift in the wind, a mistake in judgment, a fraction of error by the truck driver or helicopter pilot, and . . .

No more time for thinking. The cameras were rolling. Her sense of split second timing told her that this was the moment. A second's hesitation and the moment would be lost.

She leaped out and away from the helicopter. She became a rag doll, plummeting through space.

Almost instantly came the horrible realization that the stunt had gone wrong. She was not going to hit the air bag in the right place. A scream wrenched from her throat. There was the stunning impact of her body slamming against the side of the truck . . . white-hot sheets of pain . . . shouts of her crew . . then blackness engulfing her.

* * *

Ginger awoke with a gasping cry. She jerked to a sitting position, confused, not realizing for a moment where she was. Her body tensed, awaiting her old enemy, the pain. She looked down at her palms, saw the cold perspiration glistening there. She felt her heart pounding, nausea wrenching at her stomach.

Then she became aware of the warm sunlight bathing her body, the sensation of gritty sand under her bare legs. Reality came back in a rush. She buried her face in her hands with a sob of relief.

It had just been the old nightmare again. She must have dozed off here on the beach in the warm Florida sun. There was no more pain. The bruises had faded; the broken bones had mended.

It had all happened over a year ago.

But the nightmares were still as terrifying as ever. Would they never stop haunting her?

With a sigh, she rose and dusted the sand from her hips. She drew a deep breath, letting the tension melt from her body. She gazed out at the sparkling blue water, feeling the soft ocean breeze against her face.

Then she caught sight of a figure moving along the beach. An arm waved. She waved back.

Ginger's cousin, Lorene Parker, removed the earphones of her treasure seeker, shook out her dark hair and crossed the sand in hurried strides. Lorene was twenty-three, five years younger than Ginger and more like a younger sister than a cousin, but there was little family resemblance between them. Lorene was small and had a cloud of jet black hair. At five feet nine, Ginger towered over her cousin. Her hair was a tawny yellow brown, and her eyes matched her hair. She often thought Lorene looked a lot more like Paige, Ginger's older sister.

Ginger, in fact, looked like no one else in her family. She thought perhaps she was a throwback to some Viking ancestor who had married a Spanish noblewoman.

"Any luck?" Ginger asked.

Lorene was fussing with the dials of the sophisticated metal-detecting device with which she had been scouring the beach. She dug into a pouch and produced a rusty hatch hinge and a barnacle-encrusted nail. "Nothing much this time," she admitted ruefully.

"You can't expect to come up with a pirate treasure every day," Ginger consoled.

Lorene was usually quite successful at her hobby of treasure hunting along Florida beaches. She owned an impressive collection of old Spanish coins and shipwreck artifacts, the products of countless hours patiently scouring the beaches, listening for the electronic "beep" of her metal detector.

They crossed the tiny island to the spot where Lorene's boat was moored. Ginger was silent, lost in her private thoughts.

She felt her cousin's concerned gaze.

"You okay, Ginger?"

"Yes."

"Are you sure?"

Ginger shrugged. "I dozed off, and . . ."

"Bad dreams again?"

Ginger nodded.

Lorene sighed. "That's to be expected after what you went through."

Ginger thought about those long weeks in the hospital, then the months of convalescence.

With a determined effort, she shook off the gloomy memories. She was lucky to be alive and, more, doubly lucky that the accident had left no scars or physical impairment. As for the emotional damage, that was something she'd just have to live with.

Lorene said, "Just remember what some famous baseball player once said, 'Don't look back. Something might be catching up with you!'"

Ginger laughed. "Lorene, you're the best medicine of all."

"I try to be."

Ginger knew her cousin well enough to be sure Lorene was mentally thumbing through her inventory of platitudes in search of another that fit the situation. But then they arrived at her boat, and it commanded her attention.

It was a tiny sailboat, a Sea Snark with a Styrofoam hull just barely big enough to accommodate the two of them plus Lorene's treasure hunting equipment.

The first time Ginger had laid eyes on the fragile craft, she'd vowed Lorene would never get her in it. But she'd soon discovered that her cousin was an expert sailor. After that they had enjoyed exploring the bays, inlets and beaches of the area. Ginger thought becoming a beach bum had been a big factor in restoring her to full health.

After they shoved the boat off the sandy beach, Ginger settled in the prow, leaning against the mast, ready to duck when the sail boom passed above her head.

"Center board," Lorene called, taking her place at the tiller.

"Aye, aye, captain," Ginger said, and slid the center board into place.

Soothed by the flapping of the sail, the slap of the water against the boat and the touch of sea spray against her face, she settled back to enjoy the short trip to the mainland.

Not until they were on the mainland, carrying the Styrofoam boat hull up to Lorene's beach cottage, did Ginger notice they had company.

Lorene spotted the black Mercedes parked on the shell driveway at the same moment.

"Look, Ginger. It's your father!"

Ginger nodded. "I see."

She felt a sudden storm of emotions, as she always did when her father came breezing back into her life. She loved Derrick Lombard with all her heart, but her feelings about him were complex and not without conflict. And right now she felt her palms suddenly grow cold and damp. Derrick Lombard symbolized Hollywood—a condition—a state of mind—an industry she wanted nothing more to do with.

But of course she would be glad to see him. At the same time she wondered what on earth he was doing here at the end of nowhere.

He was waiting on the screen porch that overlooked the beach, drink in hand, and greeted the two young women expansively. "Ginger! Lorene! How marvelous to see you!"

He put his drink down and embraced them both in one sweeping gesture, then stepped back to survey his daughter. "But you look absolutely splendid,

Ginger! Brown as a berry. Eyes sparkling. Lorene you've done wonders with her!"

Ginger thought how in character he was to totally dominate this little reunion scene with his flamboyant manner and overwhelming personality. As a child she had always been a little in awe of him, this handsome stranger, matinee idol, Hollywood star, leading man. It was no different now that she was a grown woman.

She tried to see him in a truer perspective. His mane of luxurious, wavy dark hair had turned silver and was thinning somewhat. His rugged features had become lined. But his voice was still deep and resonant. His black and white checked sport coat was hand-tailored. The ascot at his throat was a shade of aquamarine carefully chosen to emphasize the deep blue of his eyes. It was pure silk, imported from India.

As always, in his presence she felt swamped by a whole range of emotions. They tumbled through her now in confused fragments: joy tinged with sadness. She remembered the old childhood hurt at his long absences when he was in another part of the world on a film location. He'd had little time for her when he was home, as he'd been busy with parties and a never-ending parade of friends. She recalled slipping downstairs to peek through the bannister, hearing his voice, hoping to catch a glimpse of him in the crowd. And, most of all, she remembered the sense of illusion about the times he did give her his direct attention, as if he were reading lines, playing a scene and all the time withholding his real self from her. With a mingling of recalled childhood bitterness and loneliness, she wished she could just once brush away the role he was playing and find the real man under the facade.

His resonant voice interrupted her thoughts. "Lorene, my dear, I hope you'll forgive me for descending on you in this way, barging in unannounced. Your back door was unlocked; I simply made myself at home." He raised his glass, eyes twinkling. "Even raided your liquor cabinet, as you see."

Finally someone else was able to get a word in. Lorene said, a trifle breathlessly, "Uncle Derrick, you know you're welcome any time. We're so glad to see you!"

"Yes," Ginger added. "What on earth are you doing way down here?"

He seemed not to hear her—another mannerism he exhibited at times that drove Ginger up the wall. "How is your mother, Lorene?"

"Just fine, except for her arthritis. But the doctor is giving her some new pills that seem to be helping."

"Arthritis, eh? Miserable affliction. Have a touch of it myself. Runs in the family, no doubt. Must ask her what her doctor is giving her. Has it kept her away from the piano?"

"No. It's more in her hips. She's getting around better now, though. She's in town this afternoon doing some shopping. She'll be so happy and surprised to see you when she comes home."

"Yes, and I'll certainly be delighted to see her." Then he changed the subject abruptly. "Most charming place you have here." He waved his drink around at the spacious, screened porch, which was festooned with Lorene's beachcombing trophies: an old ship's bell, an anchor, unusual bits of driftwood, shells, amber glass fishing floats, a ship's spoked steering wheel, fish nets. "Looks like a South Sea island film set," he said with a chuckle.

"Well, we are almost in the tropics," Lorene reminded him.

Ginger asked, "Have you seen Paige lately?"

This time she got his attention. Why not, she thought with another tinge of remembered child-hood resentment. Paige, with her incredible beauty and acting ability, had always been his favorite daughter.

"Paige is marvelous. She's very excited about doing this film for me."

"What?" Ginger asked blankly.

"My film. The one I'm going to produce, Paige has agreed to play the lead female role. Isn't that great! The part is absolutely made for her."

"You're producing a film?" Ginger asked, as-tounded.

"Yes. You're surprised?"

"Of course I am."

"I'll tell you all about it later. I knew you'd be glad to hear about Paige. We're certain to have a tremen-dous amount of box office appeal with her in the female lead role and Link Rockwood opposite her. It will be absolute dynamite."

"Link—" Ginger felt the blood drain from her cheeks. *Damn you, Derrick Lombard*, she thought furiously. *You love dropping these little bombshells, don't you?*

Now her thoughts were in total disarray. She was as angry with herself as with her father—angry that the very mention of Link Rockwood's name could still, after so many years, drive a knife through her heart.

She needed an excuse to regain her composure.

17

And she knew they weren't going to get any more out of her father, not for the time being, anyway. He loved creating an element of suspense, then teasing his audience by withholding further information until he tired of the little game.

He changed the subject, asking Lorene about her job. Ginger excused herself and went off to take a shower. While she was dressing, she heard her aunt Judy return. By then Ginger had managed to get a firmer grip on her emotions. She felt refreshed, having bathed the sand and sticky salt moisture from her body. She was dry, powdered and perfumed and wearing a comfortable, casual outfit consisting of a green halter top that suited her tawny hair and eyes and a pair of designer jeans. Her morale was somewhat improved.

She rejoined the others, who were now in the comfortable, air-conditioned den of the house. Derrick was sprawled in an easy chair with his drink. Lorene was perched on a footstool, hands clasped around her knees, her face an expression of rapt attention.

Ginger's aunt, Judy Parker, had returned while Ginger was in the shower. She had taken her place in a wicker chair beside the grand piano that dominated the den.

Judy Parker had her brother's classic features, though she was blond where he was dark. She had the same high brow, clear, wide-set eyes and a generous mouth that smiled often, accenting dimples and laugh lines around the corners of her lips. At fifty-five, she had cheerfully accepted a bit of plumpness, with the consolation that it kept her face free of wrinkles. She wore her long blond hair in a bun at the nape of her neck. Tonight she was dressed in a bright red sun dress and casual sandals.

Ginger paused for a moment in the doorway, gazing at these people who affected her life so intensely. She glanced from her father to her aunt, seeing the close family resemblance between brother and sister. Judy Parker resembled Derrick in more than physical appearance. They were the children of show people, born between whistle stops on the old vaudeville circuit of another era. They grew up in the wings of theaters. It would have been surprising had they not pursued their own careers in show business. But their professions had taken different roads. Derrick had begun with the Broadway theater and then gone on to Hollywood. His sister, Judy, blessed with a great musical talent, a bright, bubbling personality and more than the usual share of good looks, had made a name for herself as a singer during the big band era of the thirties and forties. The den walls were covered with photographs of Judy with famous band leaders of that day and with framed record covers bearing her name. The traces of her once youthful beauty lingered in her face, and her singing voice still had the husky, intimate quality that had made her famous, though she had long ago retired.

Judy had a special place in Ginger's life. She was more of a mother than Ginger's own mother, whom she'd hardly known and barely remembered. The marriage that produced Ginger and her sister, Paige, had been one of Derrick's earlier matrimonial adventures in a series of stormy marriages. Like the ones that followed, the marriage had ended in divorce. The girls' mother, also a Hollywood star, had left the children with Derrick and gone off to follow her own career. She had died in Italy when Ginger was six and Page ten. After that, Ginger had divided her time between Derrick's various households in Hollywood, with their procession of housekeepers and stepmothers, and the warm refuge of her aunt Judy's home. Unlike her brother, Judy had married once and for keeps, the marriage ending only when her husband died five years ago. Then she had settled in this Florida beach house, with its palm trees and its roomy screened porch overlooking a strip of private beach, and she vowed to remain there for the rest of her days. "The warm climate is good for my arthritis," she insisted.

In many ways, Ginger felt closer to her cousin, Lorene, than to her own sister, Paige. There was no rivalry with Lorene, And with Lorene, she was not hopelessly outclassed. While Lorene had dark hair and eyes like Paige, she did not have Paige's unearthly beauty, intense nature and natural acting ability. Lorene was uncomplicated, outgoing, funloving and somewhat in awe of her Hollywood-based relatives. She had been a star on her high school basketball team, kept a small menagerie of pets and pursued a variety of hobbies. After high school, she had taken a business course, and she now worked as a teller at a local bank.

"Ginger!" her aunt exclaimed, catching sight of her niece in the doorway. "Are your ears burning? We've been talking about you. Derrick is so pleased with your total recovery."

"Yes," Ginger's father agreed warmly. "Coming here to convalesce was obviously the best medicine for you, Ginger."

"My, you look so nice and fresh, dear," her aunt continued, giving her a hug. "Wish I could say the same for my daughter!"

Lorene, still in her beach clothes, looking sandy and slightly disheveled, blushed. "Mother! I'm going to change in a minute. I've just been so excited, having Uncle Derrick pop in like this."

"I know. We're all excited." Judy grinned. "Isn't this something, Ginger? Derrick didn't give us a hint that he was even in this part of the country. And here he is!"

"Yes," Ginger murmured, moving slowly into the room. "Here he is." She gazed at her father with a mixture of uneasy emotions. She had a premonition about this situation that made her uncomfortable. It was out of character for Derrick to appear in this fashion without some ulterior motive.

Judy said, "Derrick was just telling us he's going to produce a film. Isn't that wild!" She looked at her brother with a fond smile. "I never thought of you as a producer. I always thought you were too much of a ham to ever get behind the camera!"

Derrick made another one of his expansive gestures. "This is just too good an opportunity to pass up, sister. It's going to make us all rich."

"Us all?" Ginger questioned, giving her father a sudden penetrating look.

But he responded with his maddening habit of simply ignoring her.

"Tell us all about it, Derrick," Judy exclaimed.

"Later, sister. First I want to hear all about what you've been up to."

That's a bunch of malarky, Ginger thought. Derrick was not the slightest bit interested in what had been happening on the beach in Florida. He was, for some good reason of his own, waiting for a more opportune moment to talk about his plans.

"Ginger, why don't we hustle up something for dinner while Mom and Uncle Derrick have a chance to visit," Lorene suggested.

Ginger nodded. She was feeling nervous. It would help to get busy doing something.

The two young women headed for the kitchen. "Tell you what," Lorene suggested. "Why don't you start getting pots and pans and things out while I hop in the shower? Won't take me more than a few minutes."

"You're the one who knows how to cook," Ginger pointed out. "What are we planning to make?"

Lorene surveyed the contents of the refrigerator. "We have the makings for spaghetti and meat sauce and salad. Would that be all right with your father?"

"Sure. He likes Italian food. Do you have some Chianti? He always likes the right kind of wine with his meals."

"Check the pantry. I'm sure you'll find a bottle in there somewhere."

An hour later, they were gathering around the dining room table, Ginger marveling at her cousin's culinary magic. The meal was delicious. But not until they were sipping coffee did Derrick start talking about the film he planned to produce. "It's a splendid story," he told them. "Has everything— glamorous settings; international intrigue. Much of it will be shot on location here and along the east coast. That's one reason I'm down here, looking over possible locations. May check into the possibility of shooting some scenes in the Vanderbilt Biltmore mansion in Asheville, North Carolina. The film will be a splendid vehicle for Paige and Link Rockwood. The story is just made for the two of them."

"Link Rockwood?" Judy exclaimed. "He's top box office. You've signed him up for the lead?"

"Indeed I have. You see, we can't miss!"

Ginger realized her fingers holding her cup were trembling. She quickly put the cup down and clenched her hands in her lap. She drew a breath that hurt her throat. *Was it going to hurt like this for the rest of her life, every time she heard Link's name mentioned?*

"Isn't independent producing a pretty big risk?" Judy asked.

Derrick waved his hand impatiently. "It is if you don't know what you're doing. I do know, and I can assure you we're going to have one of the big smash hits of the year. We're all going to get rich, the whole family—Paige, myself, Ginger—"

"Wait a minute!" Ginger cried. "How did I suddenly get involved in this?"

"Well," Derrick said indignantly, "I certainly want my own daughter to be the stunt coordinator, especially in view of the fact that she happens to be the best in the business."

Ginger's face turned white. She threw down her napkin. "Oh no! Not on your life! I'm through with that stuff . . . forever!"

Derrick scowled, "Nonsense, Ginger. This is the greatest opportunity of your career."

"I don't have a career anymore. Haven't you heard?"

Derrick's expression darkened. "I simply do not

believe that. Motion pictures are your life. They're in your blood the same as in mine. You do not just walk away from a career . . ."

There was a moment of strained silence. Judy cleared her throat, interrupting the tension. "Why don't we finish our coffee in the den, where we'll be more comfortable?"

Derrick underwent one of his mercurial mood changes. His scowl vanished. He smiled. "Excellent! And I want you to sing for me, Judy."

He appeared to have dismissed from his mind the matter of Ginger's working on his film, but she was not fooled. He was sure to bring it up again, she knew with a chill certainty.

When they were in the den, Judy took her place at the piano. "What do you want to hear, Derrick? I'm afraid I'm not up on the latest hits."

"I want to hear the great songs you did before popular music turned into noise. Songs like 'I'm Confessin' That I Love You,' 'Deep Purple,' 'I Don't Want to Walk Without You' . . ."

"Okay," she consented with a grin. "You asked for it."

For the next half hour, Judy Parker's voice filled the room with the immortal melodies of the big band days. Ginger settled in her chair, her eyes closed, some of her nervousness relaxing as her emotions flowed with her aunt's lovely voice.

When the songs ended, the room was in silence, no one wanting to end the mood created by a performance that had once sold a million records. Derrick moved to the piano, bent and gently placed a kiss on his sister's cheek. "That was simply exquisite, little sister," he said huskily. "You're still in a class all your own."

Lorene and Ginger joined him, taking turns hugging Judy. "Absolutely super, Mom," Lorene said proudly.

"You're the best, Aunt Judy," Ginger nodded, her voice choked.

"Gee, it's humiliating being a no-talent member of such a talented family!" Lorene sighed. Her face lengthened into such a lugubrious expression that everyone laughed.

Judy squeezed her daughter's waist. "Honey, your talent is being a wonderful girl with a brilliant, inquiring mind and personality that won't quit."

"Hear, hear," Derrick applauded. Then, glancing at his watch, he exclaimed, "By the way, tonight NBC is doing a rerun of *Quest of the Falcon.* Should be starting about now. Would you like to see it?"

"Oh yes!" Lorene exclaimed. "That's one of my favorite movies . . . the one you and Paige were in together."

"Yes." Derrick smiled. "It was her first major role. It made her a star. And don't forget, Ginger was in the film, too. She doubled for Paige in all the stunt scenes."

Ginger felt her stomach wrench. She did not want to see this old movie or any other in which she had done stunt work. *Quest of the Falcon* had been filmed five years ago. By then she had built a reputation as one of the best stunt women in the industry. It was only natural that she would get the job of doubling for her sister in the dangerous scenes. The difference in their coloring was the principal reason they did not look like sisters. But that changed dramatically when Ginger donned a dark wig. Instantly their family resemblance turned Ginger into a taller version of Paige.

Why had her father suggested they view this old movie? She always suspected his motives when he was after something. But since Lorene and Aunt Judy wanted to see it, too, it was useless to object.

As the scenes flicked across the television screen, Ginger felt her heart pound, her clenched fists become damp. The film had a high speed roll-over in a car chase scene. When that part of the action began, Ginger felt her throat squeeze. She saw herself behind the wheel of the fast-moving car. She remembered the roadside flashing by and, with painful clarity, relived the moments, feeling the seat belts dig into her body as she went into the roll-over, heard the scream of crumpling steel, smelled burning rubber, the acrid smoke of oil spilled on metal. . . .

Suddenly she couldn't breathe.

Quietly she slipped out of her chair and left the room. She went outside, standing for a moment beside the door, feeling the warm, moisture-laden Gulf breeze against her face, hearing it stir the fronds of the royal palms that bordered the yard.

An impulse moved her away from the house. She heard the crunch of shell under her feet as she walked down the driveway to the street. She found it easier to breathe as she walked under the stars. At the end of the block, she went into an all-night convenience market and bought a package of cigarettes. Outside again, she lit one, seeing her fingers tremble in the glow of the paper book match.

Only then did she remember that she had quit smoking months ago. With a muffled exclamation, she threw the pack in a sidewalk refuse basket, but she continued to puff on the one she had lit. She walked down to the beach and leaned against a palm tree, smoking the cigarette as she stared out at the moonlight that scattered golden coins of light over the dark velvet tapestry of the restless Gulf.

She was remembering another night and another moon. It had cast its seductive light on a Mexican beach and the Pacific Ocean. It had been almost ten years ago; she had been nineteen years old and desperately in love. It had been her wedding night . . . the night she had married Link Rockwood.

Chapter Two

The first time Ginger met Link Rockwood, he was picking her—spluttering and kicking—out of a horse watering trough.

He was twenty-six; Ginger was eighteen. And from that time on, she knew she was going to be in love with him for the rest of her life.

Ginger's father was on location with a movie company that was shooting some scenes at the Alamo village on the Texas prairie near Brackettville. John Wayne had spent four million dollars constructing the village of adobe and frame building for his epic, *The Alamo*, in 1959. The crumbling replica of that famous battle shrine was the largest ever built. Since its construction, the village had been put to use as a movie set for many western films. Lining the dusty main street were saloons, general stores, a jail, an often robbed bank, hotels, a school, church, blacksmith shop, stables and other buildings.

Over the years, more than a dozen major motion pictures and television shows had been filmed there. During summer months, when the Alamo village was open to the public, tourists could visit museums where props used in making the films were on display along with photos of the actors who had performed in the films—stars like John Wayne, Richard Widmark, Raquel Welch, Chill Wills, Dennis Weaver, Dean Martin, Linda Crystal and George Kennedy.

But now it was after Labor Day, and the village was closed to the public. The main street was deserted and the buildings silent, awaiting the hustle and bustle of a new movie about to be filmed there.

Movie sets had been as familiar as playgrounds to Ginger ever since she had been a toddler picking her way between cables and film equipment. Once in a while, Derrick took Paige or Ginger with him when he went on location. On this occasion Ginger had accompanied him.

The film crew and actors were staying at a nearby town. They had leased a stable of horses for the film. The producer who had bounced Ginger on his knee when she was still in diapers let her borrow one of the horses for a late afternoon ride. At the time she was in training for a career in stunt making, and one of the things she had learned was how to handle horses.

She had picked out a frisky-looking palomino, thrown the saddle on with practiced hands and ridden out of the corral where the horses were kept.

The baleful glare the horse gave her when she pulled the cinch tight had given her a moment of uneasiness. Had she picked more horse than she could handle? As they left the corral, he humped his back a bit and danced sideways, indicating a high spirit. But she kept a steady rein and he settled down, trotting obediently as she nudged his ribs. Her misgivings faded, and she began to enjoy the ride.

She crossed a stretch of prairie, following a trail between clumps of cactus and mesquite, riding down to the Alamo village, where filming for the movie was scheduled to begin the next day. The sun was going down in a blaze of color that sent red and gold streaks across a cloud-dotted sky. The reddish brown adobe buildings cast lengthy shadows across the village street.

The place appeared as silent and deserted as a ghost town. As Ginger rode into the main street, her imagination carried her to another era. It was the 1880s, the days of the old west. She was a rancher's daughter, riding to meet her lover to warn him that tht villain was on his way for a shootout at high noon. She was totally caught up in her imaginary role-playing.

Then, just as she rode along the side of the street, a black and white border collie suddenly appeared from around the corner of a building. He spotted them and came running up, barking furiously.

Several things happened at once. Ginger's horse reared wildly. The sky and buildings spun around in a pinwheel. Ginger screamed. She had the terrifying sensation of flying through space. Then came a gigantic "splash!"

Incredibly, she was drowning!

In a fit of panic, she struggled wildly. Then strong arms scooped her up. She heard a man's robust laughter. Ginger spluttered and kicked. She blinked enough water out of her eyes to see the blurred image of a sun-tanned face grinning down at her.

"Wh-what happened?" she gasped.

His grin widened, flashing white teeth. "Well, young lady, as near as I can figure out, you just decided to go swimming in a horse watering trough."

She blinked some more water away, bringing the scene into better focus. She saw the black and white dog near the heels of the man who had scooped her out of the water. The dog was happily wagging his tail.

"I didn't dive in the trough on purpose!" she said furiously. "Your mangy hound dog frightened my horse!"

"Sorry about that. Ranger there does like to bark at strangers. But I guess you're lucky that you did wind up in the trough. The water's a lot softer than the street."

With a sudden wave of confused feelings, Ginger became aware of the fact that she was gazing at incredibly handsome male features. Suddenly self-conscious, she stammered, "I-I guess I am lucky. No damage done."

Then she remembered the horse. "My horse! Where is he?"

"Old Cactus Belly? Last I saw of him, he was high-tailing it out of town."

"You know him?"

"I ought to. I helped break him. He belongs to Mr. Davis over at the Running W. What were you doin' riding him, anyway? Horse rustling?" There was a teasing glint in his eyes.

At that point she realized she was still being held in strong arms, a situation that she was in no hurry to alter. But he appeared to become aware of the arrangement at the same time and gently deposited her on her feet.

She shook some of the water off her arms, feeling

a wave of embarrassment. She must look like a half-drowned puppy, she thought. Then she momentarily forgot her own discomfiture as she remembered the horse again. "Mr. Collier will skin me alive!"

"Mr. Collier?"

"Mr. Collier, the producer. He let me borrow the horse."

The young man gazed at her with a fresh look of interest. "Are you one of the people that's going to make the movie here? Are you an actress?"

She laughed. "No, but my father is an actor. He's Derrick Lombard. Have you heard of him?"

His eyes widened slightly. "Well, I guess I have. I've seen him in movies since I was a kid."

"I'm Ginger Lombard," she said, again feeling a wave of unexpected shyness.

"Hi. I'm Link Ireland."

"Hi." She tried to think of what to say next and felt awkwardly tongue-tied. Her eyes trailed down his lanky, six-foot frame, seeing his faded blue jeans and run-down cowboy boots. "Do you live around here? Are you a cowboy?"

He laughed. "Yes ma'm, I live around here. But I don't know if they call a fellow like me a cowboy these days. I do odd jobs on ranches when they need a hand. Depends on the season. Last winter I had a job pumping gas in town. Right now I'm working as a sort of watchman around here to see kids don't carry off the place at night." He chewed his bottom lip, giving her a thoughtful look. "I heard in town that the movie company was going to hire some local fellows who can ride. You suppose there'd be any chance I could get hired on there?"

She gazed at him. He wore his western-style hat pushed back, allowing dark curly hair to tumble over his forehead. His eyes were steel gray with swirling depths. His skin was a leathery texture, burned golden by the wind and sun. His mouth grinned in an easygoing manner that seemed to laugh at both himself and anybody who took himself too seriously. A scar traced a jagged, thin white line down the right side of his jaw.

Looking at him, Ginger felt something warm and sweet turn on inside her. Her knees became weak. She thought, *As good-looking as you are, fellah, you ought to be the hero in the horse opera they're filming.*

Out loud she said, "Sure, they always need extras for a movie like this. I'll talk to my dad about it. He's good friends with the director. I'm sure he'll put in a word for you."

"Well, thanks. That's real nice of you."

Much later, when he was no longer Link Ireland, but Link Rockwood, a top box office money maker and male sex symbol to women all over the world, Ginger would remember with an inner smile the cowhand in the run-down boots, asking for a job as an extra.

But at the moment, her concern was for the missing horse. "What am I going to do about my horse?"

"Well, I know old Cactus Belly pretty well. He's probably trotting on over to the Running W, where he's used to getting fed. Why don't you find a place in the shade to sit down, and I'll see if I can catch him for you."

Ginger found a comfortable spot on one of the

board sidewalks where she could lean against a post. Link Ireland disappeared around a building, then reappeared presently astride a huge black horse. The border collie was trotting along behind him.

Link touched the brim of his hat in a polite gesture as he rode by, his horse's hooves stirring white caliche dust in the street.

Ginger stared at the gorgeous hunk of manhood and felt all of her limbs turn weak. *No one really looks that good on a horse,* she thought, *even in the movies.* And this was real life.

She watched him ride off. Then she occupied herself with daydreams in which Link Ireland figured prominently as the hero. The plots ranged from his saving her from a band of roving Indians to his climbing a ladder to her bedroom at night so they could elope.

She was on about the fourth plot, in which Link rescued her from a runaway team of horses, when he suddenly appeared around a corner at the far end of the street. He was leading a subdued but sullen palomino.

She ran out to meet him. "Oh, thank you!" she cried. "I would really have been in hot water if I'd lost that horse!"

Link nudged back the brim of his hat with his forefinger, looking down at her with a lopsided grin that promptly turned her muscles to jelly. "Reckon it was the least I could do, seeing that it was my dog that spooked old Cactus Belly here."

He handed her the reins. "You be careful now, young lady. That palomino's got a mean streak in him."

Ginger nodded, wishing she could think of something grown up and provocative to say and wondering desperately how she could get to see him again. "Is . . . is there anything to do around here . . . you know, for fun . . . in the evenings?"

"Well," he chuckled, "there's the movie house in town, but I guess you've seen everything in Hollywood that they're showing around here. Then there's a carnival this weekend."

Her horse was stamping restlessly.

"You better get moving," Link advised, straightening and touching his hat brim again in the polite gesture that turned her all warm and soft inside. "Cactus Belly gets restless just standing around."

Ginger nodded, wishing she could kill the horse. But then she remembered that it was because of the horse she had met Link, and felt more charitable toward the beast.

"Maybe I'll see you at the carnival," she called. Then, giving in to Cactus Belly's impatience, she rode away.

That weekend she went to the carnival. She wandered down the midway, threading her way through the crowd She rubbed shoulders with men in blue jeans and western hats and with their smiling, suntanned women. She saw little brown Mexican-American boys running between the people. The air was heavy with dust and the smell of popcorn and cotton candy. The voices of barkers called out over the clanking of the machinery of rides and the screams of riders on the tilt-o-whirl. A giant Ferris wheel turned overhead, spinning its lights against the star-sprinkled prairie night.

But Ginger was not interested in the rides or the games. She walked slowly to the end of the midway,

turned and strolled back, her gaze hopefully searching the crowd for a tall, lanky figure with a sun-
tanned face, lop-sided grin and eyes with swirling
brown depths.

After her third trip from end to end of the brightly
lighted strip of booths and rides, Ginger sighed to
herself. He wasn't there. She had been childish to
daydream that she would see him there tonight.

Disconsolately she spent a dollar at a ringtoss
game, not getting close to the target and caring even
less.

A masculine voice at her elbow said, "You can
never win. Those things are rigged."

She spun around. Link Ireland was grinning down
at her. She lit up inside brighter than the carnival
midway.

"Hi." She gulped. "Gee, I never expected to see
you here."

"Small world, huh?" He offered her a piece of
gum, then took one for himself.

There was a moment of awkward silence in which
she struggled with self-consciousness. Then she remembered. "Oh, I talked to Dad about seeing if
they'd hire you for an extra. He said for you to be
down where they're shooting early Monday morning."

Ireland smiled his thanks, happily chewing his
gum. "Well, that sure was nice of you. How about
that? I'm goin' to be in the movies!"

She nodded, worshipping him with her gaze.

He said, "Guess I owe you a favor. Do you like
stuffed panda bears?"

"Huh?"

He motioned with his head for her to follow him.
They crossed the midway to a booth that offered

stuffed toys as prizes for knocking down a pyramid of wooden milk bottles with a baseball.

Link gave the booth operator a dollar, for which he was handed three baseballs. Link wound up for the throw. The ball flew so fast Ginger couldn't see it. The bottles scattered in all directions. With a look of disgust, the operator handed Link a small monkey on a string.

Ireland pointed to a large panda. "What do I have to do to win that?"

"You have to knock all the pins down three times in a row."

"Okay. Set 'em up."

A small crowd was gathering around them. Somebody laughed. "Use your spitball, Link!"

Link grinned. He waved the crowd back. He gave Ginger his hat to hold. Then he wound up, hands above and behind his head, uncoiled and the ball sizzled through the air. Pins flew in all directions. He repeated the performance a third time. The crowd applauded. Ginger gazed at him with starry-eyed wonder.

Link said, "Okay, mister. Let's have the prize."

The booth operator gave him a dirty look. "You ain't getting any prize, buster. What are you, some kind of local hotshot baseball pitcher?"

Smiling easily, Link reached across the counter, caught a handful of the operator's shirt front and lifted him off the ground. In a gentle voice, he said, "Give the little lady the panda, mister, or I'll hit you so hard all your relatives will die."

The carnival booth man looked into Link's eyes and turned pale. He grabbed the large, stuffed panda and shoved it into Ginger's arms.

They moved away from the booth. Several men in

the crowd slapped Link's back, their congratulations expressed with the hearty laughter of hard-working, outdoor people.

Ginger hugged the panda. Her emotions were running the scale from hero worship to undying love. "You . . . you seem to have a lot of friends."

"Yeah, some."

"Thank you for the panda."

"That's okay. Do you like it?"

"I love it," she said fervently, when what she meant was, *I love you, Link Ireland.*

They walked farther down the midway. Ginger said, "I've never seen anybody throw a baseball that straight. Are you really a pitcher?"

"Oh, I play a little local sandlot ball. Nothing big league. Do you like baseball?"

"Love it," Ginger said, mentally crossing her fingers because she had never been to a game in her life.

"My team is going to play Sunday afternoon down at the city park. Maybe you'd like to come watch."

"I might . . . if I'm not busy," she said, trying hard to sound casual. She knew that nothing short of pneumonia would keep her away.

They stopped at a shooting gallery booth. Link spent another dollar, hitting a moving target with deadly accuracy and winning another stuffed toy for Ginger.

They had just turned away from the booth when a young, redheaded woman dressed in tight blue jeans and a blue western shirt with the top three buttons open appeared, moving through the crowd toward them. She slipped her arm through Link's with a possessive gesture. "Hi, honey. Sorry I'm late. We had to work overtime at the diner."

"'Evening, Martha."

The redhead gave Ginger a curious look. "Who's the healthy teenager?"

"Martha, this is Miss Ginger Lombard. Her daddy's Derrick Lombard, the movie actor. They're with the Hollywood people that are making the movie. Ginger, this is Miss Martha Delaney."

Ginger's emotions had tumbled into chaos. Her stomach became a painful knot as she stared at the woman who had taken possession of Link. She was drenched with a combination of jealousy and despair.

For her part, Martha Delaney was gazing at Ginger with an expression of near awe. "Your daddy is Derrick Lombard? Gee."

"Ginger spoke to him about getting me a job as an extra with the movie they're filming at the Alamo village."

Martha's wondering gaze swung to Link. "Really? Link, you're going to be in the movies?" She gave his arm an extra tight squeeze.

At that point, Ginger could only think of escape. She mumbled, "Well, thanks for the panda," and turned and fled into the crowd, her vision obscured by tears.

Ginger vowed she would not go to the baseball game on Sunday. But Link persisted in slipping into her daydreams and her night dreams, and Sunday afternoon she went to the park and sat on wooden bleachers in the hot Texas sunshine. She watched the game, but mostly her eyes were on Link.

After the game, she was at a cold drink stand when he came strolling up, carrying a bat and glove. "Hi," he said with a smile. "I saw you in the bleachers."

"Yes. I didn't have anything else to do, so I decided to come see the game," she said with a bored tone. And with an air of great indifference, she asked, "Where's your girl friend?"

"Girl friend?"

"The one with the red hair and the shirt that wouldn't stay buttoned."

He laughed. "Oh, Martha. She's working at the diner this afternoon. But she isn't my girl friend—just a friend."

"Oh," Ginger said, suddenly feeling much more charitable toward the redheaded waitress.

"How did you get down here to the park?"

"Walked."

"Hot day to be walking. I've got my pickup. Want a ride?"

"All right," Ginger said, trying to maintain her bored tone.

The pickup truck was incredibly rusty and battered, but the engine purred. They bounced out of the park, rattled over a cattle guard and pulled onto a paved road.

Link asked, "Mind if I drop a couple of things off at the house?"

He stopped at a small grocery store, bought a loaf of bread and a six-pack of beer. Then he drove a short distance from town and pulled into a dirt driveway that led up to a dilapidated farmhouse. The structure had settled on its foundations with an air of weary resignation. The porch sagged, the roof drooped. There was a single chinaberry tree in the front yard, which was devoid of any grass. At the side of the house were several old cars in various stages of disintegration on concrete blocks.

When they parked in the yard, the black and white border collie that had frightened Ginger's horse at the Alamo village crawled out from under the porch, waving his tail. Ginger remembered his name was Ranger.

"Come on and meet my family," Link offered.

She followed him up to the front porch, where an elderly man dressed in khaki work trousers, shirt and suspenders was seated in a rocking chair.

"Uncle Jefferson, I brought you a six-pack of cold ones."

"Well, thank you, Link. How'd the game go?"

"We won. Six to nothing."

The old man slapped his knee. "Hot dog. That'll show them smart alecks from Winters something."

"Uncle Jefferson, I've got a young lady with me. She's visiting down here with the Hollywood people that's going to shoot the movie at Bracketville. Her daddy's a famous movie star, Derrick Lombard."

Not until then was Ginger aware that the elderly man was blind.

The old man said, "Derrick Lombard. Heck, I remember seein' him in movies before my eyesight went. This is sure an honor, young lady." He arose from his chair.

"Her name is Ginger, Uncle Jefferson."

"Sure pleased to make your acquaintance, Miss Ginger."

He held out a leathery hand, which Ginger grasped. His handshake was warm.

"Miss Lombard talked to her daddy about getting me a job as an extra on the movie they're making down here, Uncle Jefferson. They need some local fellows with horses."

"Now wouldn't that be something? I'd sure like to be able to see you in a movie, Link," his uncle said with a chuckle.

"Well, I guess about all you'd see was some guy riding off in the distance in a cloud of dust."

They all laughed. Then Link's uncle asked, "Can we offer you something to drink, Miss Lombard? There's more than enough beer."

"Ginger's too young for beer, Uncle Jefferson."

"Oh, sorry, miss. Well, I think there's some soft drinks in the refrigerator."

"I'm of legal age." Ginger sniffed disdainfully. "But thanks just the same, Mr. Jefferson. I had something to drink at the ballpark, so I'm really not thirsty."

When they were in the pickup and back on the road heading into town, Ginger said, "Your uncle Jefferson's a nice man."

"Yeah," Link said, "they don't make them like those old-timers any more. My folks died when I was a youngster. Uncle Jefferson took me on to raise all by himself. He's all the family I've got. He's punched cattle, rode the rails in the depression, bootlegged moonshine and once spent two years in the pen for hitting a guy too hard. But he never cheated anybody, always treated other folks fair and never backed down from a fair fight. He taught me how to pitch a baseball, how to ride a horse, how to shoot straight and how to be a man. That's about all you can ask, I guess."

With bittersweet emotions, Ginger remembered the days that followed. She remembered how Link had made his Hollywood debut as an extra in the western movie, how her father had met Link and, with his experienced eye, spotted potential star material. He'd taken Link under his wing and arranged for a screen test. From there on, Link's career was a matter of screen history, only he was no longer Link Ireland. Derrick Lombard picked a screen name for him; Link Ireland became Link Rockwood. Derrick steered him to the best acting coaches. With the help of Derrick's contacts, he began getting small roles. Then he made some of the late night talk shows, hit with a TV series and eventually worked his way up from grade-B film roles.

Link was not and would never be an outstanding actor. He was a personality, at his best when he played himself. In his most successful movie roles, he played a character who was a devil-may-care, lovable rogue. His film characters loved high adventure and fast living; he laughed at danger. In his film roles he thumbed his nose at rules, regulations and figures of authority, thus fulfilling the fantasies of an audience stifled by complex twentieth-century urban existence. Yet with it all, he was protective of women, showing a kind of rough gallantry toward the fairer sex. He rode horses, drove fast cars spent money carelessly.

That was Link Rockwood in the movies. It was also Link Rockwood in real life.

Now, on a moonlit beach in Florida some ten years after Link had scooped her out of the watering trough in that make-believe frontier village in Texas, Ginger remembered it all. And she remembered with a twist of pain that went like a knife through her heart the expression on Link's face the first time he'd met Ginger's beautiful sister, Paige. Ginger thought it must have been the way she'd looked at Link the first time, knowing she would love him forever.

Nothing could change that. Her heartbreaking marriage to Link couldn't change that. The reports in the scandal tabloids and the fan magazines, the rumors and the gossip about all the women in Link's life, were pure fantasy. There were only two women in Link's life: Ginger, who had loved him not wisely but too well, and Paige, the beautiful one, whom Link would love as long as he drew a breath on earth.

Ginger had run away from all that as much as she had run away from the emotional trauma of her accident when she'd come to Florida, seeking the quiet safety of her aunt's home. But the past had caught up with her in the guise of her father.

With a sigh, she dropped the remains of her cigarette and pressed it into the sand under her sandal.

Slowly she walked back up the beach to her aunt's home. She was approaching the screened porch when a figure moved out of the shadows. With a start, she realized it was her father.

"Derrick? What are you doing out here?"

He had been puffing on his pipe. He took it from between his teeth. "Waiting for you, Ginger," he said quietly. He took her arm. "Let's walk down the beach together. I have something to tell you."

There was a tone in his voice she had never heard before.

Chapter Three

They walked in silence for a while along the beach. There was only the soft murmur of the surf rolling on the white sand. Ginger stole glances at her father, seeing in the moonlight a frown knitting his brow. She sensed that he was wrestling with some kind of inner turmoil. Curiosity engulfed her, but she waited, knowing he would break the silence in his own time.

They approached a log. With a weary sigh, Derrick said, "Ginger, let's sit here for a moment and have a chat."

When they were seated, he fussed with his pipe nervously, frowning at it as if deciding whether or not to relight it. Finally he put it in his jacket pocket.

Ginger thought, *How sad that we have to be strangers and that he finds it so difficult to talk with me.* The situation was making her nervous, too. She had never felt completely at ease with her father.

Derrick cleared his throat. "Er . . . Ginger . . . this film I'm planning to produce. It's quite important to me. That's why I had hoped to be able to persuade you to be the stunt coordinator. I can understand how you feel about getting back into stunt work after that dreadful accident. But I'm not asking you to do any of the stunts yourself. I merely want you to plan the stunts . . . do the stunt directing."

Ginger sighed. "You don't understand, Derrick. I don't want to ever go near a movie set again. It makes me nervous to even watch an old film I worked on. That's why I had to leave tonight when you started watching *Quest of the Falcon.* I've had my share of bruises, like any stunt person. I've cracked ribs and broken a collarbone. Even had a concussion or two. But what I went through last year was different. I just can't wipe it out of my mind."

"Perhaps," he suggested, "you might feel differently if you became involved in a new film. Would you like to read the script?"

She shook her head slowly. The situation involved more than she cared to talk about with her father. How could she possibly become involved in a filmmaking project that would throw her in daily contact with Link and Paige, thereby turning the anguish of the past into a flaming agony of the present?

Derrick suddenly arose and began pacing the sand in a state of great agitation. He ran his long fingers nervously through his hair. Ginger stared at him, puzzled and concerned by his behavior.

He exclaimed, "Ginger, I must make you understand how important this film is to me. I've staked everything on it!" He sighed, looking at her with an expression of deep despair. "I can be frank with you. You're my own daughter. Ginger, my film career has hit the skids. I haven't been offered a decent part in over two years. I'm a has-been. Can you believe it? Derrick Lombard, washed up! I refused to admit it for a long time, but eventually I had to face the truth. The kind of parts I played, the image I had built for myself depended on an image of action and vigor. Suddenly I am not a young man anymore. I've seen it happen to others of my generation. From now on it will be all downhill. Perhaps a bit part now and then, a minor television walk-on role. . . ."

A wave of emotion swept through Ginger, choking her. It was the first time in her life she could remember her father speaking to her directly of his inner feelings. For the first time, he wasn't hiding behind some part he was playing. The depth of his emotion was evident in the hoarse catch in his voice.

Ginger looked at him with a rush of concern. And suddenly she was seeing him more clearly. She realized that for all of her life, when she had looked at her father, she had seen not him, but Derrick Lombard, the actor. But now she saw the man who was her father. It was true, she realized—he was growing old. How could she not have seen it before? Had it been hidden by the overpowering force of his personality? His once luxurious mane of hair was white now and thinning. His face had taken on the look of age with its lines, its hollowed cheeks. Blue veins traced patterns across his temples. His once smooth complexion now bore scattered brown spots of aging pigmentation.

But more disturbing than the physical signs were the shadows in his eyes, the haunted sense of his own mortality, a groping uncertainty, a barely concealed look of fright.

He said, "Film-making is my life! It's the air I breathe, the nourishment I subsist upon. I cannot retire. I must continue to be a part of the film industry or die. Ginger, I want to direct a great film. I have the experience. I have a statement to make, and I know what I want to say and how to say it. Most of these young punks who call themselves directors today hardly know one end of a camera from the other and, much less, what to do with a story. They're not artists; they're spoiled kids working in a media they don't understand. If they produce a box office hit, it's an accident. Overnight they become prima donnas. I know. I've had the misfortune to work under their direction. But you can be assured of this: If Derrick Lombard directs a film, it will be another matter entirely. When I walk on a set, forty years of experience are behind me. I'll produce and direct this film, and it will be the biggest artistic and commercial success of the year!"

He suddenly looked weary, as if the words had taken all of his vitality. Leaning back on the log again, he picked up a stick and slowly traced a pattern in the sand. "Ginger, during my heyday, money flowed through my fingers. I spent it as if it were going out of style. Now I'm virtually broke. I've sunk everything I have left in this film I'm going to produce and direct. I've sold all of my real estate. I'm putting whatever I have left and could scrape together into this project."

"Not the home in Malibu!" Ginger exclaimed.

"Yes, that too. Everything."

"But that beautiful home! It meant so much to you."

"True, but this is more important. Ginger, in addition to putting every cent of my own I could get together, I've borrowed all I could. You know what it costs to produce a major motion picture these days. I haven't been able to offer Paige and Link any up-front money. Instead of salary, I'm giving them a percentage of the profit.

"Y'know, Paige has had a run of bad luck lately. A few years back, she was riding the crest of her popularity, scoring some leading roles in movies and that TV series. Her picture was on the cover of every fan magazine in the country. Then there were those two awful box office flops. Now I think this movie will put her back on top.

"Link, of course, is the biggest name around. The only reason he's consented to gamble his time with me is because he feels he owes the start of his film career to me. I more or less discovered him, in a manner of speaking."

Derrick paused. He took his pipe out, looked at it again, put it back in his pocket. He cleared his throat. "The stunt work is going to be extremely important in this story, Ginger. You know how the public loves the action things Link does—the car chase scenes, the smashups, the daredevil element. No one could set those stunts better than you. Unfortunately, I'd have to offer you the same kind of arrangement that Paige and Link have—a healthy percent of the profit. But I'm sure the film will make money. Just having Link in the male lead role ought to make it big box office. . . ."

Derrick's voice trailed off. He was looking at her hopefully in a way that tightened a band around her throat painfully.

The money was not the problem, though she could use it, after all her medical expenses. Still, she had turned down numerous offers from Hollywood since her accident. It was her father's situation that had her trapped. All of her life, she had yearned to have a real father, a person with whom she could communicate, share her feelings, cry and laugh, a father she knew loved her. Now suddenly it wasn't the actor

Derrick Lombard talking with her. It was, for the first time in her life, her father. He was in trouble. He was desperate and more than a little frightened. All of the bluster and posing was gone. He had swallowed his pride and had taken her into his confidence. He had bared his soul to her.

She slipped her hand in his, felt an answering squeeze. Tears blurred her vision. She wanted to remember this moment, because she suspected that when it was over, Derrick Lombard would be playing a part again. But for the moment, the wall that had separated her from her father since her childhood had been broken.

Derrick said ruefully, "Ginger, I haven't been the greatest father in the world to you. I admit it. Always put my career before family. Dashing off to all parts of the world on location assignments. All the marriages and divorces. Hardly a stable home for a child to grow up in. I know I don't have the right to ask you to make any sacrifices for me now. Still, I do need your help, just as I need Paige and Link. Need all the help I can get. . . ."

She suspected he needed her moral support as much as her expertise, although that was not to discount the practical side of the matter. Good stunt coordinators were expensive, and she knew not many had her skill and originality.

She clasped his hand tightly. "Dad . . . I did miss having a regular father at times," she admitted frankly. "But having you for a father was pretty special, too." She smiled shakily. "Not many girls can brag about having a famous movie star for their father." She realized it was the first time in her life she had called him Dad.

She could find but one answer in her heart to his

urgent plea. She summoned all her courage and said, "All right, Derrick. I'll do the stunt coordination for you."

"Bravo!" Derrick exclaimed, his eyes alight. He arose, suddenly filled with a fresh surge of energy. "With you, Paige and Link helping me, Lombard Productions will produce a smash hit movie!" He paced the sand in a burst of restless enthusiasm.

The resurgence of his old buoyant optimism warmed Ginger's heart. But at the same time she felt an icy constriction in her stomach. How was she going to find the strength to go through with this? She couldn't disappoint her father. But the past was already closing in on her with a blanket of smothering emotions.

When they returned to the house, Ginger told her aunt and cousin of her decision to leave with her father to begin work on the film. Her aunt looked concerned. Lorene's eyes sparkled with excitement and envy.

Judy came to her room later as Ginger was packing. "Honey, whatever made you change your mind? You have been so dead set against ever going back into stunt work. Do you really feel up to this?"

"Sure. I'm okay now, Aunt Judy."

"But you've said so many times that you never wanted to go near a movie set again."

"I know," Ginger said in a muffled voice, taking a skirt from a hanger and folding it to fit her suitcase. "But this production means a lot to Derrick."

"I know it does, and I also know how persuasive he can be. When Derrick makes up his mind to have something, he usually winds up getting it."

Ginger felt a disquieting doubt. Had Derrick

really been sincere back there on the beach, or had he fooled her after all? Had he just been playing one of his scenes again, with her the gullible audience? A dark anger threatened to take control of her reason.

Judy smiled wryly. "That brother of mine is just a little insane, you know. I suppose it's the kind of insanity that goes with being a superb artist. He's enormously selfish. That, too, I think grows out of the demands of being so good at what he does. It requires an extraordinarily self-centered ego."

Ginger sighed. "You don't have to tell me about my illustrious father, Aunt Judy. Everything you say about him is true. He can be vain, self-centered, demanding, domineering. But . . . he's my father. I'm enormously proud of some of the things he's accomplished."

"Well, you should be. When all's said and done, he is Derrick Lombard, and that's saying quite a lot."

"Yes. But there are times, too, when I hate him. The usual ambivalence one feels toward a parent, I guess."

Her aunt shrugged. "Derrick is not your run-of-the-mill parent. He tends to arouse violent feelings. You needn't feel guilty about your feelings, Ginger."

"I try not to."

Suddenly Ginger realized she was close to revealing to her aunt the conversation she'd had with her father on the beach. She did not want to talk about it. She knew how much pride her father had. Their conversation had been private and confidential.

She decided she was going to believe that Derrick had been sincere. She simply could not allow herself to think he had deceived her just to trick her into working on the film with him. Derrick was capable of doing some rotten things, but she was convinced that if he had ever been sincere in his life, it had been tonight on the beach.

"Aunt Judy, my mind is made up. I've decided I want to work with him on this film. I won't be doing any of the actual stunt work myself. I'll just plan and direct the stunts and work with the special effects people."

Judy Parker gave her niece a hug. "You're just like a daughter to me, honey," she said huskily. "You've been hurt enough in your young life. If things get tough, you come running back here, understand?"

Ginger knew that her aunt was talking about a different kind of hurt from the physical trauma she'd suffered. Judy knew about the part Link Rockwood had played in Ginger's life, about their disastrous marriage when Ginger was nineteen. If Ginger worked on this production, Link would be back in her life again.

Ginger tried not to think about that now. It was something she'd have to cope with when the time came. But she knew that time was close at hand. Tomorrow she would accompany her father to the location where the first scenes of the film would be shot. Link would be there.

For ten years she had been careful to stay away from Link Rockwood. She had turned down stunt jobs on any film in which he was involved. But now she could no longer hide from him or from the past that had involved them both. Tomorrow the past would catch up with them. Tomorrow she would come face to face with Link again. Already her emotions were recoiling from the storm that was brewing.

Chapter Four

Ginger took a copy of the script for Derrick's movie to bed with her that night, but the meaning of the words on the pages dissolved as her mind persistently wandered.

Her lifetime in Hollywood, all of her years in the industry as a stunt girl, seemed to lead up to this turning point in her life. . . .

She was barely into her teens when she decided to make stunt work her career. Paige, older by four years and richly blessed with beauty and talent, had already started getting minor roles in films and was on her way to becoming a star. Ginger had had no illusions about her own chances at an acting career. But she was the healthy, active one in the family. The first requirement of the stunt profession was an athletic body.

Ginger had grown up in the shadow of her glamorous sister. As a young child, Paige had been frail and sickly, requiring a lot of special attention. That set a pattern in Paige's life, a constant hunger to be the center of attention, to be pampered and cared for, and a degree of selfishness in satisfying that need.

At sixteen, Ginger did not have the insight to analyze her own motives when she chose a career in stunt work. Looking back now, she supposed it was her method of striving for some measure of approval and attention from her father. She was convinced that Paige was her father's special daughter, making the bond between them even stronger with her acting talent. At least Ginger could be a part of their industry. She knew that as an actress she would be lousy. But she was determined to excel as a stunt person.

She had a good teacher. Wild Bill Redcloud had worked in the industry since the days the cameraman used a hand crank and the director shouted instructions through a megaphone. He had known all the great stars since the silent film era—Wallace Beery, Doug Fairbanks, Tom Mix and later Tyrone Power, Jimmy Stewart and the Duke, and he had doubled for most of them at one time or another. He had long ago forgotten how many horses he'd tumbled from, how many saloon windows he'd been knocked through, how many two-story falls he'd taken, and how many bones he'd broken. By the time Ginger served her apprenticeship with him, he was as gnarled as a weathered oak, walked with a limp, wore a black patch over one empty eye socket and grumbled at everyone within earshot.

Redcloud said he was half Comanche. He claimed he could remember visiting his grandfather in a teepee and seeing scalps hanging in the tent. He was past the years when he could do stunts himself, but he continued to coordinate and direct some of the best.

Ginger began following Redcloud around the sets

when she was sixteen. "Get lost, kid," he'd growled at her.

She'd stuck her chin out stubbornly. "I want to do stunts."

He glared at her through his one good eye. "Quit bothering me. Go play with your dolls."

"I want you to teach me," she persisted.

"I don't teach nobody nothin'!" he snapped, squinting to get her in better focus with his single orb. "You're Derrick Lombard's kid, ain't you?"

"Yes."

"Well, beat it, or I'll tell Derrick to give you a spanking."

But she had continued to follow him around, and he had continued to growl at her until one day he suddenly grumbled, "Listen, anybody that's goin' to do stunt work has got to get in first-class shape."

So she began working out on a trampoline and swimming daily. She took karate lessons.

Then Redcloud muttered, "You got to learn how to do shoulder rolls."

"What's a shoulder roll?"

"Dumb kid. I don't know why I bother. A shoulder roll is like a somersault, but instead of going straight over your head, you turn your head, give a little twist and go over your shoulder. It's one of the most important things a stunt man's gotta learn. You do a shoulder roll when you get knocked down or fall out of a window or out of a car. First you practice on a mat, then you jump off a trampoline and take your roll on the mat. If you don't break your fool neck, you work up to a higher trampoline."

Redcloud did his best to discourage her. "Listen, kid, five thousand people come to Hollywood every year wanting to break into this field. You know how many stunt people get work? Maybe two hundred. And out of them, about seventy-five are good enough to get most of the jobs. So what makes you think you're so great?"

Ginger, having by then decided his bark was worse than his bite, merely glared back at him, her eyes narrowed with stubborn determination.

The hours Ginger wasn't in school, she spent training. She learned all the varieties of shoulder rolls and used the skill in practicing falls—falls out of cars, off motorcycles, off horses and in explosions. She learned how to fight without actually hitting or getting hit—the art of taking a faked punch and making it look real and of delivering a punch that was pulled at the last moment but also looked real to the camera. She spent long months practicing high falls, beginning with a simple tumble from a trampoline and graduating to falls from first- and second-story windows. She learned how to turn a bundle of nylon into an air bag that cushioned the falls.

While most teenagers her age were taking driver's ed in order to earn their license, Ginger was learning how to get hit by a car.

"The way it works is that you'll hit the car instead of the car hitting you," Wild Bill told her.

He instructed her to walk toward the car, which was moving slowly. "Just when you reach the front bumper, instead of waiting for the car to hit you, you jump high on the hood, do your shoulder roll across the hood and go off across to the other side."

Some nights, Ginger went to bed too full of bruises and strained muscles to sleep. But she kept doggedly at it.

By the time she was eighteen, Ginger had reached her full height, five-nine, which by most standards

made her a tall girl. By that time she had also won
Wild Bill Redcloud's grudging admiration, though
he would have surrendered his own scalp before
admitting it. To her he growled more than ever. But
if someone noticed Ginger practicing a high fall and
commented that the kid had a real future in the stunt
field, Wild Bill would send a stream of tobacco juice
into the dust at his feet and nod proudly, "Taught
her everything she knows!"

Ginger spent hours on a shooting range learning
to handle rifles and pistols. Explosion gags were part
of a stunt person's repertoire. Redcloud hid a small
trampoline behind a bush. Ginger jumped onto the
trampoline. At the same instant she hit the trampoline, Redcloud set off a smoke charge. Ginger came
bouncing off the trampoline, over the bush in a
headfirst dive, using the shoulder roll as she landed.
Filmed from a camera angle in front of the bush and
with the sound of an explosion added, the result
would be a convincing scene of an actor being blown
high in the air by a charge of dynamite.

Overcoming her fear of heights was a tough
emotional hurdle. The first time she hung in a
second-story window looking down at the air bag
that would break her fall, Ginger felt sick with
dread. She was bathed in cold perspiration. Her
stomach was a painful knot. She drew a deep breath,
clenched her teeth, said a prayer and leaped out into
space.

It was a fear she never entirely overcame, which
was ironic in view of the fact that making high falls
became her forte. She was considered one of the
best in the industry for taking falls from airplanes,
helicopters and high buildings.

Her trip with her father to the Alamo village

location turned out to be a momentous turning point in her young life. First, she met Link there. Second, she did her first professional stunt in the same film that Link first worked in as an extra. She had gone to the village that day to watch the film crew shoot a scene in which Link rode into town with a group of other men. He was supposed to be just one of the dust-covered figures, but, to Ginger at least, he stood out sharply from the others in the band. He rode his big, black horse at an easy trot. She gazed at his broad shoulders in the sweat-stained shirt and felt her heart pick up the tempo of the horses' hooves that thudded into the dirt road. Her eyes were riveted on him as the scene was filmed.

The voice at her shoulder growled her name several times before she realized someone was speaking to her. Then she turned, flustered.

Wild Bill Redcloud's single eye was glaring at her like that of a malevolent cyclops. "What's the matter with you, kid? You gone deaf or somethin'?"

"S-sorry," she stammered. "I guess I was thinking about something else."

"Yeah," he muttered and grinned maliciously. "It wouldn't be that wrangler on the black stallion, I don't guess."

Ginger's face turned beet red. "Of course not!" she said furiously.

"Of course not," he mimicked. "Listen, kid, I still got one good eye. You've been hanging around the set every time he's in a scene. If you've got any sense, you'll quit mooning over him. He's nothin' but a drifting horse wrangler. I know his type. They're strictly bad news where women are concerned. Anyway, he's too old for you."

"I don't recall asking your advice," Ginger said haughtily. "You're not my father."

"Somebody has to be," Redcloud muttered. "Derrick sure don't work overtime at it."

Ginger was speechless with anger, but before she could think of an appropriate retort, the old stunt coordinator grumbled, "Anyway, I didn't come over here to discuss your love life. I want to know if you want a job in this horse opera."

Her anger evaporated. She was momentarily speechless again, but for a different reason. Finally she stammered, "You . . . you want to hire me to do a stunt?"

"Yeah. You got to start some time. The gal that was supposed to do it got sick. Ate too many enchiladas or somethin'. You're a little tall to double for the leading lady, but in a long shot action scene, nobody will see the difference. You've just turned eighteen now, so there'll be no hassle with child labor laws. There is a problem about the Screen Actors' Guild, but we can get you in this scene under the Taft-Hartly Law and then we'll see about a regular SAG membership for you."

"What's the job?"

"Nothin' complicated. A simple explosion gag. You come tumblin' through a breakaway saloon window in a cloud of smoke, do a shoulder roll on the sidewalk and run off down the street, pretending to dodge bullets. At the end of the block, you act like you get hit in the shoulder, take a tumble. Then a stunt man doubling for the hero comes galloping down the street, grabs you up and rides off with you. Think you can do it?"

"Sure!" Ginger exclaimed, beside herself with excitement now.

The crusty old stunt coordinator was eyeing her with a peculiar expression. "What if I told you," he said laconically, "that the rider that's goin' to pick you up is that horse wrangler you've been mooning over?"

Ginger's eyes widened. "You're . . . you're pulling my leg!"

"Nope."

"But . . . but why are they going to use Link?"

Redcloud shrugged. "Simple reason. Turns out he can ride better'n anybody else they've got. He's got to come down the street riding fast, bend way down from the saddle and scoop you up. Nothin' to it for anybody who can ride worth a hoot. Done it myself in dozens of horse operas. These kids they get nowadays don't know nothin' about horses. They'd probably drop you or fall off their horse and hurt themselves or you. That big Texan friend of yours does know how to handle himself on a horse; I got to give him that much."

The discovery that she was going to perform her first professional stunt before the cameras and then that Link would also be in the scene was almost too much of a thrill for one day. Ginger's heart was pounding, her hands icy.

She was turned over to the makeup and wardrobe people. When they finished with her, she was wearing a tattered shirt and blue jeans and looked very much like someone who had just barely survived an explosion.

Then the special effects people strapped a small explosive device called a squibb to her left shoulder under her shirt. A pad of lead and leather protected her body. When triggered, the device would explode outward, creating a realistic effect of a bullet ripping through her shoulder, making fabric and "blood" fly.

Redcloud walked her through the gag several times, going over her action in detail. Then she waited on the sidewalk as the camera crew completed a scene on the other end of the block.

Suddenly her heart skipped a beat as she caught sight of Link strolling toward her from across the street. "Hi," he said with one of his lazy grins that melted her insides. Then his grin faded as he got a closer look at her. His face paled. "Ginger, what happened? You're all bloody!"

She laughed. "It's makeup. I'm going to be in the next scene."

"I thought you said you weren't an actress."

"I'm not."

"You're sure made up like one."

"I'm substituting for the stunt girl."

"Really?" He looked at her with a puzzled expression. "You know how to do things like that?"

She said, "I've been training for stunt work since I was sixteen. Wild Bill Redcloud—he's the gruff old guy with the eye patch—well, he's been coaching me. He's the stunt coordinator for this film."

Link shook his head slowly. "You're full of surprises, Ginger." He leaned against a post on the board sidewalk in a relaxed, lazy manner, his arms crossed, gazing at her. She felt her heart begin its drumbeat tempo again.

"Did you know you're going to be in the scene with me?" she asked.

He looked at her with surprised interest. "They said they want me to ride down the street at a gallop and pick a stunt lady up without slowing down. You mean that's going to be you?"

Ginger nodded with a pleased grin.

Her eyes could see nothing but Link. He filled her universe. By now the lock of curly dark brown hair that tumbled carelessly over his forehead, the laugh wrinkles around his eyes and mouth, the strong, clean line of his jaw had become familiar to Ginger. She had memorized every angle of his lean, handsome features. Still, she thought she would never tire of looking at him, at being hypnotized by his luminous steel gray eyes with their swirling depths. His sleeves were rolled up on this warm day, baring sun-tanned forearms rippling with muscles. He wore a faded blue shirt, a wide belt around his slim waist, and tight jeans that hugged his rounded buttocks and muscular thighs. The exciting male smell of dust, saddle leather and healthy sweat surrounded him.

His usual casual expression had become a bit serious. "Ginger, I'm supposed to be riding fast when I grab you up. You're going to get a pretty hard jolt, and there's always a possibility my horse could stumble or something. You sure you're up to doing this?"

"Link," she said with a touch of exasperation, "I've been trained to do stunts a lot tougher than this. Stunt work is going to be my career. You just ride your horse, and let me worry about what I have to do. Okay?"

His easy grin returned. "Okay. I just want you to take care of your pretty neck."

It wasn't possible for her to stay angry with him. Back in a lighter vein again, she asked, "Well, how do you like being in movies?"

He chuckled. "I don't know if ridin' a horse with a bunch of other guys is exactly being in the movies. But it's something different. I guess I like it okay. I always wondered what went on when they make a movie. Can't make heads or tails out of what they're doin', though. Right now, they're aiming the camera at a guy kissing a girl in a wagon. But they killed off the guy this morning. He sure got well in a hurry."

Ginger laughed. "They don't film a movie in the sequence that follows the story. Sometimes they shoot the last scenes first. It's all put together in the cutting room. That's where they paste together the different scenes in the order the film editor decides on."

"Sounds like that guy, the film editor, has a lot of control over the way a movie turns out."

"Well, he does. Even if he follows the story line in a script, he can put his own ideas on a scene by choosing which takes are shown in the scene. They may shoot a half dozen different versions of a scene, and the film editor makes the decision in the cutting room about which one will go into the final version of the movie. He can sometimes turn a minor character into an important one or play down a main character. He has a lot of power. Of course, the director keeps an eye on what he's doing, so he can't always get away with murder, unless the director is outvoted by the production company."

Link shook his head. "Sounds complicated to me. Guess there are politics and personality clashes like in any business. You sure seem to know a lot about it."

"Pretty much," Ginger admitted, pleased that something about her had impressed him. "I've grown up on movie lots."

"Well, maybe you can explain something else to me." He pointed to the camera crew at the end of the block. "That guy that comes out with the little slate board and says something about scene so and so, take so and so and slams the white boards on top of the blackboard together—why does he do that? Looks to me like he's taking a chance. If he got his fingers between those two little boards when he slaps them together, he'd have him a busted finger."

Ginger giggled. "He's the marker. In European films they call him the clapper-loader. He's part of the camera crew. First there's the foreman of the camera crew, the director of photography, or the D.P. He has to be an expert in lighting. Then there's the camera operator, the guy who sits behind the camera and looks through the viewfinder. He has first and second assistant cameramen. One focuses the camera lens, the other one loads film into the camera and claps the sticks together on top of the little blackboard at the start of a take. You see, at the time they're shooting a movie, the pictures are on film, but the sound is on a separate tape. Eventually they have to put the pictures and sound together and synchronize the two. The sound of those boards slapping together gives them a point of reference. When they get the picture to match up with the slap of the boards, then the sound will be synchronized with the action in the rest of the scene."

"Well, I always wondered about that. Any time I saw a story on TV about filming a movie or a scene like that in another movie, they always have the little guy come out with that clapper. I'm sure glad to find out why he does that."

"Anything else you want to know?"

"Yeah. Whatever gave you the notion to become a stunt girl? Isn't that kind of a dangerous job for a young lady?"

Ginger shrugged. "They need women doing stunts

in movies just like they do men. I want to get in the business somehow, and I can't act. But I like action stuff. I've always been athletic. You have to be in good shape to do stunts."

Link's eyes surveyed her with a teasing glint. "Nothin' wrong with your shape, Ginger."

She reacted with a pleasant warm flush, but at the same time she felt a measure of chagrin. She would have preferred less of a big brother, teasing attitude and more genuine male interest.

She remembered Wild Bill's dour warning, *"Anyway, he's too old for you."* She longed for a magic potion that would instantly make her several years older. Maybe then Link would stop treating her like a child.

At that point, the director interrupted their conversation. They were ready to film the action scene in which she would crash through the window. For the next hour, she concentrated on the job at hand. She had never before in her life tried so hard. For one thing, she felt an urgent need to please the stunt coordinator and the director. This was her first professional appearance before the cameras. If she goofed up the stunt, it might be a long time before Redcloud would trust her again. And for another thing, she knew Link was out there somewhere across the street, watching.

They carefully went over the action sequence several times with the director and the camera crew.

The director explained, "In this shot, the heroine has gone into the saloon to find the hero. The whole town is out to get them. Somebody has set a dynamite charge to blow up the saloon. When it goes off, it knocks her through a window. On the sidewalk, she staggers to her feet. Then some men on a

roof across the street begin shooting at her. She runs
down the sidewalk, dodging bullets, still half
stunned from the explosion. We have charges set all
down the walk to look like bullets striking. There'll
be stuff flying all around you. When you reach the
end of the block—and, now, this is important—
you've been hit. That's when you press the trigger in
your hand that sets off the squibb under your shirt.
You slam into a wall, grabbing your shoulder. Remember, you've been hit with a rifle bullet. That
carries enough force to knock a person over. You
take a staggering step or two away from the wall,
then sprawl in the dust of the street. At that point, a
stunt man on a horse, doubling for the hero, is going
to come down Main Street in a gallop, also dodging
bullets. He's supposed to pick you up without slowing down much. When you see him, you pull yourself up to a crouch. He leans way down from his
saddle, grabs you and carries you with him. Have
you got all that?"

Ginger nodded, knowing the rider on the horse
would be Link.

"Think you can do it?"

Ginger swallowed hard, wiped her perspiring
palms on her jeans and nodded.

"All right, let's go, people. We're losing the sun."

The assistant director called through his bullhorn,
"This is a four-camera shot—cameras A, B, C and
D. Scene number thirty-five. Take one."

Then it was time to shoot the scene. If it wasn't
right, time would be lost in putting a new breakaway
window in the saloon and doing it over. And in
film-making, time was money.

Ginger stood behind the window on a springboard
device Redcloud had rigged up that, when released,

would hurl Ginger tumbling through the window. She concentrated on getting herself psyched up. She was perspiring from tension as much as from the afternoon Texas heat. Redcloud was a few feet away, watching her closely. The cameras were set up outside. Through the open saloon door they could hear the director call, "Action! Roll 'em!"

"Now!" the old one-eyed stunt coordinator snapped.

The muscles in her firm, well-trained young body went into action. She crouched. Redcloud triggered the springboard. The jolt threw her into the window. At the same time, she was deafened by the explosion of black powder charges and smoke bombs. She came hurtling through the window, the fake, break-away panes bursting with the splintering crash of glass around her. She had executed the blind dive through the window like going off a board at a pool. But instead of landing in water, she crashed down on a realistically designed pile of boxes and barrels made out of cardboard that cushioned her fall. She made a perfectly executed shoulder roll, then came to her feet. It didn't take much pretense to stagger. She felt half dazed and deafened from the charges that had knocked other windows and doors out of the saloon. She started her run down the sidewalk. Splinters flew around her head and feet as small charges in the walls and the board sidewalk were set off to simulate a volley of rifle bullets. Almost instinctively, she veered from side to side, dodging the imaginary fusillade.

She reached the end of the block.

Now, she thought, and squeezed the triggering device clutched in her hand. The squibb under her shirt exploded outward, giving a chillingly realistic effect of a bullet tearing through her body. She spun around, slamming against a wall, clutching her shoulder. Then she staggered two steps forward and fell into the dust of the street. She barely hit the dirt before she heard the thudding of a horse's galloping hooves. She pushed herself to her knees, looking around. In a blur, she saw the rider coming toward her at an incredible speed. She stood up in a half crouch. Link swooped down low from his saddle. The impact as he scooped her up slammed the breath out of her and jarred every bone in her body. The earth spun away before her wide, terrified eyes. She clutched at the arm holding her like it was her last grasp on life.

Then the horse slowed to a trot. Link was looking down at her, grinning. "You okay, Ginger?"

"Yes," she nodded breathlessly, feeling protected and secure in his powerful arms.

He startled her by placing a light, friendly kiss on her lips. Then he eased her to her feet.

People were suddenly crowding around her, patting her shoulder, shouting congratulations. She felt dazed as much by Link's surprise kiss as by the excitement she had been through. Her mouth tingled from the imprint of his lips.

The director came up to her. He was smiling broadly. "Nice, Ginger. Real nice." To the camera crew, he said, "Okay, that's a take. You can break down your equipment. That's the final scene."

Her heart swelled with relief and pride. She caught sight of Wild Bill Redcloud coming out of the saloon, coughing from the dust and smoke of the faked explosion.

Ginger ran up to him. "The director said I did a nice job!" she cried excitedly.

"Yeah, it'll do."

"What do you mean, it'll do? I was darn good. So was Link. Didn't you think Link was just super, the way he did that horse gag?"

Wild Bill grunted. "What do you want, an Oscar? Don't go gettin' the swell head. Jumping through a window isn't that big a deal. You still got a lot to learn."

But she knew the crusty old stuntman well enough now to discern a barely hidden gleam of pride in his eyes.

"Now maybe I can start getting more stunt jobs?"

He shrugged. "Yeah, maybe."

His gruff manner did not dampen Ginger's enthusiasm one bit. She knew now it would just be a matter of time before she would be working as a full-time stunt woman.

The filming was completed that afternoon, several days ahead of schedule, which put the producers in a generous state of bliss. They threw a party that night for the camera crew and actors. It was a border-style fiesta, tables laden with barbecued beef, corn on the cob and pinto beans under lights strung between mesquite trees on the side of a dance hall. In the hall, a western string band played for dancing. Kegs of beer and buckets of iced champagne slaked the crowd's thirst.

Derrick Lombard was in an expansive mood. He had a leading role in the movie, which promised to be a box office hit. And Ginger's initiation into film-making that afternoon was the talk of the movie company. Derrick put his arm around his daughter, waving a champagne glass in a grandiose manner, telling everyone within earshot that he now had two daughters with promising movie careers: Paige, who was sure to become a big star; and Ginger, who had a brilliant career as a stunt woman ahead of her.

Ginger's heart pumped with happiness. For this kind of attention from her father she would have dived through a saloon window made of real glass!

Then she caught sight of Link on the fringe of the crowd with the other extras who had been invited. Her heart soared even higher. But it took a nose dive a moment later when she saw he had brought a date, the redheaded waitress, Martha Delaney.

Ginger looked at them sullenly, not believing for one minute Link's assurance the other day that the redhead was not his girl friend.

She stayed away from them, eating barbecue with friends. One of the cameramen invited her to dance. She tried to work off her jealousy with fast-stepping polkas until she was out of breath. Then the band played a slow waltz. Suddenly a bronzed hand touched the shoulder of her partner. "You folks allow a friend to cut in?" a familiar voice asked.

Ginger looked wide-eyed up into the face of Link Ireland. The next thing she knew his strong arms were around her. This time it was not the dance that made her breathless. The pressure of his strong body burned through her flimsy sun dress. He danced lightly. She felt as if her feet never touched the floor.

"I watched you come through that saloon window this afternoon," Link said. "You're really good. How come you didn't get all cut up?"

"Oh, it wasn't real glass. And the window frame is made to break away easily."

"Well, it sure looked like real glass."

"I know. They used to make it out of sugar. Now they make it out of a special kind of plastic, melted and poured on top of a hot aluminum table. They make sheets of it that way. You can crumble it in your hand, and it won't cut you."

He said, "When the movie comes out, I can tell all my buddies that I knew the young lady who came sailing through that window. And I was the guy on the horse who picked her up. 'Course, they won't believe me. They'll think it was the hero who saved you."

"Yes, and they'll swear it was the heroine who got blown through the saloon window. That's the price of being a stunt person. You take the risks, and the stars get the glory."

"Then why do it?"

"I don't know. Because I'm crazy, I guess. Anyway, the pay is good." They danced in silence for a while. Ginger prayed that the waltz would never end. A question was burning her lips but was held back by a wave of shyness. Finally she could stand it no longer and blurted out, "Why did you kiss me this afternoon?"

"Oh, I don't know. Seemed like the thing to do at the time, the way we carried off that stunt so well together and all. Did you mind?"

She shook her head, looking up at him, her eyes wide. "No," she whispered. "No . . . I didn't mind."

"It was just meant to be a friendly kiss."

"I . . . I understand," she said, feeling somehow let down.

The waltz ended.

He smiled, "Well, thanks for the dance, Ginger. I guess you folks will be packing up and going back to Hollywood tomorrow. I probably won't see you again. I wanted to thank you again for helping me get that job as an extra and to tell you good-bye."

Ginger suddenly felt very sad. "This . . . this dancing has made me thirsty. Let's go outside and get something to drink."

They were under the stars. A full moon shone through the branches of a mesquite tree overhead. Ginger looked at it and then at Link.

He had brought her a soft drink and popped the tab on a can of beer for himself.

They were joined by Derrick, who was carrying around his champagne bottle. "Well," he exclaimed, "the cowboy and the stunt girl!"

Ginger blushed. "Derrick—"

He held up a hand, shushing her. His eyes were glassy, his face flushed. But his speech was clear. "Well, cowboy, now you're in the movies."

Link responded with his lopsided grin. "Just barely. But I want to thank you, Mr. Lombard, for getting me that job. I can always use a few extra bucks. Besides it was fun. I've already thanked Ginger for putting a word in for me with you."

"Yes, I understand you saved her from drowning in a horse watering trough," Derrick said, giving Link a thoughtful look. "Y'know, cowboy, I've had my eye on you. I saw some rushes of the scenes you were in. You photograph extremely well. Something about your looks and manner interests me. In some ways you remind me of the late Gary Cooper. He was before your time, but perhaps you've seen his movies on late night TV."

"Yes sir, I have. Never thought I looked like him though."

"Well, you have a touch of his relaxed, soft-spoken, polite manner and a wholesome outdoorsy quality one doesn't see much these days. But there's something else, too—a kind of casual, what-the-heck attitude, as if you're shrugging your shoulders at the whole stuffy, meaningless pretense of life. Tell me, Link, have you ever been in jail?"

"In jail?" Link raised an eyebrow. "Not exactly. The constable did break up a barroom fracas one night and put some of us in the lock-up to cool off. But he let us out the next morning. Why?"

"Nothing, really. It's just that you look like the physical type who could take care of himself with his fists if he had to. I was just curious, that's all. Y'know, son, you really ought to come back to Hollywood with us. I have a producer friend who is going to start shooting a pilot for a TV western series. He might be able to use someone like you. I could arrange for you to have a screen test made. Then I could put in a word with my friend, the producer. You might land a pretty nice part there."

"What?" Link gazed at Derrick in total amazement. "A screen test? Me? What on earth for? I don't know anything about acting."

"Of course you don't. Not all screen stars are actors, you see. Some of them are personalities. You could possibly become one of those. Oh, you'd need some stage training. That could be arranged. The thing of it is, you caught my eye in those scenes. And you look so damn macho on a horse—just what this guy needs for the TV part I'm thinking about. You'd be natural, convincing. I think a screen test would bear me out."

Ginger was scrutinizing her father, her eyes narrowed, trying to fathom this surprising development. Was it the champagne talking, she wondered. When Derrick got in one of his expansive moods, as he was over his part in the movie just completed, and went on a binge to celebrate, he tended to make outrageous statements and extravagant promises.

Someone called his name, and he wandered off to join a group of actors.

Link swung his gaze to Ginger. He looked a bit dazed. "Do you think he meant it?"

Ginger raised her hands in a baffled gesture. "It's a little hard to say what my father means at a time like this. But he knows film-making. If he says you have screen potential, there has to be some truth in it."

"D'you suppose it's the champagne talking?"

"Partly," she admitted candidly. "But at the same time, I don't think it's all hot air. Why don't you take him up on it, Link? What have you got to lose?" She was excited at the prospect of Link's coming to Hollywood, if only for a screen test. This might not be the last night she'd see him, after all.

"I don't know," Link murmured, slowly shaking his head. "My job isn't much, but it pays the beans. I'd have to give it up for what is probably a wild goose chase. Do you really think he could give me a shot at a TV part? Has he got that much pull?"

"Oh, you'd better believe it. Derrick Lombard has a lot of pull with certain studios and producers."

Link grinned. He tossed his empty beer can at a garbage can, hitting it dead center. "Then what the heck! Hollywood, here I come!"

Chapter Five

*L*ink flew back to Hollywood with Derrick and
Ginger. Derrick's promise of a screen test did not
evaporate with the champagne. The test confirmed
the Lombard eye for talent. He then introduced
Link to his friend, the TV producer. The result was a
role for Link in the pilot film, which in turn was
picked up by a major network and ran a full season.
That show became the first step in Link's rise to
stardom, the first installment in one of those legends
that keep star-struck youngsters pouring into Hollywood every year with the dream that theirs, too, will
become another one-in-a-million success story.

Derrick considered Link his discovery, his prote-
ge. Taking the broad-shouldered Texan under his
wing, he urged Link to take the stage name of
"Rockwood," arranged acting lessons, got him a
reliable agent.

Link's returning to Hollywood with them was a
miracle for Ginger, a happening like one out of the
pages of a love story movie script. She imagined all
kinds of beautiful, happy endings to the story. As
Link's career blossomed, she would become a famous stunt girl. One day she would be working the

same movie with Link. He would be the leading man. She would be in a scene, doubling for the heroine, doing some kind of car wreck. With the cameras rolling, Link would gently take her limp body from the wreckage. Just before the director yelled "Cut!" Link would gaze into her eyes, and there would be a sudden chorus of heavenly voices, a flash of realization that he had loved her from the beginning. She would be older by then, a real woman. The director would say something about the scene being over, but Link would keep holding her, and he would whisper, "Ginger . . . darling, I love you." And then he would kiss her.

But the story did not come true. There was no such happy ending.

Paige came into Ginger's love story.

It happened very early in the scenario, in the very first scene. They had just gotten back from the Alamo village location. Derrick was putting Link up at their home. At that time, "home" was a mansion in Beverly Hills. Ginger showed Link around the premises. It was late afternoon. She and Link were sitting under a large umbrella beside the pool. They'd gone for a swim and were having tall glasses of iced tea.

Suddenly Paige appeared in the gateway from the garage area, returning home after a day before the cameras at a studio set. She came in, walking toward them with just a hint of a swing of her hips. When she reached them, her huge, dark eyes swept over Link, engulfing him. Her gaze touched his curly hair, his eyes, lips and chin and then his wide shoulders, his muscular frame, the rippling muscles and bronzed skin of a man used to horses, hard work and rough play. Her face flushed, and she drew a deep breath that strained her full bosom against the sheer fabric of a flimsy blouse. As if reluctant to leave him, her gaze slowly pulled away toward Ginger.

"Hi, sis," she murmured in her sultry, husky voice. "I see you're back from the wide open spaces."

"Yes, we're back," Ginger said slowly, with an empty feeling growing in the pit of her stomach.

"How did the horse opera go?"

"Okay," Ginger murmured. She was looking at Link, and the emptiness in her stomach turned into a painful knot. Link's gaze was fixed on Paige as if he were hypnotized. Small wonder, Ginger thought bitterly. A man would have to be in the last stages of senility not to look at her glamorous sister like that. Paige was a walking charge of female allure. The combination of her long black hair, draped over one shoulder, and her enormous dark eyes made her flawless complexion glow. The tempting smooth flesh of her arms and legs with their creamy texture would surely inflame any male imagination into visualizing what her body must look like under the clinging garments.

Ginger gritted her teeth, knowing for certain Link was mentally undressing her sister. And from the bright shine in Paige's eyes and her quickened breath, it was obvious that Paige knew it, too.

Reluctantly, Ginger made the introduction. "Link, this is my sister. Paige, this is Link Ireland. He came back with us from Texas. Derrick wants him to take a screen test."

Paige ran her tongue over her lips, her wide eyes inviting. "Well . . . what they say about those big, handsome Texans is obviously true. Welcome to Hollywood, Link."

"Thanks," Link drawled, seemingly unable to pull his gaze from hers.

"You'll have to let me show you the sights."

"Okay."

Ginger struggled to keep tears from forming in her eyes. The main sights Paige had in mind to show Link were the details of her own alluring anatomy, Ginger thought furiously. From the moment Paige came into the scene, Ginger knew she had evaporated into thin air, as far as Link was concerned.

Well, small wonder. She was only eighteen, a kid to Link's eyes. Paige was a woman, with a woman's knowledge in her eyes. Paige had always been a woman, Ginger thought. Paige had skipped being a teenager. The look in her eye was as old as Eve. And Link was ready to bite the apple.

Fighting hard to keep her voice from breaking, Ginger said, "I guess I'll go in and dress."

In the doorway, she glanced back once. Link and Paige were totally engrossed with each other. He hadn't even been aware of her leaving.

For Link, it was love at first sight. He was immediately infatuated with Paige, an infatuation that became an obsession during the next year. Ginger stood by helplessly and watched with mingled heartbreak and jealousy as Paige wrapped Link around her finger.

It didn't make Ginger feel any better about the situation to worry that Link was letting himself in for a lot of grief by falling blindly in love with Paige. It wasn't just sour grapes. Ginger cared so much for Link that she wanted him to be happy even if she couldn't have him. And she had grave misgivings about his finding any lasting joy with Paige. Ginger knew all about Paige's track record with men, and although the glamorous actress was her sister and Ginger loved her for that reason, she was also realistic about Paige's shortcomings.

Paige had already been through a teenage marriage at sixteen that had lasted only six months. Since then she'd had a series of romances that she'd breezed through with careless disregard for anyone's feelings but her own.

Ginger hated to admit it about her own sister, but though Paige was incredibly beautiful and talented, she was also narcissistic, selfish and fickle.

Ginger began to wish they had never brought Link to Hollywood. In spite of his rough, macho edges, there was an element of small-town naiveté in his makeup. He had a tendency to trust people and believe the best of them. He trusted Paige. He believed in her. And she wound up breaking his heart.

As the months passed, Ginger's career as a stunt girl blossomed. She was beginning to work steadily and to build a reputation for tackling anything.

"You take too many chances," Wild Bill grumbled. "You're not going to live to be an old lady at this rate—or even a young lady."

"Live fast, die young and make a good-looking corpse," Ginger quipped breezily.

Her mentor's single eye regarded her thoughtfully and for once looked sad instead of glaring at her. "Kid, he isn't worth it. No guy is worth it."

Ginger felt her cheeks redden. "I don't know what you're talking about," she stammered.

"Sure you do. I'm talkin' about that cowboy and your sister, Paige. What do you think—I took so many falls on the head I don't know what's goin' on? Remember, I helped raise you. I know what you're thinking half the time before you do. I saw you tumble for that horse wrangler back in Texas. You never got over him, right?"

Ginger said furiously, "You nosey old—"

"Yeah, I know. Go ahead and call me names. Won't change anything. Link's had the hots for your sister, Paige, ever since he laid eyes on her. And you're eating your heart out over it. She's gettin' to be a big star, while you're grinding your face in the dirt doin' risky stunts, doubling for her and other prima donnas. Meanwhile, Link's career is taking off. Latest thing I heard is that he's tooling around town in a fancy sports car, wearin' imported Italian shoes instead of scuffed cowboy boots, and he just bought Paige a diamond engagement ring as big as the baseballs he used to throw on the sand lots back home."

The anger went out of Ginger. Her shoulders slumped, and she blinked quickly to clear the tears from her vision. She didn't feel like fighting with the old stunt man anymore. She just nodded numbly. "Yes, they're engaged. . . ."

Wild Bill growled something deep in his throat. Clumsily, he patted Ginger's hand. It was the first time in her life he had made any gesture of affection. "You got your own life to lead. If you're goin' to do stunts, you can't have your mind on Paige and Link, or you'll wind up dead."

Then he muttered a string of expletives that turned the air blue, sent a charge of tobacco juice sluicing into the dust at his feet and stomped off.

It was to be a June wedding. The studio publicity department pulled out all the stops. PAIGE LOMBARD TO WED LINK ROCKWOOD. Big news for all the fan magazines. The studio offered to pick up the tab for an elaborate ceremony. Link, and Paige were on late night talk shows, telling the world about their plans.

Ginger wished she could avoid them. Every time she saw them together, the knife in her heart twisted. But they were too much a part of her life for her to hide from them. She saw Paige at home every day. Link had been almost like a member of the family ever since Ginger's father had brought him to Hollywood. He had a key to their home and breezed in and out as casually as if he lived there. Derrick was pleased about the wedding plans. He had taken a special liking to Link from the beginning, treating him like the son he never had. He welcomed Link into the family circle with open arms.

Link's attitude toward Ginger hadn't changed from the time he'd picked her spluttering and kicking out of the horse watering trough. He displayed an amused, tolerant, protective big brother feeling about her. He never guessed how she felt about him. And she took pains to keep it hidden from him.

One afternoon, she ran into him at their swimming pool. He'd gone for a dip and was sitting on the edge of the pool, dangling his feet in the water. Drops of moisture still clung to his shoulders and glistened like diamonds in the curly, dark hair on his broad chest.

Ginger gathered her strength and forced herself to walk up to him. It was one of the rare occasions he was not with Paige.

"Hi," she murmured. "Working on your tan?"

"Hi, Ginger. Yeah. Why don't you get into a swimsuit and join me? Great weather for it."

She swallowed the hurting lump in her throat. His soft drawl never failed to awaken the soft, glowing feeling inside her. But she tried not to think about that now. She had a painful task to do.

"Link, I haven't had a chance yet to . . . to congratulate you and wish you happiness."

"Well, that's sweet of you, Ginger. I know I'm going to be happy. I guess I'm about the luckiest guy around. Y'know what I was sitting here thinking about when you walked up?"

"No. What?"

He smiled his slow, lopsided grin. "Just how crazy life is. How one little day can change the whole thing and start you off on a whole new ball game. For me it was the day that you rode into the Alamo village and my silly old dog spooked that palomino you were riding. If that hadn't happened, I'd still be back there working at some piddling job, drinking beer on Saturday night and pitching baseball on Sunday. Now here I am, making more money than I ever dreamed there was in the world, with a part in a weekly TV series, my picture in fan magazines and people coming up asking for my autograph. And now about to marry a movie star who is one of the most beautiful women in the world. It all seems like a dream. I swear I keep thinking I'm going to wake up any minute with a hangover back in Uncle Jefferson's old frame house."

Ginger nodded sadly. "Life can get pretty screwed up," she agreed softly.

But Link was too absorbed in his euphoria to notice the sadness and irony in her reply.

Link did wake up from his dream with a cold shock. Ginger heard the rumors on movie sets even before the scandal magazines got the story. Paige had suddenly become involved with an Italian director. Ginger went home one night to find her glamorous sister in a frenzy of packing. She was taking an early flight to Rome, she explained. She had been offered a role in a movie to be directed by her latest romantic interest. It was a major role in what promised to be a large-budget, important motion picture.

Ginger gazed at her sister. Paige's dark eyes were sparkling, her face aglow and animated. Ginger had never seen her more beautiful. With a flash of insight she realized that Paige lived from one of life's peaks to the next. Only in these moments of exhilaration was she truly alive. She demanded the most intense highs life could offer and became bored and restless with anything less.

"What about Link?" Ginger asked quietly.

Paige hesitated in her packing. Was there a flash of guilt in her eyes? "Link was a mistake, Ginger," she stammered. "I . . . I don't think it would have worked."

"He's . . . going to be badly hurt," Ginger said, unable to disguise a tremor in her voice. "He's very much in love with you."

"I know," Paige sighed. She suddenly sat on the edge of the bed, her eyes filling with tears. "I don't mean to hurt him, Ginger." She gazed at her sister with a helpless expression. "But he'd be hurt even more if I went on seeing him, feeling the way I do now. You understand that, don't you?"

Ginger swallowed a painful lump. She sighed, engulfed by a strange mixture of emotion. Then she sat on the bed beside Paige and impulsively put her arm around her sister. Her feelings toward Paige were conflicting, ambivalent. At times she almost hated Paige for her fickleness and selfishness. Then a wave of love swept aside the negative emotions. She supposed it could only be explained by the old cliche that blood was indeed thicker than water.

Paige was not an evil person. She was just Paige, one of those incredibly beautiful creatures that fate allowed the world to have from time to time to satisfy its hunger for sex goddesses. Paige was the dream men dreamed of sexual perfection.

But Ginger's memory, going back to when they were children, bound them together in ways denied to the adoring fans. No matter how much Paige's worshippers wanted to search out every hidden corner of her daily life, they could never share the childhood memories Ginger had of herself and Paige growing up together.

Accepting her sister with all her shortcomings, however, did not soften Ginger's concern over the present situation. "Have you told Link?" she asked, well aware that Paige's usual method of handling an awkward situation was to simply hide from it.

"Link is making things very sticky," Paige sighed.

"Then he knows."

"Oh, sure. He can certainly be unpleasant."

"Well, you can't exactly blame him."

"He's the physical type, you know, and very jealous. When he found out I was seeing Alberto Mastroni, he threatened to beat him up."

Ginger grinned in spite of herself. "Well, I suppose that's what men tend to do back where Link comes from."

Paige didn't think it very funny. "I'm really afraid of what he might do. He's going around drinking and making all kinds of threats. That's why I want to get away from here. I was so relieved when I was offered this part in Italy."

"Paige, just how have you handled this situation with Link?" Ginger demanded.

Paige's gaze slid away. "I don't know what you mean."

"What I mean, is have you had a talk with him, tried to explain how you feel? Link is a reasonable, sane man. He's not going to break your neck or anything, although I can understand why he'd like to."

"I'm not too sure about that," Paige said nervously.

"Well, you haven't answered my question."

"No, I haven't had any kind of heart-to-heart talk with him, if that's what you mean," Paige said sullenly. Again she looked at Ginger with an expression of helplessness. "I don't know what to say to Link. I still care about him, too, Ginger. I don't know. I'm all mixed up. I guess the truth is I'm in love with two men at the same time."

"That's exactly what I thought!" Ginger exclaimed. "Now I'm beginning to get the picture. You've been stringing Link along while you've been seeing your Italian friend at the same time." Ginger pointed at Paige's ring finger. "You're still wearing Link's engagement ring!" she cried. "No wonder Link is mad and jealous and threatening to sock the other guy."

Paige bit her lip. Suddenly she twisted the diamond ring from her finger and thrust it into Ginger's palm. "I just can't confront Link. I never was any good at breaking off an affair. You're very close to Link, Ginger. You're like a kid sister to him. Will you please give him the ring and explain things to him for me?"

Ginger felt a wave of anger. "I don't know why I should have to do your dirty work."

She tried to give the ring back to her sister, but Paige pushed her hand away. "Please, Ginger. You're not involved in this like I am. You can talk with Link in a calm, reasonable way."

Tears stung Ginger's vision. *Not involved!* It was so typical of Paige to be too wrapped up in her own interests to be totally blind to the obvious—that Ginger was in love with Link, too.

"I thought you said a minute ago that you couldn't make up your mind between Link and Mastroni . . . that you were in love with both men."

"Yes, but I don't want to be engaged to Link anymore. He's too possessive. Ginger, I have to be free for a while to find my own mind. Tell Link that I'm going to Rome to get away to think things through . . . to get my own feelings sorted out."

"You know he won't believe that for a minute. When I hand him this ring back and tell him you're going to Italy with your director friend, it's going to be obvious that you've made your choice—that you've run off to have an affair with Mastroni."

"Well, perhaps it's best that way after all." Paige sighed. "It's what I want to do. Right now I have to be with Mastroni. He's all I can think about. Ginger, he's the most dynamic man I've ever met. You should see the way he takes control of a film set. When he's directing, actors come alive. He can bring out talent in me that I never dreamed I possessed. Link arouses me physically, it's true. I can be very passionate with Link. He's all man, very sure of himself, yet tender. But he knows nothing, really, about acting and film-making. With Mastroni directing, coaching, teaching me, I can become an actress, a real actress, a star.

"Link's future is very uncertain, you know. He has this role in the TV series, but the network ratings haven't been all that good. It looks as if the series is going to be cancelled after the first season. Link will be out of a job. I . . . I don't want to be tied down to a loser, especially when this great opportunity is opening up for my own career."

Ginger stared at her sister, struck anew by the extent of Paige's selfishness and ruthless ambition.

Early the next morning, Ginger was awakened by a banging on the downstairs front door. She was alone in the house. Derrick was away for the week. Paige had taken a cab to the airport.

Groggily, Ginger slipped into a robe and went downstairs. She peered through a magnifying eye-piece in the door. With a cold shock, she recognized a disheveled, unshaven Link Rockwood.

Hastily, she unlocked the door.

Link thrust his way inside, brushing past her. "Where's Paige?" he demanded thickly.

Ginger stared at Link. She found it hard to believe the man she was looking at was Link Rockwood. His face was haggard, deeply lined. His eyes were blood-shot.

"Link, for heaven's sake, take it easy. Sit down. I'll make some coffee. You look like you could use some."

Her words didn't appear to register. "Ginger, I have to talk to Paige. Right now." His voice was harsh, demanding. There was a look in his eyes that reminded her of the time at the carnival in Texas when the carnival man tried to get out of giving her the panda bear prize.

Trying to sound calm, Ginger said, "That's impossible, Link. Paige isn't here."

"Where is she?"

Ginger bit her lip. She knew there was no easy way to break the news to Link. "I would say," she told him, "that right about now she's getting ready to board an airliner."

Link's face paled. His jaws knotted. "Then what I heard is right. She's going to Italy with that director."

Ginger made a helpless gesture.

Link turned and stormed out of the door.

Ginger ran after him, grabbing his arm. "You wait just a darn minute, Link Rockwood. Where do you think you're going?"

"To the airport. Gonna try and talk some sense into her," he mumbled. "I'm not going to let her get on that plane."

"You're in no shape to drive a car!" she cried. "Look at you. You haven't been to bed all night. You've obviously spent the night in a bar. I'm surprised you made it this far in one piece."

He tried to shake her hand from his arm, but she held onto him stubbornly. "No, Link!"

"Ginger, don't make me get rough with you," he said, his face growing dark with anger.

"Just try it," she retorted. "I have a black belt in karate, and as drunk as you are now, I'd flatten you."

Their eyes locked. Some of the rage in Link's eyes softened. "You might just at that," he muttered. Then he said, "Ginger, I'm sorry. I have no business taking out my feelings on you. You're a good little kid."

I'm not so little, and I'm not a kid, she thought

bitterly, *and I wish to heaven you'd stop thinking of me that way.* Aloud she said, "Now, be reasonable, Link. Come in the house and let me make some coffee."

But he remained stubborn. "No, I have to get to the airport. I have to talk to Paige . . . try to get her to change her mind."

"Well, I don't think you could possibly get there before the plane takes off. But I can see you're too stubborn to listen to reason. At least, I'm going to drive."

"I can get there faster by myself," he said and walked unsteadily toward his sports car, which was parked half on the driveway, half in a flower bed.

"Oh yeah? You seem to forget that part of the way I make a living is by driving cars fast."

She finally succeeded in talking Link into the passenger side of the sports car while she got behind the wheel. She knew the trip to the airport was futile. By now Paige's plane would be taking off. But in Link's condition, the best approach seemed to be to humor him. So she used her driving skill to whip the fast little sports car through traffic at record speed. As they drove, Link took a bottle from under the seat.

Ginger's heart wrenched to see him in this condition, but he was not the kind of man who took orders from anyone. The best she could do at a time like this was to try and keep him from killing himself.

She prayed Paige's flight was not delayed. She shuddered at the kind of scene that would take place in the airport if Paige and her Italian friend were still there when Link stormed in.

Her prayers were answered. The plane had departed on time. Paige and Alberto Mastroni were airborne and on their way to Italy.

Back in the car, Link slumped in the seat with a look of total defeat. His silence gave Ginger a worried chill. She would have preferred to hear him curse and rage. Instead he just stared blankly into space and gulped drinks from his bottle.

Ginger's heart ached for the pain she saw in his eyes. She loved Link. She thought she should be happy that Paige had jilted him. But she couldn't rejoice over the pain he was feeling. Right now her mood toward her sister had gravitated to fury.

She drove them back to the Lombard home at a more legal speed. There she was able to talk Link into the house, but he refused to eat anything or drink the coffee she made. He seemed determined to drink himself into a state of oblivion.

Ginger tried talking with him, explaining the conversation she'd had with Paige last night. She even made an attempt to explain Paige's actions as they related to her personality and character. She had the eerie feeling that she was talking to a zombie. Link seemed to have shut himself off in a private world where he was wrestling in some kind of emotional life-or-death struggle.

In as kind a way as she could, Ginger got the engagement ring from a drawer and gave it to Link. He stared at it for several minutes without a word, then shrugged and thrust it into a pocket.

A bitter smile twisted his lips. "Just like in the movies. Boy meets girl. Boy loses girl. Except this story doesn't have a happy ending. Boy doesn't get girl back in the end. Looks like my Cinderella Hollywood success story will fizzle out, too. I got word that the network has cancelled the western TV series. The ratings were good, but not good enough. We shot the last episode yesterday."

"Oh, Link, I'm sorry."

"Heck, it's no big deal. I can always go back to Brackettville and find a job herding cows. At least I'll go back something of a local celebrity."

Suddenly a change came over him. There was a reckless glint in his eyes. His lips moved in a wry expression. "Oh, what the hell," he said. "It won't make any difference a hundred years from today, right? Y'know what let's do? Let's go have a party!"

"A party?"

"Sure. Why the hell not? Why sit around and. mope over a two-timing little tramp like Paige. Uh . . . sorry. I forgot she's your sister."

"That's all right. At the moment, I'm not sure I want to claim her."

Link was gazing at Ginger, making an effort to focus his eyes. "Y'know something else, little Ginger? In this whole rat race I got myself into here in Hollywood, you're the only real friend I've got. Oh, I got plenty of buddies that hang around and drink my booze. But you're real. You're genuine. When you say something, I know you mean it. Nobody else in this crazy business says what they really mean. Come on. Let's find a place that serves martinis for breakfast."

Ginger wasn't sure she liked the sudden reckless mood he was in any more than the depression that had swamped him earlier. "Link, I can't just go chasing off on some kind of crazy binge," she laughed uneasily. "I have a whole day of stunt work ahead of me, shooting a car chase scene for a TV commercial."

Link snapped his fingers. "Of course. Forgot you were a working lady. I'll just go on by myself—"

"No, wait" she cried, aghast at the thought of Link driving on the freeway in his condition. "I'll . . . I'll call the studio. Maybe the stunt coordinator can find somebody else."

The stunt coordinator was furious. "Ginger, how dare you call me this time of the morning and say you can't work today? You know what the producer will do if I tell him we have to cancel the day's shooting? He'll break a chair over my head and then personally kill you!"

"Marty, this is an emergency. You know I wouldn't do this to you unless it was a matter of life or death. I can get a substitute. Linda Mavis could do the gag. She's great with cars, and she isn't working today. I'll call her."

"Well, if you can get Linda to do it . . . ." the stunt coordinator grumbled. "But if it was anybody but you, Ginger, I'd have you blackballed for pulling something like this."

"Yeah, but you love me, right?"

"I love the way you do stunts. Of course, if you want to discuss a more personal arrangement . . ."

"You wouldn't respect me in the morning, Marty."

"I'd respect you. I'd respect you."

Ginger grinned, relieved that she'd gotten the stunt coordinator over his anger. "I'll call Linda," she promised and hung up.

She made the arrangement for her substitute and quickly changed into slacks and a blouse. Considering the mood Link was in, she didn't want to leave him downstairs alone too long. She was afraid he might take it in his head to drive off without her.

She hastily applied a touch of makeup, then ran downstairs. Link directed her while she chauffered him on a round of his favorite haunts, where he consumed several bloody Marys. She drank coffee and worried about him.

He was behaving strangely, staring at her with a moody expression. Suddenly he said, "Ginger, I've got a great idea. Let's go to Mexico."

"Let's go to where?"

"Mexico. You know. 'Sou's of ze border.' Tamales. Enchiladas. Sombreros. Tequila. Lots of tequila. Do you know how to drink tequila, Ginger? See, you drink it straight, and then you suck on a lemon and lick some salt you put on the back of your hand. There's a little worm in the bottom of the bottle. Or is that mescal? I forget."

She laughed in spite of herself. "Link, you're acting crazy. I can't go to Mexico."

"Why not? Give me one good reason?"

She could think of a dozen, but when she looked at him, they didn't really matter that much. She was struggling with a storm of emotions stirred up by the implication of what he was suggesting. Alone with Link in romantic old Mexico. Suddenly she felt herself caught up once again in a Hollywood fantasy. It was all happening too fast. She couldn't keep up with the plot. Yesterday Link was engaged to marry her sister, Paige. Ginger had long ago buried her heartbreak in a secret corner of her being. Now, overnight, the producer had decided on an entirely new scenario. Paige was flying off to Italy. Ginger and Link had been thrown together. He was asking her to go to Mexico with him.

She wanted to say, "Okay, Link, so you're lonely and heartbroken because the woman you love walked out on you, and you're in the mood to fly off somewhere and do crazy things so it won't hurt so bad. Right now you need someone to talk with, to hold onto, and I happened to be a female who is handy and willing." But that was okay, she thought, swallowing her own pride and tears, because she was so crazy in love with Link that the only thing she cared about was being close to him. If her being with him would ease his hurt and make him feel better, that was okay. Because she'd be doing it for selfish reasons, too. She would pretend they were just a girl and her best fellow going on a wild weekend date, and she wouldn't count the cost until later. If he wanted her to sleep with him . . . she'd just have to cross that bridge when she came to it. But loving him the way she did. . . .

Those were the things she thought to herself. As she gave her head a reckless toss, she said aloud, "I might just take you up on that offer, Link. Where would we go? Tijuana?"

"Oh, heck no. That's where all the tourists go. I made good buddies with an actor on the TV series we just finished. He owns a place down on the west coast of Mexico not far from Acapulco. Said I could use the place for a weekend anytime I wanted. A regular villa. Or do they call it a hacienda down there? Anyway, it's a comfortable house overlooking the Pacific. Has a swimming pool. Hot and cold running servants. How about it? I'll promise to be a perfect gentleman, little Ginger. You don't have to worry about me makin' any passes or anything like that. This isn't a proposition. I've got too much respect for you for that. Heck, you're just like my own kid sister; you know that. It's just that I'm lonesome, and I can't think of anybody I'd rather pal

around with. We can go swimming, lie in the sun, go
into town and buy things in the markets—you know,
those little straw figures on burros and sombreros
with tassles—and maybe see a bullfight or something."

Ginger swallowed the lump in her throat, feeling
ridiculous and embarrassed at the romantic, sensuous fantasies that had flooded her mind moments
before. She didn't have to be concerned about
making any moral decisions about going to bed with
Link down in Mexico. Nothing had changed. As far
as he was concerned, she was a child, his kid sister,
as he said. He felt no more physical attraction for
her than for his horse! All he wanted now was a
buddy, a pal.

Well, all right, she thought, swallowing her tears.
She'd settle for that. She'd settle for just about
anything to be with him. And a persistent hope
whispered secretly that perhaps in a romantic
atmosphere . . . with them alone together . . . maybe—just maybe—the chemistry between them would
start to boil.

Ginger hastily packed an overnight bag. Then they
were on the freeway on their way to the airport.
"Why were you pounding on the door this morning?" Ginger asked. "You have a key to the house."

"Lost my key somewhere between bars last night.
Here, want a nip?"

He offered her his bottle.

"No thanks. I think one of us had better stay
sober. How much of that stuff are you planning to
drink?"

"Depends on how much there is. I've discovered
an interesting physio . . . physio . . . medical fact.

After you drink a certain amount, your brain turns off. You don't feel anything anymore. Very important discovery. Remind me to tell the medical profession about it."

"I'll remind the medical profession to check your liver when we get back," she said grimly.

They drove with the top down. The sun was warm on her shoulders. The wind blew her hair. Ginger tried to get an emotional grasp on the events that had abruptly turned all their lives upside down. She was alone with Link. They were going to Mexico for whatever reason. Link was running away from the pain of rejection. What was her reason? To be with Link, of course. What would happen in Mexico? She would have to wait until the next scene was played.

She smiled, realizing how her thought patterns had been conditioned to think in story terms: scenes, lighting, scenario, character, happy or sad endings. Dreams were the product of Hollywood. She had lived in the midst of making those dreams so many years that they had become ingrained in her thought processes.

Their plane landed in Mexico late that afternoon. Link had finally eaten a meal on the plane and then had slept during most of the flight. When they landed, Ginger was relieved to see him wake up reasonably sober.

At the Mexican airport, eager taxi drivers approached them. A smiling young man in a loud sport shirt, his hair thick and luxuriously black, his teeth flashing white against his bronze complexion, beat all the others to their bags. He told them in broken English that his name was Ramón, and he assured them that he had the best taxi in town, knew more about the area than all the other drivers put together and would be happy to take them anywhere and serve as their guide for a price that was negotiable.

Link, having grown up along the Mexican border, could speak Spanish as fluently as Ramón. The young taxi driver's grin spread even wider, and the two of them exchanged a rapid barrage of words, not one of which Ginger understood. But she assumed a bargain had been struck, because Ramón happily deposited their bags in his cab and opened the door for her with a flourish.

A half hour's drive took them out of town, over a winding, narrow mountain road fringed with palm and banana trees. The road stopped at a sprawling stucco home on a bluff overlooking the blue Pacific.

The view took Ginger's breath away. "It's beautiful!" she said with a gasp.

"Yeah," Link agreed with an expression of surprise. "Joe told me his place was pretty lavish, but I thought he was exaggerating."

"I don't know what he told you, but it would be hard to exaggerate this!"

The structure was a sprawling ranch-style home built of native adobe brick, its whitewashed surface blinding in the bright sunlight. It was surrounded by a wall covered with bright red bougainvillea. The roof was of rust-colored tile. From this vantage point, there was a steep slope to a beach of crystalline white sand onto which gentle breakers rolled.

They entered through a courtyard filled with lush tropical plants. The floor of the entrance hall was of gleaming tile.

Link's friend and host had called ahead to alert the servants. A tall, matronly woman with dignified

Aztec features, her jet black hair styled in a thick bun, greeted them. She was obviously the house-keeper. Again Link's ease with Spanish proved to be an asset, for none of the servants spoke any English.

Before leaving, Ramón assured Link in rapid Spanish and Ginger in fractured English that his cab would be at their beck and call day or night and gave a phone number by which he could be contacted.

The housekeeper led the way upstairs to their respective bedrooms.

Ginger was entranced with her room. The furni-ture was beautiful—dark, hand-carved mahogany in heavy, traditional Spanish style. It contrasted with spotless, white plastered walls. From her window, she had a view of the Pacific below.

She thought of the proximity of Link's bedroom, just across the hall, and felt a warm blush suffuse her body. She firmly put romantic daydreams aside and took a shower in the modern bathroom. It was a spacious chamber. In Mexico tile was a popular building material, she decided. The bathroom was in gleaming pink and white tile, obviously built by craftsmen who were artists at their trade.

Link's actor friend was apparently affluent to be able to afford such a lavish vacation home. But that was not surprising. He had a leading role in the TV series they had just completed and had numerous other major screen and TV credits.

Ginger reveled in a shower that caressed her body sensuously. She lathered herself from head to foot with a delicately scented soap, then let the water trickle down her body, between her breasts, gently washing away the rich lather. The warm, trickling stream mingling with the foaming soap gave her flesh a feeling of intimate pleasure. Then she switched the shower to stinging, cold needles and danced and giggled in the deluge. She emerged from the bath, pink from head to toe, tingling all over and feeling incredibly refreshed.

She added to the glowing pinkness of her body with a vigorous toweling. Then she splashed on cologne recklessly and dressed in a peasant blouse, skirt and sandals.

Ginger found Link downstairs. Bathed and shaved, there was a hundred percent improvement over his appearance from the hungover, disheveled character who had banged on her door early in the morning. He was dressed in form-fitting tan slacks that outlined his muscular thighs and hugged his firm backside and waist. A short-sleeved, knitted white shirt molded his broad shoulders and deep chest.

"You sure look cool and pretty, Ginger." He smiled.

"And you look like my favorite leading man," Ginger quipped, keeping her voice light to cover the real meaning of her words.

It suddenly struck her that the past months in Hollywood had made a lot of changes in Link. He still had the healthy, easygoing air of the horse rider from the Texas prairie, but some of his rough edges had been smoothed. He had a touch of sophistication now, a bit more of the self-assurance and polish of an urban man.

The housekeeper, Señora Alvarez, ushered them into the formal dining room, where they were served a meal that Ginger would have classified a banquet. A gleaming white linen cloth covered the long table. The centerpiece was an arrangement of lush tropical flowers. The place settings were fine china and sparkling crystal.

The meal, served by a beaming servant, consisted of avocado salad, shrimp cocktail and soup followed by a main course of several kinds of meat and fish and delicious vegetables and finally a dessert of delicate pastries and a huge bowl of tropical fruit.

Ginger ate with a healthy appetite. She exclaimed over the exquisitely prepared dishes. "Your actor friend who owns this place sure knows how to pick a good cook!"

Link nodded. "He told me he hired a man who used to be a chef at a big restaurant in Mexico City. The man is semiretired now. He lives nearby and comes over to cook whenever the house is open for guests."

Link had been silent and withdrawn during most of the meal. He ate little and barely touched his wine. Ginger's heart ached to see him so sad. Since this morning she had seen his moods swing erratically from feverish highs to spells of despondency.

After the meal, Link wandered outside. Ginger sensed that he wanted to be alone. She returned to her room. From her window, she watched the sun set over the Pacific. It was a breathtaking sight, a mingling of ruddy splashes against darkening clouds and shafts of pure gold streaking across the heavens.

She caught sight of Link strolling along the beach. He paced back and forth for a while, then took a seat on a dune and sat there staring at the sunset.

It grew dark, and Ginger could no longer see him. She felt a cold draft of apprehension. Considering the mood he was in, she became worried about what he might do. Finally she could no longer bear the thought of him all alone out there in the darkness. She left the house, moving down the bluff to the sea.

By then a full moon was rising, imparting a ghostly illumination to the beach setting. With a sense of relief, she spotted Link. He was still on the sand dune. Then, as she drew closer, she saw that his face was buried in his hands and his body was shuddering. His choked sobs, carried by the evening breeze, reached her ears.

She sank to her knees in the sand, her own eyes burning with tears. Her heart wrenched at the agony he was suffering. Her instincts screamed at her to rush to him, to comfort him in any way she could. But better judgment held her back. To a strong man like Link Rockwood, tears were a private thing. Like a wounded animal, he had stolen off to be alone with his pain. She had no right to intrude on him at a moment like this. Some deep female knowledge warned her that this was one of those times that a man had to be by himself. A woman might welcome a companion at a time like this so they could cry together, but a strong man broke down in solitude.

After a while, he seemed to grow calm. He rested his chin on his knee and traced his finger in the sand.

Ginger decided to take a chance and call his name as if she were looking for him. That would give him the opportunity to ignore her if he didn't want company.

But he replied at once, "I'm over here, Ginger."

She moved to his side and took a seat on the dune beside him, curling her legs under her. His face was masked by night shadows. She knew he was thankful that the darkness hid his reddened eyes from her.

"You . . . you look kind of lonely out here."

"Oh . . . I'm okay. I was just sitting here thinking."

"About what? Or maybe it's none of my business."

"No, I don't mind talking to you about it, Ginger. I was just thinking about Paige and me. I . . . I cared a lot for her, Ginger."

"I know you did," she said, her voice muffled to hide her own heartache.

"But, y'know, I got to thinking. I guess I just got the swelled head or something. I stepped way out of my class, thinking I could hold onto a beautiful woman like Paige. Heck, what am I? Just a small-town horse wrangler who happened to get a lucky break in Hollywood. I don't fit in with the kind of international, jet-set crowd that Paige runs around with. She probably thought she could still smell horse manure on my boots!" He nodded. "Yep, that was it. I was out of my class with Paige."

Tears filled Ginger's eyes. She swallowed a hurting lump. Slowly she shook her head. She slipped her fingers through Link's. "No," she said huskily. "It was the other way around, Link. Paige was out of her class with you."

He laughed in a way that let her know he didn't believe her. "You're one heck of a sweet kid, y'know that, Ginger? I know you're trying to make me feel better, and I sure appreciate it. And you know what? I'm going to stop this moping around! This sure isn't any fun for you! We're going to get a good night's sleep, and tomorrow I'll call that taxi driver, Ramón, and we'll get him to drive us into town, and we'll have a ball. Okay?"

He jumped up, as if resolved to throw off his

mantle of depression, and helped Ginger to her feet. "Okay," she agreed, forcing her response to match his new lighthearted air.

On an impulse, she stood on tiptoes and touched his lips with a fleeting good-night kiss. "See you in the morning!"

She hurried back to the house, knowing that it was going to be her turn to shed a lot of tears in her own privacy before she finally went to sleep tonight.

They slept late, had a combination breakfast and lunch and then Link sent for the taxi.

They arrived in the small Mexican town early in the afternoon and wandered through the central village area.

They roamed around the square, looking into curio shops, and they watched the people. Here the past rubbed shoulders with the present. Burros pulling two-wheeled carts crowded past modern Japanese-made cars on narrow streets. Old women, their heads covered with black shawls, fingered vegetables in the marketplace. A street-corner peddler mixed orange and pink cold drinks and sold the sticky, sweet concoction by the glass. Goats wandered in and out of sun-baked dirt yards. Adobe walls topped with bits of colored broken glass guarded old-world-style patios from the outside.

And over all of it was a film of white dust, settling over the square, over the wilting mesquite trees, the yards, the streets, the rusting, broken-down old cars that were parked in the yards.

In the market place, Link bought Ginger a black lace mantilla, a pair of maracas and a silver bracelet.

When the sun went down and the awful heat faded, they went to a little cafe and ate enchiladas and tacos. Link could bite the end off a *jalapeño* pepper with his straight white teeth and suck the juice out of it without batting an eye.

Ginger picked one up. "Don't try it," Link warned, grinning. She took his warning for a dare, made a face at him and took a healthy bite. She thought the top of her head would come off. She gasped. Tears streamed from her eyes, and she gulped water frantically. Link laughed until he almost rolled off his chair.

"You sadist!" Ginger said in a strangled voice.

"I warned you!" Link reminded her, wiping tears of laughter from his eyes. "Where I come from, kids are weaned on those things."

"I'll bet!" Ginger gasped out, her voice still hoarse. "My mouth will never be the same."

"Sure it will."

They watched the Mexican *señoritas* and *hombres* stroll around the square. Neon signs were flashing. Music was coming from bars and nightclubs.

They wandered into a small dirt-floored cantina on a back street.

To Ginger there was a sense of unreality about what was happening. She couldn't actually be here in this romantic setting alone with Link. It had to all be part of a scenario. She felt as if she had been thrust into the scene of a film in which she was playing a lead role opposite Link. She thought that surely, if she looked around, she would see cameras rolling, see the director watching from his vantage point on a crane, looking down at them. Any minute now he was going to yell, "Cut!" and the fantasy would end.

The Mexicans stared at them curiously—this was not the kind of place American tourists usually came into—but they were very polite.

Link and the waiter conversed fluently in Spanish,

and the waiter beamed, bowed politely and brought the bottle of tequila Link had ordered.

Link showed Ginger how to drink the clear, fiery liquid straight: a bite of lemon, a swallow of tequila and a lick of salt sprinkled on the back of the hand.

The potent liquor had the same effect on her palate as the *jalapeño* pepper. Link took pity on her eye-watering, gasping discomfort and ordered Margaritas for her instead, a drink also made with tequila but somewhat more civilized. After a few sips, Ginger felt a glowing warmth steal through her being and a feeling of reckless abandon take over her mood.

They sat in the adobe-walled, dirt-floored bar, drinking tequila and laughing together for no reason except that for the moment it was good to be alive. Everything Ginger said seemed very funny. She knew the bitterness and heartbreak must still be eating at Link, but he certainly had covered it well. Perhaps this was his form of coping, his defense mechanism. Or perhaps it was simply the tequila.

A handsome young Mexican came into the bar with a guitar slung over his shoulder. He sat at a table talking with the bartender for a while. Then he placed the guitar on his hip and played the most exciting flamenco guitar Ginger had ever heard. The wild, abandoned rhythms made her pulse pound.

When he finished, Link called him to their table and tipped him generously. *"Gracias, señor,"* the young musician said with a smile. He was staring at Link with open curiosity. In halting English he said, "I come back from Los Angeles last week. I work there two years, till the *inmigración* catch me and send me back. My cousin in Los Angeles has the television. We watch every night. I see an *hombre* on

the show 'Sagebrush' that look just like you, *señor.*
Are you that man?"

Link nodded.

Immediately the musician rattled off an excited
stream of words to the others in the bar. Everyone
seemed to start talking at once, gathering around the
table to get a closer look at Link.

"I told my friends you are a famous American TV
actor," the musician explained.

Ginger found herself in the center of a burgeoning
party. Toasts were offered in Spanish and English.
Much tequila and *cerveza* were consumed, overcoming initial shyness. The musician told his friends that
on TV, Link was *muy hombre,* very much a man,
very macho. That combined with Link's easy use of
their language made him the hero of the evening.

At one point, Link borrowed his admirer's guitar.
He surprised Ginger by striking some resounding
chords, then breaking into a medley of country and
western songs in a rich baritone. He sang, "Your
Cheatin' Heart," "Please Release Me" and "Born to
Lose." Then he almost caused a riot with "El
Rancho Grande," sung in Spanish.

*"Allá en el rancho grande . . . Allá donde
vivía. . . ."*

At the appropriate spot in the song, the audience
let out whoops and yells that rattled the windows.

Ginger's habit of role-playing turned Link into the
leader of a band of Pancho Villa revolutionaries who
were about to storm the federal stronghold. She
would be on his horse behind him, her arms around
his waist, her heart pounding against his strong back
when he rode triumphantly into the palace of the
governor.

Instead, an hour later, they were in the taxi of the

patient Ramón, who had waited all evening outside the bar, and were on their way back to the villa overlooking the sea. Link kept her entertained all the way home by singing seventeen different verses of "It Ain't Gonna Rain No More."

Ginger laughed until her sides ached.

When Ginger stepped out of the taxi at the gate of the villa, she found her senses drenched with the beauty of the evening. A great full moon overhead had cast a silver patina over the tropical setting. The whitewashed adobe walls of the house had become luminescent. Below them, the gentle breakers of the surf were scattering diamond droplets that sparkled on the white sand. The perfume of tropical flowers and plants sweetened the air.

"Hey, how about a midnight dip in the ocean?" Link exclaimed, weaving slightly.

Ginger raised an eyebrow. "That might not be a bad idea. You're listing pretty heavily to starboard. A cool dip in the ocean might sober you up."

"Oh yeah? Well, I'll just show you who's steady on his feet. Last one to get into the water is a cross-eyed armadillo!"

Ginger ran giggling into the house and up to her room, where she stripped and donned a brief bikini. Minutes later, she was hurrying outside. She felt as if she had defied gravity and were flying as she sped down to the beach. Somewhere behind her, she heard Link's cry, but she didn't stop until she plunged into the waves. The cold water was a shock, but then she felt invigorated and alive, tingling in every fiber of her being.

Suddenly a hand grasped her ankle, pulling her below the surface. She came up gasping. "You rat!" she cried.

Link laughed. He chased her through the water, but she swam hard, then ran through the breakers.

He caught her on the edge of the surf, and they sprawled in the sand. They were both laughing at first, rolling arm and arm in the shallow foam-flecked water. But then the laughter died.

Ginger was suddenly furiously aware of the contact of their bodies. With a rushing sheet of flame that blazed through her, she felt the touch of Link's strong thighs against hers, his arms around her bare back, her bosom pressed against his powerful chest. Her heart awoke with a thudding awareness, sending blood coursing through her arteries. She quivered, feeling her flesh cling to his with starved hunger. Their bare skin, gleaming with salty drops, slightly gritty with sand, was pressed together, tighter and tighter.

She could barely make out Link's features in the shadows cast by the moonlight as he looked down at her. But she could discern the burning intensity in his eyes, an intensity that matched her own.

His breathing had become swift and deep. She, too, found it hard to catch her breath. She wanted to whisper his name, but speech had become impossible.

Then his mouth crushed down on hers hungrily. She responded eagerly, welcoming the savage demand of his kiss, the thrust of his tongue, forcing her teeth apart. Her body arched up against his.

It became a moment of total madness, blotting out reason and consciousness of their surroundings, creating a universe of its own, a universe of consuming passion where the only reality was touch and feel and sensation.

She felt his trembling fingers pull the flimsy, wet

covering from her bosom. Her breasts gleamed in the moonlight. The exploring caress of his lips brought fire to her eager nipples.

His hands moved over her, mapping the tender curves of her thighs, searching under her suit to fondle her hips and gently explore forbidden territory.

Sensation mounted on sensation in a cascading crescendo that rampaged through her entire being, causing her to shudder from head to foot.

Her breath had become gasping moans. His name blazed across her chaotic thoughts like streaking fire. *Link, I love you . . . I love you . . . I love you . . .* came the achingly silent chant from her throbbing heart.

Then, like the sudden shock of a dash of ice water thrown in her face, Link tore his lips from her, pulled away to a sitting position in the surf. He buried his face in his hand with a sob. "Ginger . . . Ginger, forgive me." He choked. "I didn't mean . . . it was the tequila. I was drunk. I . . . lost my head. Honey, please forgive me."

With a strangled sob, he struggled to his feet and ran unsteadily back up the hill to the house, not looking back.

Ginger sat up, shaking with a violent chill. Her body was a torment of unfulfilled desire and bitter pain. She began crying uncontrollably.

Losing all track of time, she sat there crying until there were no tears left, and only dry sobs wracked her throat. She felt humiliated, degraded, stripped of every shred of pride. She was so hopelessly, blindly in love with Link that she was ready to give herself to him here, anywhere, under any circumstances. "The world's easiest pushover," she told herself bitterly.

She had known it wasn't love that fired Link's passion. Brokenhearted over Paige's jilting him, inflamed with tequila, he had simply needed a woman.

What stung the deepest was the shameful realization that she was crying not so much because of the circumstances, but because Link had come to his senses before his desire was consummated.

Wearily she dragged herself to her feet, slipped her bikini top back in place. "Yes, Link," she whispered into the night wind, "I would have been yours tonight, even under these circumstances. I'm so much in love with you I stopped counting the cost or using any reason."

The next morning, Ginger was on the terrace picking at a breakfast of *juevos rancheros*, orange juice and bowls heaped with tropical fruits when a contrite and hungover Link joined her.

His eyes were downcast. He looked embarrassed and self-conscious. "Ginger, about last night . . ."

She shrugged casually. "What about it?"

"What happened on the beach. I . . . I feel terrible about the way I acted. I wouldn't blame you if you took the earliest plane back home today. I promised I wouldn't make a pass and then . . . well, we started playing tag, and when I grabbed you . . . all the tequila I'd been drinking and the skimpy bathing suits we were wearing and . . . I'm supposed to be taking care of you, looking after you and . . . instead I treated you like one of the girls from the village red light district."

Ginger had dreaded facing Link this morning.

She'd known it was going to be a painful and awkward moment for both of them. She had spent most of the night staring at the ceiling and wondering how to handle the situation. She knew she had her own humiliation and heartache to cope with, and she had expected Link would try to apologize. Finally she'd come to the conclusion that the only way she could preserve a shred of pride was to make light of the whole situation.

"Link, for heaven's sake!" she said breezily. "Stop sounding like some villain out of a melodrama who just compromised a maiden's virtue. So we both had a little too much to drink and got into a steamy necking session on the beach. What's the big deal? You're not the first boy I've kissed!"

To herself she remarked that Paige couldn't have played a more convincing scene. If she could just keep a silly grin pasted on her face and restrain from bursting into tears, she would earn her own private Oscar!

An expression of immense relief spread over Link's face. "Ginger, you're terrific!" He took a seat at the breakfast table. "I just knew you'd be hurt or mad or both. I practically attacked you last night."

She managed a light shrug and a casual toss of her head. "Oh, I seem to recall it was a pretty even wrestling match. It was a great evening. I enjoyed every minute." She patted his hand with a reassuring gesture, forcing herself not to allow her fingers to turn the touch into a caress. "Now stop worrying about it. I'm having a great time."

"Okay," he said, reaching for a cup of coffee. "You're a swell sport about it. And I do promise not to get out of hand again."

Ginger didn't answer, the pain being too great.

Had she really expected him to say the kiss they'd shared last night had meant something to him? Perhaps, far back in that secret part of her heart that generated impossible dreams, that tiny hope had been there. She had even allowed herself the fantasy that he would come downstairs, take her hands in his, gaze into her eyes and tell her that the moment of passion had awakened him to the real feeling he had for her—not that of a friendly big brother, but that of a man for a woman he loved. What fools fantasies make of us, Ginger thought. The cold reality was exactly what he'd said: He had treated her like one of the prostitutes from the village. Their embrace had meant no more to him than that.

She quickly looked down into her cup of coffee to hide the sting of tears.

Then she heard Link say brightly, "Hey, I've been talking with the housekeeper, Señora Alvarez. She told me about a real, authentic fiesta going on in a little village far back in the hills—not the sort of thing tourists usually see. Would you like to take a trip out there? I'm sure Ramón, the taxi driver, will be happy to drive us there."

"Sure," she said, forcing a smile. "Do you think his beat up old taxi will make it that far?"

"Oh, I think so. If not, maybe we can hitch a ride on a burro. Señora Alvarez said she'd be happy to pack a picnic lunch."

This was a day Ginger wanted to stretch out forever. Just to be close to Link, to have him smile at her, touch her . . . to hear his voice . . . The director had not yet called, "Cut!" Let the fantasy go on. Reality would come back all too soon.

Yes, Ramón said cheerfully, he would be happy to drive them to the village for a price they could negotiate. It was, as Señora Alvarez had described, the authentic Mexico few tourists had the good fortune to see. He had many friends and cousins in the village who would welcome them if he were their guide.

They drove on a narrow dirt road that wound precariously around narrow ledges and dipped into rocky gorges. Several times Ramón stopped to clear brush and large rocks from the road.

The only living soul they passed was an old man pulling a small burro that was almost lost beneath a load of sticks. He stared at them with a startled expression as they drove by.

As they bounced over the primitive road, Link reached for Ginger's hand. His fingers laced through hers. "You're a heck of a great sport, Ginger, you know that? Why haven't we ever been out on a date before?"

He was back to his friendly, big brother, half teasing manner, she thought. She couldn't let anything he said get her hopes up. She replied lightly, "We were once. Remember the carnival when you threw the baseball and won the panda bear for me?"

He laughed. "That wasn't a real date."

He slipped his arm around her. She let herself relax against him, loving the comfort and security of feeling close and protected.

She thought sadly that Link was in the mood to drink tequila and do crazy things to keep from thinking about Paige. If holding her would comfort him, it was all right. She would just pretend that there wasn't any Paige and that they were out to have a good time together. She wouldn't count the cost until later.

She clasped his hand in an answering squeeze and

sat close to him, feeling her body throb every place they touched.

She was beginning to wonder if the taxi driver really knew where he was going. Her faith in him was restored when they wound out of the foothills and saw the village below, a tiny cluster of adobe buildings huddled together around the traditional central plaza and church.

The village was exactly as Ramón had described it, a remote, isolated town, hardly touched at all by the twentieth century. The church was one of those old missions built by Spanish padres four centuries ago, where mass was still held regularly. The narrow streets were unpaved. The adobe walls were crumbling with age.

Ramón parked his taxi on the outskirts of town and they entered the *pueblo* on foot, mingling with the crowd.

The plaza was jammed with people. Most of the men were dressed in white cotton pantaloons and loose white cotton shirts. The women wore blue or black rebozos—scarves over their heads. The men who were taking part in the dances wore masks, and some were dressed in costumes for the pageant.

The costumes were the most incongruous sight Ginger had ever seen. It was a typical kind of village play performed in villages like this, often combining medieval history with religion. Ramón explained to Link, who translated to Ginger, that this pageant told the story of the ancient war between the Castilians and the Moors. The people in this remote Mexican village dressed in clothes of the Middle Ages and acted out a war about people they did not know, who had lived in a land and a time they had never heard about. It was simply one of the

Spanish legends they had absorbed into the Indian-Mexican culture.

In booths at the plaza, table cloths, napkins, rebozos, straw toys, silver talismen and amulets were sold. There were oranges and sweet limes and roast pork and barbecued goat and tortillas roasting over glowing coals. Vendors peddled homemade candies.

The tequila and the drive through the hills had made Ginger hungry again. They ate tostados, a delicious mixture of chopped meat and onions topped with green lettuce and red radishes all on a toasted tortilla. It was the most delicious delicacy Ginger had ever put in her mouth.

The people, curious but friendly, stared at them as they wandered about. There was a happiness in these peoples' eyes and a harmony with their isolated world that Ginger found delightful.

Late in the afternoon there were cock fights. Then night fell. There was no electricity in the village. A full moon spread a silver glow over the countryside. Above, stars were like hot sparks in a velvet canopy. A meteorite flashed across the sky. Ramón said something in Spanish. Link translated his words to Ginger—God had struck a match across the heavens.

The plaza was lighted with torches and candles. About ten o'clock, fireworks lit up the sky. It began with rockets swishing up into the night and bursting into plumes of colorful sparks. The tequila gave Ginger a sense of dreamy unreality. She was aware that Link was having two drinks to her one. He seemed capable of holding his liquor well. Except for a slight unsteadiness when he walked and a slurring of some of his words, he did not appear intoxicated.

Suddenly, in the confusion of the crowded plaza,

Ginger couldn't find Link. She looked around with a feeling of panic. She saw Ramón nearby. She asked him if he'd seen where Link had disappeared. He smiled and nodded and said something she couldn't understand. His meager supply of English appeared to have suddenly deserted him. But when she said Link's name, he nodded reassuringly, making a gesture that she took to mean she was not to worry.

The main part of the program consisted of men and boys running from the churchyard, carrying large frames that were loaded with fireworks. The frames, Ginger later found out, were called *toritos*. They were roughly in the shape of a bull and covered with hide. The superstructure of slender sticks held the fireworks.

Each bearer came running out, with all the firecrackers, sparklers, pinwheels and rockets on his *torito* fuming, spluttering, smoking and exploding as the crowd applauded. He ran around looking like an animated Mount Vesuvius.

One of the masked *torito* bearers towered a head above the others. There was something strangely familiar about him. When he dashed out of the churchyard and scurried around the crowd with his flaming, exploding inferno, Ginger suddenly screamed, "Link!"

The *torito* had blazed into a climax of sparks and pinwheels and fizzled out. Link came over to where Ginger and Ramón were standing. He pushed back his mask. "How did I do?" he asked with a grin. "I paid a guy five bucks American money to let me carry his *torito*."

Ginger stared at Link and the smoking framework and could only shake her head in speechless amazement. Then both of them began laughing. Ginger doubled over laughing. Tears streamed down her face and hysteria threatened to engulf her.

It was a night made for laughter, a night not meant for tears or regrets or serious concerns.

From an adobe cantina lighted by a kerosene lamp that spread shadows over a bullfight poster on a wall, Link purchased a bottle of mescal. "It's made out of the maguey cactus plant," Link explained. "First the natives ferment the plant into a beer called pulque which has the kick of three mules. That's refined into mescal, which has the kick of two mules. Refine it some more, and you get tequila, which has the kick of one mule."

Ginger let him talk her into sampling the fiery liquor, after which her memory of the night became hazy.

She could vaguely recall the trip back through the mountains. Ramón and Link sang Mexican songs in harmony. Ginger thought they sang beautifully, and Ramón's wild driving over the corkscrew mountain road seemed more amusing than terrifying. Perhaps it was because Link's arm was around her. Nothing could frighten her when Link held her this way.

Once he kissed her and she responded eagerly.

"You're a terrific little girl, Ginger. You're fun and a great sport. Did I ever tell you what a terrific girl you are?"

She shook her head, suppressing a giggle.

"Well, you are." He nodded gravely, as if confirming his own evaluation of her.

Then he kissed her again and said, "Let's get married."

"Let's," she said with a giggle, thinking it was part of the game they were playing.

She didn't for a moment dream he was serious.

But he stopped singing and began a long, complicated verbal exchange with Ramón.

Finally he settled back, his arm giving her a fresh
squeeze. "It's all settled. Ramón knows a government official in town who can do it. We'll have to
wake him up, but for a few hundred pesos he'll
forgive us for that."

"Government official?"

"Yeah. The mayor or something. He can do it."

"Do what?"

"What we were talking about—marry us."

Ginger's laughter faded. She swallowed hard. "I
thought you were joking."

"No, I wasn't joking."

"You . . . you really meant it?"

"Sure. I asked you and you said yes."

"I know, but I thought you were just teasing."

"Well, I'm not. Want to back out?"

"N-no." Ginger said in a small voice. Suddenly
she felt totally sober. She stared at Link's profile,
trying to see what was in his eyes, but it was too
dark. They kept bouncing from side to side on the
primitive road, and Link held her in a protective way
to keep her from being thrown against the side of the
rattling old car.

"Why . . . why do you want us to get married?"
Ginger asked, still in a small voice.

"Seems like a good idea. You're the greatest,
Ginger. Look how much fun we've had tonight. And
after that kiss in the surf on the beach last night, I'd
say we wouldn't have any trouble with our sex life,
d'you think?"

"No," she murmured, glad it was too dark for him
to see the blush that made her cheeks sting.

It was a night of madness, somewhere between a

fantasy and reality. Getting married under these circumstances was sheer insanity.

Should she grasp this moment and say to heck with any second thoughts Link might have tomorrow? Could she marry him like this, knowing she was getting him on the rebound, knowing he was running away from his broken heart over Paige? Somehow her pride didn't count for much where Link was concerned. She had loved him too deeply and too long for logic or pride to stand in the way.

A faint voice of better judgment cried out a warning in the back of her mind, but it was drowned by a torrent of emotions. She leaned her head against Link's strong shoulder, closing her eyes, her throat filled, her eyes moist. With every beat of her heart, her pulse said, "Link, Link, Link. . . ."

She was tired of struggling with her conflicting emotions. The battle between reason and feeling had exhausted her. She just wanted to feel the comfort of Link's strong arms around her and drift along with whatever script was being written for their future. She'd leave the ending up to the director.

Later she remembered, as in a dream sequence, the drive through the dark, narrow streets of the village in search of the government official's home, the mumbled words in a language she didn't understand by the grumpy and half-asleep official, the signing of documents, not a word of which she could read, and Link's stuffing a bundle of pesos into the man's eager fingers.

Ramón, grinning from ear to ear, rattled off a burst of exuberant words.

"He hopes we will live together happily and have

many, many children," Link translated. "At least a dozen."

Ginger was in a daze. She clung to Link's hand as he led her back out to Ramón's car. She stared down at a split washer on her ring finger. Ramón had found it in the toolbox in the trunk of his car. It was the closest thing they could find to substitute for a wedding band.

"Are . . . are we really married?" Ginger asked, confused, her grasp on reality a slender thread.

She looked up at Link. His hair, blown by the wind coming through the missing window in Ramón's car, tumbled over his forehead. His eyes were definitely not in focus. His grin was lopsided. "Yep, sweetheart. How does it feel to be Mrs. Link Rockwood?"

"It . . . it feels wonderful," Ginger whispered, doubting that he heard her. She was fighting back tears. This was not the kind of wedding she would have chosen to become Link's bride. But that did not alter the fact that a miracle had taken place. She was actually married to Link! She repeated that fact to herself several times, trying to grasp its reality.

On the drive back to the oceanfront villa, Ginger said the words over and over, "Mrs. Link Rockwood."

Still the reality eluded her.

They entered the house and went upstairs quietly so as not to awaken the servants.

"Hey, wait," Link murmured. "Gotta carry the bride across the threshold."

With that, he scooped Ginger up in his powerful arms and carried her into her bedroom. She snuggled against him with the feeling that nothing in the universe could harm her here in the strong circle of his arms.

He sat in a chair with Ginger on his lap. A silver shaft of moonlight poured through a window, touching them with its romantic aura. The fragrance of tropical flowers tinged the air with perfume. Down at the foot of the hill, the breakers washed against the shore with a gentle murmur. Somewhere off in the tropical jungle, a night bird sang.

"Ginger, I haven't really told you this right . . . but you're a heck of a terrific kid, you know that?" Link mumbled softly.

Ginger touched his strong jaw with loving fingers. "Link, honey, right now I think it's the mescal talking. But the words are pretty anyway. Do you think I'm pretty?"

"You better believe it." He nodded gravely.

She smiled and kissed his chin. "No, I'm not really, Link. But that's okay. I'm healthy. That counts for something. And"—she suddenly felt choked—"and, honey, I'm not a kid; I'm a woman, and I love you. Okay?"

"Okay." He nodded.

"Give me a few minutes, and I'll prove it to you."

She slipped her arms around his neck, gave him a lingering kiss and winked. "Be back shortly."

She kicked off her shoes and walked across the cool tile floor into the bathroom. She felt gritty from the long drive over the dusty mountain road. A shower was in order, but she did not wish to spoil the romantic mood by turning on a light, so she bathed in the dark, working up a foaming lather with a bar of scented soap and then turning around and around in the shower, letting the lather pour down her body to her ankles and finally disappear down the drain.

She stepped outside, her body like a gleaming marble statue in the moonlight that poured through a high window. She gazed at a mirror, wishing she were as beautiful as Paige, so Link would have a beautiful bride tonight. Her unusual coloring, yellow brown hair and tawny eyes to match, was, she supposed, her best asset. "Tiger eyes," she had been told. And her tall body was in great shape—long slender legs, a high, firm bosom, not an ounce of flab. She was strong for a girl and in the top condition her profession demanded.

But nobody could call her beautiful. Her nose didn't have the aristocratic, patrician lines that Paige's had. It was more of the turned-up, pug variety. Her chin was too square, her mouth too wide. *Wholesome* was the term reserved for her kind of looks. Beautiful she was not. She wasn't even sure she was pretty.

She sighed. Well, it was dark, and in Link's condition tonight, any woman would look good to him.

She suddenly shivered. What would the morning bring when Link compared her to her beautiful sister? Would he spend the rest of his life feeling cheated?

A moment of panic seized her. Could she go through with this wedding night? She twisted the split washer on her ring finger, looking at it through a mist of tears. All of her life, she had gotten Paige's leftovers. She knew it was Paige her father cared for the most. Ginger got whatever crumbs of his affection were left over. Link had given Paige a huge, expensive diamond engagement ring. Ginger's wedding ring was a split washer out of Ramón's toolbox. And she was getting Link on the rebound.

Then she squared her shoulders and raised her chin. Well, she just wasn't going to think about that tonight. She was going to give Link so much love that she'd wipe Paige from his memory. They would honeymoon here in this beautiful, romantic setting. Neither one of them had any deadline that would make them hurry home. Link had filmed the last episode of his TV series. And Ginger had no immediate stunt work scheduled. They could forget about time and just make love and get to know each other. She would show Link that she was no child. She was a woman with a woman's body and a woman's love to give him without reservation. The time, the setting, the mood were all on her side. Even the fates seemed to have joined forces with her.

Yes, she told herself bravely. She was going to make Link glad that he had married her. He would love her and they would be happy together.

She found a towel and dried herself briskly. Then, in lieu of a nightgown, she wrapped the large bath towel around herself, fastening it under her arms, and stole softly back into the bedroom.

Link was in bed, fully clothed, the empty bottle of mescal cradled in his arms. He was dead to the world.

Ginger stared down at him with a mixture of chagrin and exasperation. "Well, a fine bridegroom you turned out to be!" she exclaimed.

She felt a strong impulse to get a glass of cold water from the bathroom and splash it right in his face. But then she had second thoughts. Better let him sleep it off. They had all of tomorrow for lovemaking.

Gently she removed his shoes. She slipped into bed and snuggled close to him, resting her head on his shoulder. He stirred, mumbled something in his sleep, then was quiet again. Ginger felt a glow of contentment, savoring the warmth of him so close to her. She let her arm fall across his chest, felt the steady rise and fall of his breathing. "Link . . . my husband," she murmured. How wonderful it would be to sleep this close to him every night, to feel his breath against her cheek, to awaken during the night and know he was there and then to greet him when dawn sent rosy light through the window.

She wanted to stay awake to enjoy this closeness with the man she loved, but suddenly sleep became overpowering. The excitement of the day, the rough drive over the mountain trail, the tumult of emotions had exhausted her. She fell into a deep sleep and dreamed about Link.

When she awoke it was with a start and a frightening awareness that something was wrong. Instead of the soft, rosy light of dawn, glaring sunlight poured through the window. With wide-eyed dismay she stared at a clock on the wall. The hands pointed to ten o'clock!

She looked around with a feeling of panic. The pillow beside her was vacant. She was alone in the room. The only evidence that Link had been there last night was the empty bottle of mescal, now in a waste basket beside the dresser.

A dreadful sense of loss filled her. Had she only dreamed that Link had married her? Had it been some kind of hallucination brought on by the drinks they'd had?

She started to scramble out of bed. But then there was a soft tap at the door. It opened and the housekeeper, Señora Alvarez, entered with a breakfast tray. *"Buenos dias, Señorita,"* she said. She followed that with a stream of Spanish, not a word of which Ginger understood.

Realizing she was clothed only in a bath towel, Ginger clutched the bedsheet around her as the housekeeper placed the breakfast tray on the bed, smiled and departed.

Ginger stared at the tray. In the center was an envelope addressed to her in Link's handwriting.

With trembling fingers, she tore it open.

"Dear Ginger. Please forgive me. Guess I just can't handle this Mexican booze. I wish there was something I could say to apologize. I feel like a dirty dog. Wouldn't blame you if you hated me. I woke up early and decided the best thing I could do was get my tail back home before I cause you any more trouble. I'm catching an early plane back to Los Angeles. There's another early this afternoon. I told Ramón to take you to the airport. Sorry. Hope you'll understand. Link."

Stuffed in the envelope was a wad of Mexican pesos for travel expenses and an airplane ticket for Los Angeles.

Ginger stared at the note for a long time, her eyes dry, her face frozen. And then the flood of tears came.

Chapter Six

G inger had returned from Mexico with her spirit broken. Her dream of Link falling in love with her had turned to cold, bitter ashes, dead forever.

The love story she had been acting out had ended in cold reality. She had to face the fact that Link was a one-woman man; and his woman was Paige. No matter how Paige had treated him, he could not stop loving her. Some men were like that.

When he awoke that morning, sober, all his love for Paige must have come back in a rush, filling him with fresh heartache.

As for Ginger, her pride and self-confidence had been devastated. She was crushed with the humiliation of knowing that when Link had awakened that morning, she was snuggled half naked beside him, his for the taking. He had found her so unappealing that he'd fled back to Los Angeles without wanting to consummate their Mexican marriage.

What an ultimate blow to a woman's self-esteem!

A few days after returning to Los Angeles, she heard that Link had gotten a part in a movie that was filmed on location in Arizona. It was his first major

Hollywood role following the TV series. It typecast him as a guy who drove fast cars and loved women with equal skill. He was tough in a barroom fight and tender in the bedroom. From then on he was stuck with that image, and it pushed him to the heights as one of the big box office names of the decade.

For a while, Ginger fled Hollywood. She spent some time with her aunt Judy, who had taken the place of the real mother she never had. To her aunt she tearfully confessed the painful and humiliating story of her impetuous marriage to Link. For several months, Ginger looked like someone who had been through a debilitating illness. She was withdrawn. She cried herself to sleep almost every night. She lost weight. Her feelings toward Link swung from grief to hatred. Eventually hatred won out. She never wanted to have any more to do with him, never wanted to talk to him, never wanted to see him again.

She recovered from her depression and returned to Hollywood and took up her stunt career. But she wiped Link Rockwood from her life. If one of his movies was shown on TV, she switched to another channel. When she saw his picture on the cover of a fan magazine, she quickly turned away. She refused to accept any stunt assignments on any film with which he was even remotely connected.

Several times Link had tried to phone her, but he soon got the message that she wanted nothing more to do with him. She hung up when she heard his voice. And she gave strict orders to anyone else answering the phone that she was accepting no calls from Link Rockwood.

As for her sister, Paige married her Italian director and was divorced a year later. There followed several romances and another short-lived marriage. Like Link, her career flourished. But then two box office flops in two years dropped her career several rungs down the ladder. She was in dire need of a hit role.

Ginger had thought all of her teenage romantic muddle with Link Rockwood was far behind her. Sometimes memories of Link stole into her dreams, but for the most part, she believed she had successfully eradicated him from her life.

And now her father had come to Florida with his bombshell that was going to demolish her peace of mind, thrust Link Rockwood back into her life and tear open old wounds.

After a restless night haunted by memories and dreams of the past, Ginger struggled out of bed and had a cup of strong coffee and a piece of toast for breakfast. Then she spent the morning in her room, forcing herself to concentrate on the script of her father's movie, *Thunder at Dawn.*

The script was an adaptation of a fairly successful novel that had been published a few years before. Obviously Derrick had bought screen rights and hired a screen writer to adapt the story for the movies.

Ginger remembered reading the novel when it was first published. She had been moved to tears by the tender love story that ran like a golden thread through a tapestry of events and lives.

In the film adaptation, the first love story took place when the couple met during the Civil War. He was a dashing Confederate cavalry lieutenant, she a lovely plantation belle. They fell desperately in love, but he was killed in battle before they could be married.

The time shifted to the prohibition era of the Roaring Twenties. The same actors would portray the couple, who met again in another lifetime, feeling that somehow they had known each other before. In this story he was a World War I flying ace who returned after the war to become a race car driver. He got involved with a bootlegging gangster gang. Needing money for an operation for his sweetheart, he agreed to smuggle contraband liquor across the border from Canada. He eluded the police but then wanted out of the gang.

However, he knew too much about the gang's secrets. In his next big dirt track car race, they tampered with his race car, and he had a fatal crash.

The time shifted again, to a battle scene during the Spanish Civil war in the 1930s. The hero was an American volunteer fighting on the side of the Republican forces against the fascists. He met a lovely Spanish girl. Again the lovers would be played by the same actors. In the few hours before Franco's forces attacked their village, they fell in love, drawn together by a sense of familiarity and longing they could not explain. They spent the night before the attack making love. The next day, in the height of battle, they died in each other's arms.

Finally there was a scene that took place in today's world in the strife-torn Mideast, where the characters were foreign news correspondents. Later, on an assignment that took them through some southern states, they visited an old cemetery and felt an odd fascination with the names on two ancient stone markers—of the names the Civil War cavalry lieutenant and his sweetheart, who had been portrayed in the first sequel. They walked away, hand in hand. The story would leave the audience with the feeling that the love that existed between these two people had been stronger than time or death, but the question as to whether fate would ever allow them to live out the love story remained unanswered.

The story was epic in scope, revolving around historical moments that had shaped the world of the twentieth century. But the central theme dealt with love and fate. It made the statement that lovers facing death could experience love more intense in a single night than many know in a lifetime. And it left the reader wondering if the love of the couples in the story was so powerful it had survived even death.

Ginger had wept when she read the book, because of the power and sweep of the author's style. Now she laid the movie script aside with a mixed feeling of excitement and apprehension. A multitude of questions assailed her. Could the story be successfully told in a visual media? The simple outline of the plot sounded corny and melodramatic. It would be the acting, the directing, the mood and tone of the scenes, the musical score, that would save the story. As for the directing, she had a lot of confidence in Derrick. Though he had never directed before, he had the experience and skill to pull it off. Could Paige, who had something of a sex goddess image, handle a serious, dramatic role like this? Probably she could. Whatever shortcomings her sister had in her private life, Paige was a born actress.

What about Link? As Derrick had long ago pointed out, Link was more of a screen personality than an actor. This would be his first really dramatic role. True, the parts he portrayed—the Civil War cavalry lieutenant, the race car driver, the soldier and the foreign correspondent—fitted his dashing, macho image. But this story was going to take some strong, dramatic acting. It wasn't going to be enough for his manly swagger, his infectious grin and his winning personality to put this role across.

By noon she laid the script aside with a mixed feeling of excitement and apprehension.

She changed into a halter top and shorts and went in search of her father. She found him on the screened back porch having a sandwich.

"Good morning," he greeted her, obviously back in his usual self-confident, expansive mood. He nodded at the script in her hand. "Well, what do you think of it? Fantastic, isn't it?"

"That's putting it mildly," she murmured.

"I told you it was going to be a blockbuster," he exclaimed. "Don't you agree?"

"I'll tell you what I think in a minute. Where is everybody?"

"Well, your cousin, Lorene, left early this morning for her job at the bank, of course. Sister Judy went for a stroll on the beach. Oh, she said if you're hungry for lunch, there are some cold cuts and things in the refrigerator. As you see, I've served myself."

Ginger disappeared into the kitchen and returned shortly with a glass of orange juice and a bunch of grapes.

She plopped into a rattan sofa, fixing a speculative look on her father. "This," she said, holding up the movie script, "is no low budget film."

"Never said it was." Derrick smiled confidently.

"Derrick, this is going to cost a fortune to produce." She pointed to the thick manuscript. "It starts with a Civil War battle scene. My Lord, you have cavalry horses, cannons, a whole army, a plantation mansion being blown apart! And that's only the beginning. The next scenes, the 1920s sequel, car chase scenes, the Mideast location shots and the Spanish Civil war battle scenes. . . ." She threw up her hands in a gesture of despair.

Derrick shrugged. "I told you it's going to be one of the big movies of the year."

Ginger was gazing at her father with a wide-eyed expression of amazement and confusion. For a moment a chilling thought assailed her. Was her father becoming senile, losing his judgment?

"Derrick, I know you had some valuable real estate holdings. But you can't raise the money it will take to produce a film of this scope."

"Quite true, Ginger. I have other backing in addition—private investors, loans, et cetera."

Ginger felt somewhat relieved. "I'm glad to hear that."

"Yes, the money is there. Nevertheless, it will be touch and go. No running over budget."

Ginger frowned. "Derrick, I am not getting any stunt people hurt just to save a buck. I want the best special effects people money can buy. A stunt person's life often depends on how well the special effects are engineered."

"I know, I know," Derrick said impatiently.

"I want Nick Davidson to do the special effects."

It was Derrick's turn to frown. "He's the most expensive in the business."

"Right. And the best. I refuse to get involved if you can't afford Nick. He's tops at what this script calls for. He can set up the explosions, the fire scenes, the car crashes so they look good but people won't get hurt or killed doing them."

"All right, Ginger. We'll trim costs somewhere else if need be. The effects are all important. This is

an action picture as well as a powerful love story. We
need top quality stunts and effects."

With that resolved, Ginger allowed herself to
express some guarded enthusiasm. "Derrick, it really is a fantastic story. It has everything, just as you
said."

The old actor's eyes took on a fresh gleam.
"Thunder at Dawn is going to be a film classic. I can
see definite possibilities of Academy Award nomina-
tions."

"Yes, it does have that possibility," she said
aloud, while thinking grimly to herself, *or a good
chance at being the year's greatest flop.*

Then, addressing herself to her father again, she
said, "I see you had Alex Carter write the screen-
play."

"Yes. He did a great job, don't you think?"

"Oh, he's a terrific writer, one of the best. And
also hard to get along with sometimes. He's got the
notion that tampering with his script is like daring to
revise the Bible. I can already see some changes that
may have to be made."

"Yes, so do I. But we'll cross that bridge when we
come to it. Let me deal with Alex. I can handle
him."

In the following weeks, Ginger found herself
thrust headlong into the hectic world of motion
picture production. She quickly discovered that
when her father begged her to become stunt coordinator for the film, he actually needed her for much
more than that. He desperately needed her help and
support in almost every phase of his venture. She
became his right hand in the tremendous job of
creating a motion picture.

Again she was made aware of the difference in relationships between her father and his two daughters. Paige was the artist, the prima donna whose only function was to walk on the sets and display her talent as an actress. Ginger, on the other hand, was able to deal with all the practical nuts and bolts of putting a motion picture together. She could help pick out costumes or roll up her sleeves and wield a hammer right along with a set construction crew. Having grown up in the industry and having worked in it for ten years, Ginger knew almost as much about motion picture production as Derrick.

It soon became apparent to her that Derrick was depending on her help, that it had been a major factor in his wanting her involved in the film. Of course she would enhance the movie with her talent in the stunt field. But Ginger suspected that in spite of his bluster and posturing, Derrick Lombard was haunted with the gnawing fear that he might have bitten off more than he could chew. He would be in his element when he took on the role of director. But he would be running himself ragged as executive producer. Ginger could take a tremendous load off him. She had become his associate producer as much as stunt coordinator!

Again she might be settling for the crumbs, but Ginger felt a deep emotional hunger fulfilled in just knowing that her father depended on her and needed her.

Putting together a motion picture, Ginger knew, was an undertaking of staggering proportions involving hundreds of people. The preproduction stage, before a single footage of film was shot, could take months and involve such things as vast paper work in the budgeting department.

Casting was another major undertaking. Although Derrick had signed Paige and Link to play the leading roles, there were dozens of other parts ranging from secondary to very minor that had to be cast. Unlike a major studio that had a casting department, Derrick went about the matter by hiring an independent casting consultant, who worked closely with him to hire the necessary actors, using the Motion Picture Academy's guide to Screen Actors' Guild members.

The major studios took care of casting, budgeting, costumes, props and location scouting through departments specializing in such matters. Going it as an independent, Derrick had to deal with these problems directly. Ginger found herself arguing with the art director over the way the sets would look and then discussing with set designers how to put the ideas into reality, utilizing their engineering and architectural know-how.

She spent hours with the costume designer, who selected clothing and in some cases designed original creations for the cast.

Ginger flew all over the country with Derrick, helping him scout locations.

The Civil War settings would take place in a southern mansion in Georgia. For interior shots of the gangster era, they arranged to use the Biltmore mansion in Asheville, North Carolina, one of the most elegant structures in the world and often used in movies. Derrick closed a deal with a landowner friend in Spain to lease some property for the Spanish Civil War set. An entire village would be constructed. Derrick believed in authentic location scenes when possible. As for the Mideast sequel,

Derrick planned to use locations in Israel for authenticity, actually shooting some footage in the streets of Jerusalem.

There were times when Ginger felt caught up with the excitement of the film's possibilities, its tremendous sweep and scope. But there were other times she was awake half the night worrying. No one could predict for certain if any motion picture would be successful, mediocre or a total flop.

At last the preproduction work was behind them. The entire production crew was on location in Georgia, prepared to film the Civil War scenes.

Up to this point, Ginger's phobic anxiety of being near a movie set had been buried under all the preproduction detail work.

But now she faced the cold reality of a confrontation with her nightmare fears. Her stomach was in knots, her hands icy as she talked with her stunt people, outlining the action of the battle scenes. The special effects people had set up explosive charges in the battlefield. Hundreds of squibbs were in place, wired to explode as "bullets" flew. Some of the stunt people were outfitted with squibbs under their uniforms. Derrick wanted stark realism—close-ups of Rebel and Yankee troops being wounded. The field was a mass of blue and gray uniforms.

One group of soldiers was set up to go tumbling head over heels in the dust and smoke of an explosion as a "shell" struck in their midst.

In a cavalry charge, a number of stunt riders specializing in falls would crash to the ground with their horses.

Ginger had spent days with the special effects people, going over every detail meticulously, checking and rechecking. The possibility of somebody getting injured in this scene was very real. And she felt the responsibility would be hers.

After holding her final conference with the stunt crew, she quietly headed for the nearest bathroom, where she lost her breakfast. She bathed her face with cold water. Then she caught sight of herself in a mirror. Stark white features like a stiff mask gazed back at her.

She wanted nothing in the world so much as to go hide in a closet until they were through filming the battle scene. But she drew a deep breath and somehow pulled herself together. She was going to be right behind the cameras as every foot of this scene was shot.

She stepped outside. There was a mass of noise and confusion, dust in the air, the whinny of horses, hundreds of extras in blue and gray uniforms milling about, the creaking of cannon being rolled into place, Derrick's assistant director yelling through his bullhorn at the camera crews.

Then she heard the creak of saddle leather and the rustle of hooves right behind her. She turned and looked straight up into the steel gray eyes of Link Rockwood.

Chapter Seven

He was astride a big, fierce-looking black stallion. He was in costume, the flamboyant uniform of a dashing Confederate cavalry officer, complete with sash, boots and heavy gauntlets. At his side was a saber and a heavy pistol.

He crossed his arms, resting forward on the horn of his saddle, fixing his gaze on her in a long, searching look.

Ginger felt the strength melt out of her legs. Time evaporated. She was a teenager in a dusty western movie set in Texas, seeing Link all over again for the first time.

The momentary fantasy evaporated. She clenched her fists at her sides, trying to pull her eyes away from his, but failed.

Then he said, "Hello, Ginger."

His words were soft, but somehow distinct in spite of all the noise and confusion around them.

She tried to swallow but found her throat paralyzed. Finally she managed a cold, "Hello."

Ten years of hating him boiled up in her, turning her emotions into a more violent battleground than that about to be filmed.

"You're looking super," he went on, his gaze trailing down her body slowly and back to her face in a way that made her cheeks flame. "All grown up now."

How did he look? Her confused eyes tried to take the sight of him in all at once. First there was the dashing, masculine impact of his glamorous image in the gray uniform, the sight of a tall, handsome soldier on a giant horse. That would overwhelm any female heart. But she tried to see beyond that, to the real Link. Ten years had changed him. There were lines in his face now that made him appear even more ruggedly handsome. The streaks of gray at his temples had not been touched up by the makeup department. She sensed a sureness about him now, a worldly polish that had replaced the small-town uncertainty of those early years.

She was locked in his gaze for another agonizing moment, and then she managed to overcome the hypnotic effect of his steady look. "I have work to do," she said shortly and turned away.

She walked toward a distant camera crew, feeling his gaze burning into her back every step of the way. She felt badly shaken. Ever since Derrick had broken the news of the production company he was forming and the film he would make, Ginger had been dreading the moment she would come face to face with Link again. She had spent sleepless nights rehearsing her reaction, preparing herself, steeling her emotions against exactly the way they had reacted. Yes, her emotions had betrayed her! She was swamped by memories, torn apart by heartache as fresh as the morning Link walked out on her in Mexico. She hated Link, hated herself for her weakness. Could she never rid herself of the curse of Link

Rockwood? Was she damned to suffer the after-math of her teenage infatuation for the rest of her life?

That was all it had been! she told herself furiously. A silly, blind teenage infatuation. She had never really loved him. It was no more than an overpower-ing physical attraction. A chemistry that somehow came to a boil when he came near her. Had it happened again today—the overwhelming primitive desire set afire in an instant by his presence, wiping out her rational thinking processes, turning her emotions into chaos? Was that what had shaken her so badly, that mixed with a torrent of nostalgic memories warring with the bitterness she felt toward him?

It was more than she could cope with now. She had enough of a struggle on hand with her own private demons of fear to overcome as the filming of the action scene began. She had to put Link Rock-wood out of her mind.

That was not so easily done. Not ten minutes passed before a violent argument between Derrick and Link erupted. Ginger saw Derrick seated high on a crane where he could get an overview of the battle scene. Link was below him on his horse. They were shouting at each other, but there was too much confusion for Ginger to hear what was being said.

At that point the assistant director ran over to Ginger, his round face gleaming with perspiration. "Ginger, you'd better come over here," he said panting. "Link wants to do that fence jump himself. Derrick is having apoplexy."

Ginger swore under her breath. She accompanied the agitated A.D. to where the heated discussion was taking place.

Derrick yelled at her, "Ginger, talk some sense into that idiot. He appears determined to break his damn neck in the first scene we shoot, thereby ruining the entire production!"

"What seems to be the trouble?" Ginger asked, surprised at how calm her own voice sounded.

Link shrugged, sending one of his careless grins her way. "Derrick is turning into a fussy old maid. He wants me to ride out to the field and then have one of your stunt guys take my place to jump that little old rail fence out there."

"That's the way it's set up," Ginger said coldly. "We've rehearsed the stunt. I have a good man all set to do it."

"But that's plain silly. Back home, I jumped fences that small on a pony."

"Derrick's the director," she snapped. "You'll do it his way."

Link didn't answer. She saw his jaw take a stubborn set. He reined his big horse away. "All right, start shooting the damn scene!" he snarled.

Taking that to mean he had capitulated, Derrick nodded to the assistant director, who bawled orders to the camera crews. The marker was snapped. "Action . . . roll 'em!"

Pandemonium broke out on the battlefield.

The crack of rifles firing blanks mingled with the roar of cannon and the explosions that threw dirt and dust high in the air. The piercing cry of the rebel yell was heard as the lines of gray charged the flanks of blue.

Then, into the melee rode the cavalry led by Link. Ginger watched, her body rigid with tension. At this point her stunt man was to run out and take Link's place on the horse. The cameras would keep rolling.

The cutting room would eliminate the change in riders.

But Link did not stop his horse. Instead, he spurred the beast to a faster run. Ginger heard Derrick's furious cry. She gritted her teeth. "Link, you darn fool!"

He cleared the fence easily. The script called for the hero to receive his fatal wound on the other side. Link slumped forward, seeming to lose control, and then tumbled to the ground, where he sprawled still and lifeless."

"Cut!" Derrick shouted.

The noise on the battlefield died down to a hush. Dust and the smoke from black powder hung like a dark cloud over the scene. All eyes were riveted on Link, who hadn't moved. Derrick came down from his crane and strode to where Link was lying. Ginger, her heart pounding in her throat, was one stride behind her father. Her fury at Link had been washed away by icy fright. She knew she should be terrified at the thought of what a serious injury to Link would mean to the rest of the film, but fear for Link's life somehow pushed that aside.

They hurried up to the prone, still body. Link was on his back. His uniform was torn and stained, his face smeared with dirt. His eyes appeared glassy, fixed on the clouds above. There was no sign of life. No breath moved his chest. *My God, he's dead,* she thought in terror.

Derrick was swearing with every breath.

They were almost at Link's side.

Suddenly Link leaped to his feet, laughing uproariously. "How'd I do?"

Derrick froze, staring at Link with an expression of cold fury.

Ginger felt an overwhelming surge of relief, followed immediately by a blinding wave of anger. "You darn fool!" she cried. "What kind of smart aleck grandstand idiot are you, anyway?"

Link only grinned at her in an infuriating manner. "Well, see, it was this way. I tried to stop the horse so your stunt man could take over, but that fool animal just wouldn't whoa. I guess all the shooting and explosions got him spooked. He kept right on going over that fence, so I figured I'd just have to stick with him and then fall off where the hero was supposed to get shot."

Ginger stared at him, tight-lipped. "You expect us to believe that story?"

He shrugged. "That's the way it happened."

Derrick Lombard turned on his heel and strode away without a word.

Ginger started to follow him, but Link caught up with her. He removed his gauntlets, slapping the dust out of them against his legs.

"Hey, wait up, Ginger, I'll walk with you."

"I'm in a hurry," she said in a muffled voice.

His long strides brought him to her side.

"What's the rush? They've finished shooting the scene."

"I have other things to do. We're trying to put a motion picture together, in case you hadn't noticed."

She felt his hand touch her arm. It sent a quiver racing through her body.

"Take it a little easy," he said with a smile. "You'll have an ulcer before we're through. I'd like to talk to you."

The truth was, she thought, the main reason she had been hurrying was to get away from him. But his hand on her arm brought her headlong rush to a halt.

"I . . . I don't have a thing in the world to talk with you about, Link. My job is stunt coordinator. The only people I have to communicate with are the stunt people. If you have anything to discuss, go talk to Derrick or the assistant director."

His maddening smile continued to taunt her as his gaze trapped her eyes again and brought fresh torment to her hurting emotions. "You were communicating with me pretty well a few minutes ago when you were chewing me out for taking that jump."

"I had good reason to!" she retorted, feeling a fresh wave of anger. "That was a problem involving my job as stunt coordinator—a problem, incidentally, that you caused with your egotistic grandstand play!"

Her barbed words seemed to glance harmlessly off his cool surface. He infuriated her further by appearing more interested in looking her over than listening to her words.

"I heard about the accident you had last year, Ginger," he murmured, his face growing serious. "I was concerned about you. I stopped by the hospital one day when I was in the city, but they weren't letting you have any visitors. Did you get the flowers I sent?"

"Yes," she said coldly. "I told the nurse to give them to somebody else."

He gazed at her in a speculative way, as if searching for something in her eyes. What he was looking for made her uncomfortable. She tried to pull her gaze from his.

"I know you hated me for a long time, Ginger. I

can't blame you. Do you still feel the same way now?"

Her gaze became chilled. Through pale lips she choked, "Yes, I do. I don't want to have anything to do with you, Link. All the money in the world wouldn't have gotten me to work on a film you're involved in. The only reason I gave in and consented to do it was because my father needed me."

"But what happened between us took place ten years ago. You were a child then. Now you're a grown woman." His eyes again verified that fact with a bold glance at the curves distinctly outlined under her blouse. "D'you suppose we could let bygones be bygones and be friends again?"

Her cheeks were stinging. Her body felt flushed from the scrutiny of his gaze. *How is it possible you can make me feel this way, Link Rockwood, when I hate you like I do?* she asked her warring emotions. But no answer came.

Tears were rising dangerously near the surface. "No, I don't want to be your friend. I don't want to have anything more to do with you. I just want you to leave me alone!"

"I'm not sure if I believe that, Ginger. There was a time when you were my best friend."

"That was before I found out what a rat you are!" she hurled back at him.

He countered by throwing his head back and laughing uproariously, which only brought her closer to tearful frustration. Then he said, "Ginger, seriously, I do want to see you and have a long talk with you, and obviously a movie set is not the place to do it. Look, they're not going to do any filming over the weekend. I have to fly to Denver to do a benefit show on Saturday night. Why don't you come with me? It would give you a break. You're under a heck of a lot of pressure here. It would be good for you and give us a chance to visit."

Her immediate response was a firm "No," although inwardly she felt less sure of her answer.

He looked at her in a teasing manner. "What if I make a deal with you. I'll promise not to jump any more fences if you'll go with me."

Her eyes narrowed. "Is that some kind of blackmail?"

"Could be. Y'know, there'll be a lot more action scenes before we're through with this movie. Stuff like car wrecks, high falls, explosions. . . ."

"I don't believe you'd try another silly thing like you did today—jeopardize the whole film just to show off."

"But you're not sure, are you?" he challenged.

Now her emotions were torn in several new directions. She knew Link had a reputation for doing wild, unpredictable things just for laughs. Was he threatening to sabotage the film just to get his stubborn way?

For several long moments, no words were exchanged. Only their eyes locked in a fierce struggle, testing for strengths and weaknesses in their opponent. Mostly Ginger was searching for the truth, or lack of it, in Link's threat.

Her uncertain mind weighed the consequences—a weekend in his company against the possibility that he might pull another hair-brained trick that would add to Derrick's already staggering burden of worry. The reasoning part of her mind told her that Link wouldn't do that—his loyalty to Derrick was too great. But there was an answering warning that Link Rockwood was also impetuous and volatile. He might do something crazy on the spur of the moment just out of stubbornness or on an impulse.

It wasn't fair! her heart cried out. Because confusing all her attempts at calm reasoning in the matter was the power of traitorous emotions that were melting her resistance. *Damn you, Link Rockwood,* she thought tearfully. *Just being near you again has demoralized me.*

It was true! She could feel his presence like a force field, reaching out and engulfing her. The very essence of her being had become acutely tuned to his vibrations. Her senses were like radar, picking up the rustle of his uniform, the creak of his wide leather belt, the smell of horse leather, dust and sweat, the design of his rugged, sun-tanned features, his steel gray eyes, his lips, strong chin, broad shoulders and powerful, broad hands.

But more than all that was something deep inside, the very essence and soul of Link Rockwood. The ten years had changed his outer appearance somewhat, just as they had changed her. But another part was unchanged, their inner beings. The ten years were swept away in the wink of an eye, and he was the same Link who had lifted her from the horse trough in his strong arms, who had won the panda bear at the carnival for her, who had awakened her young body to a woman's passion that night in the surf on the moonlit beach.

Would the memories never give her any peace?

Perhaps they would if Link would stay away from her. She had avoided him for ten years, but now fate had thrown them together again and he was showing a strange persistence. The way he looked at her was different now, a way that touched her with a feeling of chilled anxiety followed by a wave of uneasy excitement.

One thing was for certain. He no longer gave the impression of a big brother's protective attitude, seeing her youth and innocence as a barrier between them.

No, she had no protection against him now, or against her own weakness for him. Even as these chaotic thoughts were racing through her mind, that very weakness was taking control of her—wanting so much to give in and say yes to him.

She swallowed hard. "When . . . when would we leave?"

The flush of triumph on his face made her bow her head. He said, "How about early Saturday morning? My jet is at the airport in Atlanta. We can be in Colorado in a few hours. I have a ranch there now, you know. Up in the high country. It's beautiful up there. Snowcapped mountains all around. Trees, flowers, streams as clear as crystal. Remember my uncle Jefferson?"

She nodded, recalling clearly the crusty, blind old-timer who had been Link's only family.

"Well, I bought the place partly for him. The high, dry climate up there is good for his asthma. He loves to sit on the porch all day in the sunshine. I go there whenever I can between film and TV jobs. It's my hideaway, a place I can relax, go hunting, ride my horse. I have a landing strip there. We can land there and drive into Denver for the benefit show."

Ginger shot a look at him, wondering how all his success had really affected him. Perhaps she would find out if she spent the weekend with him. The Link she had known ten years ago had been a ranch kid, raised in poverty, who had dropped out of high school to go to work to support his blind uncle. Now he talked about his private jet, a ranch of his own. His was one of the best-known faces in the country. He couldn't go out in public without being mobbed by autograph seekers. His movie contracts earned him millions.

Standing here, talking to her, he seemed in most ways to be the same Link, but was he really?

She thought about the fan magazines that had linked him romantically with numerous glamorous women. Were those accounts true? Had he simply decided to make her another one of his conquests? But her own involvement in the industry made her aware of how those tabloids could exaggerate gossip just to please readers and sell copies.

There was no way of knowing the truth about Link . . . or about his motives. She could be taking a blind chance on a fresh heartbreak worse than she had already suffered.

Then she thought, he might be ten years older, but so was she! He might still have an overpowering physical appeal, the same old charm that could melt her resistance. But on the other hand, she was no longer the naive teenager blindly in love with her hero. She was no longer in love with love. She distrusted love now as much as she distrusted Link.

Finally, though filled with misgivings and doubts, she said, "All right. I'll pack and be ready early Saturday. We have to be back by Sunday night, though, because we're shooting again early Monday morning."

She said, "I want it clearly understood that in exchange for my going with you, I'll have your solemn promise you won't try to do any more of your own stunts, that you'll follow Derrick's orders and you'll leave the stunt work up to me and my people."

He nodded, gravely holding up his left hand. "Scout's honor. I promise, Ginger."

She was uneasily aware that this time he made no promises about not making a pass or trying to take advantage of her as he had that time ten years ago when he'd begged her to take the trip to Mexico with him.

Chapter Eight

On the flight to Colorado, Ginger tried to adjust to the changes ten years had made in herself and in Link Rockwood. He appeared to have accepted quite comfortably the affluence his screen success had brought him. He had arrived at the airport dressed casually in a western shirt, blue jeans and cowboy boots. He was at ease in the luxurious private jet, joking casually with the flight crew before takeoff. It appeared, at least on the surface, that he had taken his sudden wealth in stride without letting it go to his head.

He was in a jovial, lighthearted mood, but Ginger was not interested in casual chatter. She was withdrawn and uncommunicative, preferring to sit beside a window, gazing down at the countryside below, busy with her own thoughts.

After several unsuccessful attempts to strike up a conversation, Link fell into his own silence. He sprawled comfortably in his seat, occupying himself with a stack of outdoor, hunting magazines.

Ginger was attempting to deal with all the threatening implications of this new turn in her life. She relived the times she had spent with Link ten years ago, when her love was fresh and innocent. The flood of memories brought waves of nostalgia mingled with bitterness.

With agonizing clarity, there flashed across her mind's screen the picture of Link's face the first time his eyes drank in the sight of Paige's beauty. And she remembered with a stabbing twinge that night in the Mexican resort villa when she'd seen Link in the sand dunes, sobbing over Paige's rejection of him.

On their "wedding" morning, when she'd awakened to find herself a deserted bride, she had been convinced that Link was and would forever be a one woman man. And that woman was Paige. He would never again give his heart to another woman with such total devotion, she had believed then.

Did he still feel the same?

He had come back into her life something of a mystery. The fan magazines had linked him with Paige romantically from time to time in the past ten years. Was Link's infatuation with Ginger's beautiful sister still a major factor in his life?

The fact that he had remained single was evidence that he had never given up hope of someday winning Paige. He hadn't even been seriously involved in one of those "relationships" that made such juicy reading in the scandal tabloids, though he was often reported seen out on the town with beautiful women. That seemed to Ginger convincing evidence that his torch for Paige still smoldered as strong as ever.

Then why had he twisted Ginger's arm into making this weekend trip with him to Colorado? Perhaps for the same reason he'd talked her into going to Mexico with him. Link was a gregarious man. He did not like to be alone. But there had also been that avid look of male interest in his gaze that had taken inventory of her from head to foot, a look that had filled her with confusion and made her cheeks burn.

Her thoughts continued to go in circles, leading nowhere and giving no answers until her head throbbed. She was actually relieved when Link tossed his magazine aside and made another attempt at conversation.

"What do you think of your father's production?"

Ginger shrugged. "You've studied the script. What do you think?"

He frowned thoughtfully. "I dunno. Looks to me like Derrick is going way out on a limb on this one. It could bomb out."

"Yet you agreed to play the lead role."

"I owe Derrick a bunch, Ginger, as you know. Besides, I have a lot of confidence in him. If he says he can pull this off, maybe he can. And it gives me the first shot I've had at some real acting. Up to now all I've had to do is drive cars, get in barroom fights and act charming. This one can be a challenge."

Ginger nodded slowly, feeling a stab of worry, wondering if the part might be more than Link could handle. "It certainly doesn't fall into the genre that Hollywood is grinding out these days—the car smashing, blood and guts shockers, the sci-fi or suspense-porno flicks. It has the broad sweep of an epic covering turbulent periods of the past hundred years, while at the heart is a tender love story . . . and something else. I'm not sure just what Derrick has in mind, but I know he's going to want to make a statement with this film. Before he's done with it, there are going to be some changes made in the script; you can bank on that."

Link said, "Well, we'll have a chance for some of the first nationwide prepublicity tonight."

Ginger looked surprised. "You mean the benefit show?"

He nodded. "It's being carried by a major network on prime time. It's a kind of variety show format with some talk show and interview segments. They're going to ask me what I'm working on now, and that'll give me the opportunity to talk about *Thunder at Dawn*. I want you to be there with me. I'll introduce you as the stunt coordinator and the director's daughter. You can talk a little about the way the stunts in the film will be handled. People are interested in stuff like that."

Ginger looked dismayed. "Well, thanks for telling me. I get a terrible case of stage fright in front of TV cameras."

"After all the movies you've been in?"

"But those were different. I was always anonymous, just doing a stunt, not talking to a TV audience!"

He dismissed her concern with a casual shrug that was maddening. Then he changed the subject abruptly, nodding at a window. "There's the Rockies up ahead."

Ginger looked out. The sweep and grandeur of the great mountain ranges were breathtaking. Although it was late spring, many of the peaks were still snowcapped, some of them lost in low-hanging clouds.

They flew on for another half hour, then the plane began circling. Link straightened, his eyes lighting with eager anticipation. "There's my spread!" he exclaimed with boyish pride.

Ginger could see an area of rolling terrain, a beautiful green valley nestled among the towering mountains. The white ranch house looked like a child's toy from this height, and fences seemed from here to be made out of match sticks.

They buckled their seat belts. The plane came down for a smooth landing on a strip near the house.

Then they stepped from the plane to the firm earth. A plume of dust followed a speck that took on the form of a four-wheel-drive vehicle racing toward them from the ranch house. It slid to a gravel-slinging halt near the runway, and the driver hopped out, waving a broad-brimmed western hat in an exuberant greeting. "Señor Rockwood!" the Mexican-American ranch hand called.

He came striding toward them. For a heart-wrenching moment, Ginger thought it was Ramón, the taxi driver who had driven them to the Mexican village the night they were married. But when he drew nearer, she saw it was not.

"Hi, Enrique." To Ginger, he said, "Honey, this is Enrique Garcia, my ranch foreman."

Then, to the foreman, Link said, with a wicked twinkle, *"Enrique, esta es mi esposa, Señora Ginger."*

The foreman's face reflected surprise, then he bowed politely. "Welcome to your home, *Señora.* Please, I take your bags."

The foreman walked ahead of them to the vehicle. Ginger shot Link a narrowed look. "Why did he call me *Señora*? That's Spanish for a married woman, isn't it?"

Link shrugged.

"Just what was it you said to him in Spanish?" she demanded.

Link grinned. "I said, 'Enrique, this is my wife, Señora Ginger.'"

Ginger froze in midstride. Her face was flaming. "How dare you tell him that?" she raged.

"Well, it's true, isn't it?"

"It is not!"

"I seem to remember a certain night in Mexico, ten years ago. I was pretty looped on mescal, but not so much that I don't remember us getting married."

"That was a farce!" Ginger cried, dangerously close to tears now. "It was a cruel, mean thing for you to do to a nineteen-year-old kid. It wasn't a legal marriage, and you know it! And I think it's pretty rotten of you, Link Rockwood, to turn it into a joke now!"

Link's face grew sober. "You're right, Ginger. I shouldn't treat it lightly. And I didn't mean to make a joke out of it. But as for it not being a legal marriage, I'm not so sure about that. That taxi driver, Ramón, assured me the official we went to was legitimate. Do you remember Ramón?"

"I . . . I don't know," she lied. Of course she remembered Ramón. She remembered every moment of that weekend in Mexico with Link, every word that was spoken, every emotion she had felt, every sensation when he'd touched her. She'd fooled herself into believing she had forgotten, but being with him again brought back every aching detail.

As if wishing to extract himself from a touchy subject, Link waved his arm at the scenery around them. "Well, what do you think of my place?"

It was almost more than her senses could take in. The mountain ranges that surrounded Link's valley were awesome. The air, as pure as the crystal streams that tumbled down rocky gorges from the melting snow above, was delicately scented by the blossoms of a thousand spring wildflowers. The mingled hues of white and pink larkspur, bright red Indian paintbrush and the white, red and yellow tuliplike flowers of mariposa blanketed the countryside.

She drank in a lungful of the pure, sweet air. The altitude gave her a heady, slightly intoxicated feeling.

"Oh, Link, it's beautiful!" she cried, forgetting for the moment the bitterness that had made them strangers.

He made no attempt to conceal his joy and pride at his land. She could see it filling his eyes, and his gaze made a sweep of the valley. "Best way to really see the place is on horseback," he said. "Tomorrow morning, we'll go for a ride. But now we're going to have to hustle to get to Denver in time for the benefit show."

Enrique drove them to the ranch house with such reckless disregard for the dirt lane's limitations that Ginger grasped her seat and asked, "Is he related to that taxi driver, Ramón, down in Mexico?"

Link responded with a happy laugh. One booted foot was propped in an open window and he appeared totally unconcerned by Enrique's hair-raising driving style.

Considering Link's affluence, Ginger had halfway expected that his home here in the mountains would be palatial. But the ranch house was a white frame structure of modest design and construction. The rambling front porch extended across the entire front of the house. Its posts were made of stripped and polished cedar logs.

Seated on the porch in a rocker, his cowboy boots

crossed and propped against one of the posts, was
Link's uncle Jefferson, his sightless gaze directed
toward the distant mountain ranges. There was an
expression of peace and contentment on his leathery
countenance. Ginger saw with a pang that the ten
years had left a deep mark on him. His hair was
snow white; his voice was soft when he greeted Link.

"Uncle Jefferson, I have a young lady with me,
Ginger Lombard. Remember I brought her around
to the place when we were living in Brackettville just
before I went into the movies?"

The elderly man arose stiffly with an air of old-
fashioned courtesy. "I can't say I remember, ma'm.
You'll have to forgive me. Lately my memory isn't
very good. But you're certainly welcome. Link, you
see that your young lady friend has something cool
to drink, you hear?" Then he settled back in his
chair with a sigh, seeming to slip back into a world of
his own.

"He's getting pretty feeble," Link said, when they
had entered the house. "Has spells when his mind
wanders and he gets the notion he's back in Texas
punching cattle. But at least he isn't in any pain.
Doctor says he'll just sit out there dreaming away his
last few years and probably slip peacefully away one
night in his sleep. Kind of a quiet ending for an old
reprobate who led a violent life."

"You're . . . very kind to him," Ginger murmured, feeling a twinge of admiration for Link
despite her antagonism. "I suppose a lot of guys
would have just left a relative like that alone in his
shack back in Texas. But you brought him out here
to take care of him."

Link did have some admirable qualities, she
grudgingly admitted. An example was this benefit

performance tonight. He was known in the film industry as a soft touch where any charity was concerned. He spent much of his free time doing benefit shows around the country.

But that had nothing to do with their personal conflict, she reminded herself grimly.

The main room of the rambling old house was spacious, with a large stone fireplace at one end. The furniture was a western mixture of rough hewn oak and cowhide. A Navajo rug covered the hardwood floor. On the wall were game trophies and a collection of modern cowboy art by such painters as James Bama, John Clymer and James Reynolds, a collection that Ginger suspected had not come cheap.

Link showed her to a guest bedroom where Enrique deposited her luggage.

"Think you can be dressed and ready to go in thirty minutes?" Link asked, glancing at his watch.

"That's asking a lot of a woman, but I'll do my best."

Under the circumstances, with an imminent appearance on a nationally televised benefit show, Ginger knew her sister, Paige, would carefully plan an effect with a gown custom designed for shock or sex appeal.

Ginger's wardrobe included nothing so exotic. She preferred the casual—usually shorts, slacks or sports outfits. Her stunt career had not called for glamor, and she didn't spend a lot of money on high-fashion garments. But fortunately she had brought along one slightly extravagant outfit designed with a cowl-neck collar, full sleeves, a wide bronze-colored obi belt and divided skirt. Ginger thought it made a rather dashing, adventurous statement in keeping with her career as a stunt person, and the shiny knit material in a plum hue gave a flattering accent to her yellow brown hair and tawny eyes.

Her high heels, bronze-hued to complement the garment's belt, added inches to her proud height. But beside Link's towering physique, her being a tall woman would present no problem.

She met the thirty-minute deadline. When she entered the living room, Link gave a soft, approving whistle that brought heightened color to her cheeks.

As for Link, he had made the transformation from cowboy to formal attire. The event called for a black tie. Ginger thought, with a tremor in her stomach, that it wasn't fair for one man to look so devastatingly handsome in a tuxedo. It draped smoothly from his broad shoulders, tapered to his tight waist. The trousers were just snug enough to outline his firm posterior and muscular thighs.

The fast drive over winding mountain roads in Link's sports car was breathtaking. But Ginger felt secure with his strong, tanned hands on the wheel. When Link drove, he seemed to become part of the machine. It responded eagerly to his skillful handling. He was as good with a car as he was with a horse. And probably with a woman, Ginger's simmering hostility reminded her with a knife's burning twist.

The benefit show was well planned. It was a spectacular event including a parade of stars and celebrities interspersed with musical and dance acts. Just as Link promised, he got in a plug for *Thunder at Dawn*, and Ginger was on camera briefly to answer questions about the special effects and stunt work planned for the film. She nearly suffocated from stage fright but somehow survived.

Their spot in the show had come on late. Ginger

was exhausted when they left the studio. Link looked tired, too. On the drive back through the mountains, Ginger curled up on her side of the seat and dozed.

When they drove into the ranch yard, Ginger stumbled groggily into the guest room, shed her clothes and fell into bed. She was fast asleep within minutes. Perhaps it was the high, cool air. She couldn't remember when she'd slept so soundly. She awoke the next morning feeling totally rested and filled with energy.

She was halfway out of bed when she realized that what had awakened her was a tapping at her door. "Yes? Who is it?"

"Link," he answered through the door panel. "Are you hungry?"

She became aware of the tantalizing fragrance of bacon and coffee and was suddenly ravenous. "Yes, I'm starved."

"Okay if I come in?"

She drew back into bed, clutching the cover in front of her. "W-why do you want to do that?"

"Because I have your breakfast, silly," he said with a chuckle.

"You . . . you do?"

"Sure. Guests here at the Double L Ranch get the VIP treatment—breakfast in bed. Now can I come in?"

With a wave of panic she drew still more of the cover up around her neck, then said, "Y-yes."

Link pushed open the door. He entered with a breakfast tray that was laden with a hearty meal of biscuits, scrambled eggs, bacon, toast, fruit and coffee. He carefully placed the tray across her lap.

"It looks delicious," Ginger exclaimed, her appetite for the moment overriding the conflicting emotions she felt at having Link enter her bedroom.

"Hungry?"

"I sure am!"

"This climate will do that to you." He sat on the edge of the bed, watching her. "Well . . . go ahead. Don't let it get cold."

Nervously she wondered if he intended to stay and watch her eat the entire meal. She supposed she could order him out of the room, but that seemed a bit harsh after his apparent display of warm hospitality. Perhaps, he was just waiting to see if she found the meal satisfactory, then he'd leave. She hoped so.

One bare arm ventured from under the cover. She took a sip of the coffee. It tasted even better than it smelled. Then she sampled a crunchy strip of bacon and licked her lips in ecstasy. Next she tried a golden brown biscuit. It brought an exclamation of delight. "That has to be the best biscuit I ever tasted—so light and fluffy!" she exclaimed.

"Try it with some of that homemade preserve," Link suggested.

That required exposing two bare arms, but she took the chance and ladled a generous spoonful of the peach preserves on a biscuit and popped it in her mouth. "Ummm," she murmured. "Wherever did you find homemade preserves like that?"

"Enrique's wife makes it," he said.

"And she baked the biscuits," Ginger concluded.

"No," Link corrected. "I baked the biscuits."

"You!" She gazed at him in wide-eyed amazement.

"Sure. Why do you act so surprised?"

"Well . . . you look like the type who would be

more adept in a horse corral than in a kitchen. I have this mental picture of you plowing through a kitchen, knocking over pots and pans and dropping dishes."

"Well, I do break a dish now and then," he admitted. "But do I look that inept?"

"No, just the outdoor type," she observed, wolfing down another biscuit and following that with a sip of steaming coffee. "What else do you cook—quiche, chateaubriand . . . ?"

"Whoa! Now you're getting out of my class. My cooking repertoire is strictly confined to cowboy chuckwagon fare. After Uncle Jefferson went blind, I had to cook for both of us. I learned how to fry bacon and eggs and bake biscuits. I make a mean rabbit stew, and I can fry catfish. Nothing fancy, just plain, hearty food that sticks to a man's ribs when he has to go dig fence posts all day."

"Well, I don't plan to dig any fence-post holes, but I'm really enjoying this."

"I'm enjoying the view," he teased. "Do you always sleep in the buff?"

She had become so absorbed in the delicious meal that she'd totally lost track of the cover she'd had tucked under her arms. She looked up, saw a flaming glow in his eyes and at the same instant realized with a horrified shock that the cover had slipped away, exposing considerably more than her bare arms and shoulders. She gasped and jerked the sheet over her breasts. "Link Rockwood, you miserable polecat!"

He held up his hands in a gesture of defense. "Don't get sore at me. I'm just sitting here minding my own business."

"The heck you are!" she cried. "You . . . you Peeping Tom! Get out of my room!"

"Okay, okay!"

He arose and headed for the door. She angrily hurled a biscuit after him, then regretted the impulsive action because it was the last one on her plate. And she'd die before asking him for any more.

Through the closed door, Link said, "After you finish breakfast, get into something comfortable and we'll go for a ride. I want to show you around the place."

Her first reaction was to tell him she was locking her door and staying in the room until it was time to fly back to the filming location. But a glance through the window at the incredible scenery outside advised her that she'd be cutting off her nose to spite her face. She managed to simmer down and finish her breakfast. Grudgingly she admitted to herself that it wasn't Link's fault the cover had slipped down.

A dark question bubbled up from some subterranean level of her mind to embarrass her. Might letting the cover slip have been the result of a subconscious act of deliberate negligence?

Her cheeks flamed as she furiously denied the charge of her own conscience. She hated Link Rockwood! The last thing she wanted to do, consciously or unconsciously, was anything that could be construed as flirting with him.

She moved the breakfast tray aside, took a quick shower and dressed in a faded shirt, blue jeans and boots. She felt a lot more at ease in this outfit than she had in last night's glamorous attire.

She found Link in the main room, comfortably sprawled in a chair, reading a newspaper. He put it aside when she walked in, leaned back, laced his fingers and gave her the kind of head to toe survey that brought a burning wave of self-consciousness and anger. He never used to look at her in that bold, appraising way when she first met him. Was it because he had grown egotistical and callous about women? Or was it because she'd been a teenager then and he'd had a big brother, protective attitude?

She certainly didn't have that protection now. She felt as if his gaze was searching out every curve of her bosom, which filled the old, worn shirt she was wearing, and every inch of her long legs, clearly outlined by the tight jeans.

His look angered her because she knew there was no love involved. He kept that reserved for the one woman who had forever captured his heart—Paige Lombard. But for some reason, he had worked up some kind of male interest in Ginger's body since seeing her again. She supposed that should give her wounded pride some satisfaction, considering how he'd rejected her that night in Mexico. But the victory was hollow. She was no longer a child as she'd been that time in Mexico, willing to settle for any crumb Link Rockwood was willing to toss her way.

"Well," he said, breaking the unpleasant tension, "I'm glad to see you're all dressed for a ride. Good! I already told Enrique to saddle up a couple of horses."

Ginger followed Link out to the corral. She found it impossible to remain in an angry mood. The crisp mountain air and spectacular scenery were therapy her emotions couldn't resist.

Link's ranch foreman led a beautiful bay mare toward her. "Good morning, *Señora,*" he said politely. "I hope you slept well."

Ginger's cheeks burned as she remembered that Link had introduced her to Enrique as his wife.

Evidently Link hadn't bothered to correct the situation, because Enrique was still calling her *Señora*.

She was about to get that little matter straightened out when Link rode up on his own horse, a spirited palomino. "Let's go," he said impatiently. "I have a lot to show you before we have to fly back this afternoon."

Ginger swung easily into her saddle. She always got a feeling of exhilaration when she was astride a good mount.

"What do you think of her?" Link called.

"She's beautiful! I just love her!" Ginger cried, reaching forward to pat the sleek neck of her steed. The animal gave a frisky toss of her head in response.

"Well, she doesn't have a mean streak like that cayuse that threw you in the watering trough back in Texas." Link chuckled.

That awoke a flash of hurting memories that Ginger forcibly put aside. She was determined not to let all the old bitterness spoil this beautiful day. This would be her last breathing spell before plunging into the demanding work ahead of them, made all the more demanding because of the fear that haunted her constantly when she had to be around stunt work. And Paige was flying in sometime today and would be on the set with Link tomorrow. The minute they were together, the old flames would ignite, and Link would forget Ginger existed.

So why not make the most of this peaceful moment and savor all the day had to offer? She lifted her face to drink in the beauty that surrounded them as they rode across the wildflower-carpeted valley. All of her senses seemed acutely sharpened. Colors were almost painfully vivid. Sounds were like a symphony—the creak of saddle leather, the rustle of grass they rode through, the distant call of a bird. She felt in tune with the universe, a part of nature.

Was it because Link rode beside her, so tall and handsome, his steel gray eyes sweeping across the panorama that extended for miles around them, then gazing directly at her?

No! her cautious mind shouted. Being with Link had nothing to do with the strange mood that had come over her. And even as she told herself that, she knew she lied. How was it possible to hate a man and yet feel so in tune with his being? They had not spoken a word since they rode out of the corral. Link seemed to have the sensitivity to know that conversation would spoil the fragile beauty of the golden morning. The silence between them was comfortable and relaxed. Gone for now was the ugly tension she'd felt around him since he'd come back into her life. There was something good about having him riding beside her.

She had never outgrown the habit of role-playing. As they rode, her imagination took over, creating a beautiful scenario with a frontier setting. They were living in the past century, a couple who had made the grueling journey across the plains in a covered wagon. Now they had found the land they'd staked out for their homestead. Link would cut down trees with his ax and build a log cabin. They would raise cattle and horses, fight off outlaws, have a family, build an empire. They would live close to the land and nature, making friends with wild animals, be in tune with the seasons.

She was still lost in the reverie of her story when they reached the foothills. Link swung down from his horse and indicated that she was to do the same.

He tied both animals to a bush, then led the way through a grove of towering pine trees. They came to the bank of a stream. Ginger gasped with delight at the incredible beauty of this hidden glen.

The glaciers of the Pleistocene Age had left their scars behind in the ravines and tumbled boulders around them. The icy clear mountain stream raced down a bed of stones washed smooth and white, splashing here and there over waterfalls, then resting in deep ponds where trout swam. The area between the boulders was carpeted with soft grasses and wild flowers.

"Link, this is just . . . just breathtaking!"

"Thought you might like it. Beats a Hollywood make-believe set, right?"

She found a comfortable spot in the grass beside the stream. Link walked back to where the horses were tied, then rejoined her carrying his saddlebags. From them he took several packages and a thermos bottle. "Did the ride give you an appetite?"

"You know, after that breakfast, I didn't think I could possibly eat again all day, but, incredibly, yes, I am hungry. I'm afraid if I spent much time up here, I'd wind up as plump as my aunt Judy."

"Oh, you'd ride it off."

For the moment, she sensed that her emotions had made a kind of truce with him. The day was too beautiful to spoil it with negative feelings. In a few hours they would be flying back to join the others with the movie production company. She decided she would stifle her emotions about Link for the time being and treat him with cool politeness.

Link was busy laying out a picnic lunch of imported cheeses, jars of sweet pickles, caviar and crackers. He placed a bunch of huge, red grapes in the icy water of the stream to cool. Then he produced two plastic thin-stemmed wine glasses and uncorked the thermos.

Ginger watched in amazement as he filled the wine glasses with champagne from the thermos.

"It was the only way I could think of to keep it cold," he explained, handing her a glass.

She sipped the bubbling wine. It tingled in her mouth and made her nose tickle. Then she sampled the cheese and realized she was more than hungry— she was ravenous. The simple lunch became a king's banquet.

Link lifted the bunch of grapes from the stream. Tiny beads of moisture clung to the purple globes. He asked Ginger to open her mouth and popped one between her lips. She bit into the succulent fruit. Her taste buds were flooded with sweet nectar. She made sounds of ecstasy.

"I have a friend in California who raises superb grapes," Link said. "Once in a while he sends me samples."

The food, the champagne, the altitude and scenery combined to give Ginger a feeling of languid relaxation. She lay back in the soft grass, hands behind her head, and gazed at patches of blue sky peeping at her through the pine branches overhead. A soft breeze whispered through the boughs to the gurgling brook, which passed the message on to a humming insect that touched its surface.

Then Ginger became aware of Link's face moving into the perimeter of her vision. "You look very contented," he murmured.

Instead of intruding on the gentle sounds around them, his low, masculine voice blended in, lulling her even more into a dangerous sense of security.

There was a vitality about him that seemed an extension of the wild setting, the giant boulders, the towering pines, the restless energy of the stream pouring down through the great chasms in the mountainside. The strength in his arms was like that of the branches above her that could whip back at the force of a gale. And she saw in his steel gray eyes a reflection of the winter blizzards that raged through these mountains. Something about Link Rockwood would forever be as untamed as this wilderness, she knew with a growing, uneasy feeling of excitement.

Her senses that had been so aware of nature suddenly became focused on the big man stretched in the grass beside her. The mingled masculine scent of saddle leather, shaving lotion, healthy perspiration and tobacco swept away all other smells. He was propped on an elbow, gazing down at her, and she lost sight of the forest.

Suddenly she became acutely aware of their isolation here. With a touch of panic, she sat up. "Ready to ride again?" she asked nervously.

"The horses need a rest," he said calmly. "Besides, I like it here, don't you?"

There was more to his words than the surface meaning. He was looking at her in a way again that made her instinctively cross her arms over her breasts as if to keep him from seeing through her blouse.

"The horses have had plenty of rest," she said sharply.

But her protest made no impression on him. He appeared determined to stretch out this interlude. "This is the first chance I've had to really talk with you, y'know that?"

"I don't see what we have to talk about," she said coldly, all of her defenses aroused now.

"Oh, I can think of a lot of things. It has been ten years since I've seen you." He was silent for a moment, then disconcerted her by asking abruptly, "How about your love life?"

Her cheeks burned. "That's a very personal and impertinent question!"

"Really? I didn't mean to insult you. I just wondered if there's been any special man in your life since we parted company."

"I don't think that's any of your business," she said, her voice as cold as the mountain stream.

"I think a husband has a right to know who his wife has been running around with."

There was a twinkle in his eye, but that attempt at humor rankled her.

"You're contemptible, you know that?" she retorted. "Don't you feel any shame over what you did in Mexico? And stop referring to yourself as my husband!"

Her scolding had little effect on his good-humored teasing. "You're evading my question. Does that mean you have a boyfriend?"

"Several," she snapped. "A whole male harem."

He chuckled. "Why is it I don't find that convincing?"

She shrugged. "I don't care if you do or not. Of course there have been some men in my life. Do you think I've been sitting home knitting for the past ten years?"

He frowned, and for the moment his eyes darkened. Aha, she thought with a feeling of triumph. His male ego had been nicked.

He said, "Well, I notice you didn't marry any of them."

"What, and commit bigamy?" she asked, with a raised eyebrow, deciding to counter with his own game.

"It would have been bigamy." He nodded. "That Mexican marriage was legal, you know."

"Oh, I doubt that," she retorted, although feeling somewhat shaken by his positive tone. "Those quickie Mexican marriages are not considered legal."

He gazed at her steadily, his steel gray eyes unnerving her. "I wouldn't be too sure about that. Have you ever discussed it with a lawyer?"

"N-no. I . . . didn't think it was necessary. Anyway, if there was any legality about the marriage, it could be annulled. It was . . . was never consummated, you know," she said, aware that her cheeks were flaming.

He nodded soberly. "Yes, I've thought about that a lot since seeing you again, Ginger. And I think we ought to do something about that."

She tried to swallow. "Wh-what do you mean?"

Panic suddenly raced through her. She was on her back. He was propped on an elbow, looking down at her in a way that put her in a trapped, helpless position. "Just this," he said softly, and bent and kissed her.

She was too surprised to move. She stared up at him, her eyes wide. It had been a light kiss, but it left her temporarily paralyzed.

Before she could catch her breath, his lips touched hers again, this time more firmly. She lay rigid, her thoughts flying in the wind. Her emotions lost all sense of direction. His kiss was a slow, lingering caress, almost as if his lips were fondling hers, loving them, savoring the contact as if enjoying a sample of heady wine.

She tried to raise her arms, to push him away. But her muscles were like water. Her breathing had become ragged. With a supreme effort, she turned her face away. "No," she whimpered.

"No?" he asked, as if surprised. "But why not, Ginger. "You don't like kissing me?"

She looked up at his face, only inches away, her eyes filling with tears. "Why . . . after ten years, are you doing this to me? You used to be so nice to me . . . so kind and protective."

"Don't you think the situation is a little different now?" he challenged. "Back then you were a youngster, a teenager. I was a lot older than you. I felt like I would have been a dirty rat, taking advantage of you. But now you're grown up, a woman. A very sexy woman, I might add."

"I don't think the situation has changed at all," Ginger whispered, fighting hard to battle down her tears. "I'm not sure I buy all that chivalrous talk, Link. The simple truth is that you were so hopelessly in love with my sister, Paige, that no other woman on earth could turn you on."

She saw at once she had struck a vulnerable spot. She could almost feel sorry for Link at the flash of pain from an old wound in his eyes, a wound she had just touched. "It's true, isn't it?" she murmured.

"Now I'll repeat what you said a while back," he replied almost harshly. "That's none of your business. It's a personal matter, Ginger."

But she felt compelled to strike again at his vulnerable spot. "Furthermore," she said, "I think you are still in love with her as much now as you were then. I notice you haven't married either. And I seriously doubt it was because of any worry over committing bigamy!"

If she had hoped to see a reaction, she was in for a disappointment. Something like an internal door slammed closed in his eyes, keeping his feelings shut away from her searching eyes.

"Ginger, honey," he said, his voice softening. "let's not spoil this moment by dredging up a lot of things out of the past. I know I hurt you in Mexico, and I'm sorry. But that was then and this is now. And you can't convince me you find me all that repulsive."

To prove it, he kissed her again, and her traitorous emotions sided with him. She might hate him and curse him with the reasoning part of her mind, but reason had nothing to do with the chemistry that his touch brought to an instant boil.

His kiss became more searching, more demanding, asking that her lips part, and finding the rim of her teeth with his tongue when they did. The gentle probing sent scorching waves of heat rising from deep within her. Her breath rasped.

She fought the rising tide of passion. It was like trying to push back the ocean with a child's sand pail. She had loved him too long. Yes, loved him! For ten years she had been telling herself the lie that she hated him, wanting nothing more to do with him. Now one kiss from him stripped bare the lie and made her face the truth. She had never stopped loving Link Rockwood, had never stopped wanting him.

Every pounding heartbeat reaffirmed it.

When his kisses trailed down her cheek to the

hollow of her throat, then to the valley of her bosom, the hunger in her body responded with mounting waves of heat that made her feel flushed all over. She felt herself trembling.

And she was aware of the trembling of his fingers as he opened the buttons of her shirt and pushed the bra straps down from her shoulders. She felt the cool mountain air caress her bare bosom, and then she gasped as his kisses rained a trail of fire over the creamy mounds. His tongue toyed with nipples that were now throbbing points of fire. Her arms went around him instinctively. Her fingers caressed his hair and then trailed around to his shirt front and shamelessly opened buttons and pushed the garment back from his shoulders, baring his broad chest. She pressed her palms against the thick mat of hair on his chest, then dug her fingers into the tight curls.

Somewhere among her chaotic thoughts was the prayer of thankfulness that her accident last year had left no scars. She might not be a raving beauty like her sister, but her body was strong and supple, with long, clean lines and healthy curves. Her breasts were as high and firm as when she was eighteen. Her legs, conditioned with running and swimming, had the long, slim lines of a model.

His arms became steel bands around her. She throbbed with the exciting contact of their bare flesh, her soft breasts yielding to the pressure of his hard, muscular chest. She felt the hair on his chest tickle her skin.

Then he drew back from her, his gaze hungrily drinking in the lovely vision of her figure. She felt mounting waves of excitement at the intimacy of the moment, of allowing him to see her this way. His caresses moved down to her waist, opening the fastenings on her jeans, caressing her stomach, sliding the waistband over her hips.

It was the touch of grass and earth against her bare back that brought a cold dash of sanity to her. Somehow she found the strength to struggle away from Link, to slide her jeans back in place and close fasteners and buttons with shaking fingers. She drew a deep breath, then said unsteadily. "Link, please don't rush me. I'm not ready to go to bed with you."

"Are you sure about that?" he asked, his gray eyes stormy. "It seems to me you want me as much as I want you."

"All right," she admitted, turning her flushed face away. "Maybe I do want. But I'm not going to let it happen just yet. I've had heartbreak enough from you. I want to know more about what I'm letting myself in for before I give in to that kind of commitment. I'm sure in the past ten years, you've become very adept at seducing women. Now you've seen me after all this time, and for some reason I look good to you. You have the day off, so why not have a little fun. That's about the size of it, isn't it? A one-night stand? Well, thanks but no thanks. I need more than that before I'm going to sleep with you, Link."

"Dammit, Ginger," he exploded. "We're not having an affair. You're my wife! It's perfectly legal. We're just ten years late having our honeymoon!"

She glared at him. "Boy, I've heard some great lines, but that has to be a classic!"

"It happens to be true, doesn't it?"

"It wasn't my fault we didn't have a honeymoon ten years ago," she said cuttingly. "If you'll recall, I was available. But apparently you didn't find me attractive enough to want me. Why you have suddenly changed your mind and want me now is beyond me."

"Ginger, you've got it all wrong! I didn't find you unattractive. Any sane, healthy man would have wanted you. I've told you—but you don't seem to listen—that I didn't feel right taking advantage of you when you were so young. I married you when I was drunk. The next morning I sobered up. There you were, a trusting little kid, curled up beside me. You might think I'm a rat, but I do have something of a conscience. I thought the best thing for you was for me just to leave before I messed your life up even more. There've been plenty of times in the past ten years when I wanted to see you, to explain. But my acting career was taking me all over the place, and every time I tried to contact you, you refused to talk to me. When you were in the hospital, they wouldn't let me see you. I sent you flowers, and you said you gave them to somebody else. Now this film we're working on has thrown us together. And seeing you again well, you looked damned good to me. Maybe it's occurred to me how much I've been missing the past ten years."

"And I don't suppose Paige had a thing to do with the reason you left in such a hurry that morning after we were married," Ginger said pointedly.

His refusal to give her a direct answer was all the answer she needed. "Ginger," he said with a gesture of frustration, "you're asking tough questions, questions I don't have all the answers to. I was a very confused, heartsick, distraught guy that time we went to Mexico together. You know that. I was drowning, Ginger, going down for the third time. All I can tell you is that I didn't think it was right to drag you down into the emotional muddle I was in."

"But now you do?"

"This is altogether different. It's a different time in our lives, a different place."

Was it really? Ginger wondered with a touch of sadness. Link seemed to be under the impression that because she was older, a woman now, she would be more immune to heartbreak. That wasn't true, but she had no way of explaining it to him.

She was weary of trying to explain it to herself. Once before in her life, the opportunity to realize the fulfillment of her love for Link had been denied her. Now life was giving her another chance. The temptation was almost overpowering for her to grab the chance and count the cost tomorrow. But reason and fear held her back, fear of even more pain than she had suffered over him in the past. Loving him had caused her nothing but heartache. Why would it be any different now?

"I don't understand exactly what it is you want from me."

He smiled crookedly. "You don't?"

She flushed. "Besides the obvious, I mean. You keep bringing up that Mexican marriage . . . saying I'm your wife. Are you implying that you want us to start living together openly as man and wife?"

He gazed at her thoughtfully. "Ginger, I'll be honest. I hadn't thought that far ahead. I felt a powerful attraction the minute I laid eyes on you again. I guess I've been sort of playing it by ear ever since, letting things happen naturally. Right now, the most natural thing in the world seems to be to take you in my arms, to hold you, to make love to you. And you can't tell me you don't feel the same. You responded like a woman very much in love."

Damn him, she thought hopelessly. How could

she defend herself against him when her infatuation with him was so obvious?

To gain time, she moved away from him. She kicked off her boots, sat on the bank of the stream and let her bare feet dangle in the crystal-clear water. It swirled around her ankles. The icy chill of the water cleared her head. She drew her left foot up and rested her chin on her knee, hugging her leg and staring down at her right foot in the stream. "Link," she sighed, "why the heck did you have to come back into my life right now? You couldn't have picked a worse time!"

He moved to her side, looking at her questioningly. "I don't know what you mean."

"Oh"—she waved her hands in a gesture of despair—"it hasn't been enough that I'm going through hell trying to cope with this grandiose production of my father. Now I've got the problem of what to do about you, too!"

"I don't think I understand exactly."

She sighed. "Link, something happened to me inside when I took that bad fall from the helicopter last year. I'm not just talking about getting busted up physically. That part eventually healed up okay. But it's left me scared inside. It . . . it was so bad I couldn't stand even to watch a movie on TV that I'd done any stunt work in. My hands would get sweaty, my stomach would knot up, I couldn't breathe. The walls closed in on me. I swore I'd never go near another movie set again as long as I lived. Then my illustrious father breezed back on the scene and dumped this little blockbuster in my lap. I'm supposed to plan and coordinate all the stunts. And yet every time we get ready to shoot a stunt scene, I'm still sick with fear."

She could feel his troubled gaze. Gone from his eyes was the passion of a few moments ago. She had the feeling he was looking at her with the caring, protective concern he had shown toward her when they first met, when she had been in the uncertain stage between childhood and young womanhood and he'd been a small-town horse wrangler with an air of old-fashioned frontier chivalry about him.

"I didn't realize you were under that kind of strain, Ginger. You do a good job of covering up. And I didn't make it any easier on you the other day with my grandstand ego stunt. I'm sorry. But why on earth did you take on this job if it's going to be this rough on you?"

She shrugged. "I didn't have a choice. Dad has everything he owns sunk in this production. And more than money, his life is riding on this film. He hasn't been getting parts any more, Link. He feels he's over the hill as an actor. He has to make it as a producer-director or get out of the film industry altogether. And that would kill him. He needs me, but more than just to coordinate the stunts. The whole thing is more than he can take on by himself. These past months I've practically been his associate producer. I need to take a lot of the details off his hands so he can concentrate on directing now that we're actually going into production."

Link's arm went around her in a way that was comforting and strong. Gone was the passionate fury of the stormy moments a short while before. Ginger welcomed the quiet security of his strength. She rested her head against his shoulder, feeling very close to tears.

He gently stroked her hair and kissed her forehead gently. It was the kind of masculine tenderness she had hungered for from her father when she was a little girl but had never received. Now she felt tired and lost from the battle she had been fighting. For a few minutes, she wanted to be that little girl whose father had been too busy, too wrapped up with his own life, to understand the needs of a young daughter.

She was dimly aware of a growing tenderness between herself and Link. A sweetness took the place of fire and passion. He reached for her hand. He gently kissed each fingertip. It was not a moment for words. She only wanted to be close to him, to be lost in the security and safety of his strong arms.

She was tired of struggling with thoughts and emotions. She just wanted to be taken care of, to be made to feel whole.

The act of making love, when it happened, was a slow and tender discovery of each other, an unhurried touching and melting together, a kind of poetry of the joining of their bodies and inner beings. A camera would have pictured them through a softly focused hazy lens, their movements attuned to a musical score whose theme was created by the wind in the trees, the rustle of the wild flowers, the sweet song of a bird. Through the mist of the special camera lens, their bodies would show pale in the crushed grass, beautiful with the line and symmetry of human form.

Afterward, Ginger snuggled contentedly against Link's shoulder, her arm across his broad chest. She felt close to tears and couldn't decide if they were tears of joy or sadness. She felt at ease in their nakedness, unashamed and relaxed.

She gazed at him for a long time, memorizing each line and curve of his face. Something deep within her, conscious and fearful of the fragility of time, wanted to imprint this moment indelibly in her mind so it could be called back up and replayed for the rest of her life. For, she thought sadly, the present was gone almost the instant it took place, and all that was left was memories.

She turned and gazed up at the trees and sky above. She felt lazy and languorous. She breathed deeply, causing her breasts to rise and fall. Softly she said, "Link . . . it was so good."

"Yes," he said, his breath stirring her hair. "Yes, it was. I knew it would be."

A squirrel scampered across a branch in the tree above her and stopped, looking down, flicking its tail nervously. She watched it for a moment, thinking about the night she had married Link in Mexico. In a way, for right now, she did feel they were married, just the way the papers they'd signed down in Mexico said they were. What had happened between them was something that had seemed right for the moment, and she was Link's wife.

Her fingers trailed down to his chest, where they traced a pattern in the swirls of hair. In the mingled afterglow of lovemaking, she felt a mixture of contentment, happiness and a bittersweet tinge of sadness.

This beautiful hideaway, this private Garden of Eden, was only an island between emotional storms. Making love with Link today had solved nothing. No mention of love or permanent commitment had passed Link's lips.

Today Paige would be flying in from Europe. She was probably already with Derrick at the film location. She'd had the movie script for several weeks, long enough to learn her part. Tomorrow they would

begin shooting the scenes with Link. The two of
them would be thrown together every day for many
weeks to come. They would be acting out passionate
love scenes before the cameras. Nothing Link could
say would convince Ginger that he had ever gotten
Paige out of his system. The torch he carried for her
was smoldering, ready to burst into flames again.
Ginger felt certain that he had fallen as hopelessly in
love with Paige from the first moment he'd laid eyes
on her as Ginger had fallen in love with him. And
she was convinced that Link was the kind of man
who loved a woman for a lifetime.

As much as it hurt and as bitterly jealous as she
might feel, Ginger knew she had nothing to gain by
using today's intimacy with Link as some kind of
hold on him. Nothing had really changed. Her love
for Link was as hopeless as ever. There was no real
change in the scenario. When Paige came back on
scene, they would be back in the roles that fate had
assigned them.

Ginger sat up and began dressing. She felt a
sudden chill in the air. The birds had stopped
singing. The sun had gone behind a cloud.

Chapter Nine

$\mathcal{L}$ ink's private jet flew them back to Georgia that night. For Ginger it was like leaving a movie theater where she had been lost in a beautiful make-believe story. Now she was being thrust back into the world of harsh reality.

As she expected, Paige had arrived during the day. She was in Derrick's motor home on the film set, having a drink with her father when Ginger got there.

Paige was as breathtakingly beautiful as ever. She was wearing her raven hair in a sweeping style over one shoulder. Her complexion was flawless. Her eyes were luminous, dark pools, her lips full and sensuous, and as always she was dressed in a way that displayed her stunning figure in a subtle, yet provocative manner. She was wearing black designer hostess pajamas that clung silkily to every delicate curve and svelte line of her body. One glance at her, and Ginger's childhood inferiority complex returned in a smothering wave.

Ginger knew Paige and her father had been sharing one of those special close chats that had always made Ginger feel like an outsider.

Paige greeted Ginger with a dazzling smile. "Hi, sis," she said brightly. She put her drink down and jumped up to give her younger sister an impulsive hug.

They had not seen each other in six months. Now she stepped back and surveyed Ginger with a sweep of her huge, dark eyes. "You look wonderful, Ginger!"

"Didn't I tell you?" Derrick grinned. "Completely recovered—no scars. Good as new!"

"Yes, and something else," Paige said with a smiling, quizzical look. "You have a sort of radiant glow, Ginger, darling. Do I detect the look of a woman in love?"

Ginger blushed furiously, feeling a wave of unreasoning anger at her sister's female intuition. She tried to mutter a denial, but Derrick put his two cents in at that point. "She just flew off to Denver with Link over the weekend. Maybe that accounts for it," he said with a wicked twinkle in his eyes.

Paige's appraisal of her sister suddenly became coolly speculative. "Is that it, Ginger? You and Link? Really? I always thought he treated you like a kid sister."

"Oh, don't be ridiculous," Ginger snapped, acutely defensive for reasons she couldn't explain. She wasn't ready to announce to the world that she was in love with Link Rockwood. The emotions she was experiencing were too personal, too fresh, too fragile. Besides, she'd had no assurance from Link that he shared her feelings. She had already faced the fact that what had been so important to her might well have been no more than a weekend fling for Link, quickly forgotten. She had finally surrendered to the insanity of the moment, but with enough grasp on reality to accept facts.

She had no intention of letting the world know what had happened between her and Link, only to face humiliation subsequently.

"Of course I'm not in love," she said firmly, hoping she sounded convincing. "Right now I'm too wrapped up in this production to get involved with any man."

She could tell by Paige's cool, searching look that her glamorous sister didn't quite believe her. It wasn't easy to fool another woman, especially Paige, who'd had so much experience in matters of the heart.

"Well, children," Derrick announced, arising and placing his empty glass on a counter with a flourish, "it is late and I am facing a difficult day tomorrow, so it's off to bed for me. You may stay up and talk if you wish, although, Paige, I would remind you—not as your father, but as your director—that you have an important scene in the morning in which you must look extremely beautiful."

He kissed them both on the forehead and retired to one of the bedrooms at the rear of the large motor home.

"How does he do that?" Ginger muttered. "He can't say good night without making it sound and look like a scene from a sophisticated drawing room drama."

"The word is elegance." Paige smiled fondly. "A few men have that air. He makes you think of Peter O'Toole, doesn't he? Or Noel Coward perhaps?"

"Yes." Ginger nodded. "What do you think of the story he's shooting?"

Paige lit a cigarette, blew a plume of smoke through pursed lips. "Unusual. Daring. Different. How intense love between a man and woman can be under stress . . . when they have to live a lifetime in a few hours. Fascinating, don't you think?"

Absentmindedly, Ginger took a cigarette from the package Paige had carelessly tossed on the table, lit it, then frowned at it. "I keep forgetting I quit smoking." She puffed on it a few times anyway before crushing it in an ashtray, then sighed. "Yeah, it's all those things, Paige. It could be an artistic triumph or a box office disaster. I'm not sure yet if he can make it commercial enough to sell."

"Oh, I have faith in Derrick. If anyone can do it, he can."

"He has a lot riding on this production," Ginger said with a frown, rubbing her fingers together nervously. "He sold all his property, you know."

"Yes. He told me. But I think he'll get it back with a huge profit."

"I hope so."

There was a moment of silence as Paige smoked thoughtfully, gazing at Ginger. "You're uptight, darling. I don't remember you ever being nervous. Still have the jitters from that accident?"

"Yes," Ginger admitted. "I don't like being involved with stunt work again, even as coordinator. I wouldn't have done it for any other reason except that Dad needed help."

Paige leaned over and patted her hand. "You're going to be all right, Ginger. You're made of tough material."

It was a rare moment of closeness between them. She tried to examine her feelings about Paige and found them as confused and ambivalent as those for

THUNDER AT DAWN

her father. Sibling rivalry struggled with family
blood ties. Over the years her emotions toward
Paige had run the gamut from love and admiration
to envy and hostility. At this point in life, it was
impossible to unravel their tangled relationship. As
a result there was always a certain element of tension
between them.

"How was Europe?" Ginger asked, wanting to
change the subject.

"Oh, you know. I was in Scotland, shooting that
blasted made-for-TV-movie thing. Most of the time
I was cold and miserable and bored."

"Bored" in Paige's frame of reference meant that
she was between love affairs, Ginger thought uneasily, a situation that would make Link all the more
interesting to her.

As if tuning in on the direction Ginger's thoughts
had taken, Paige asked casually, "What took you
and Link to Colorado? Just a pleasure jaunt?"

"He was doing a benefit TV spot in Denver. He
just asked me to go along for the ride . . . to get
away from the pressure here."

Paige touched the flame from her gold lighter to a
fresh cork-tipped cigarette. "Did you get to see his
ranch?"

Ginger felt her defenses rise. "Yes."

"Lovely, isn't it? The sunrises over the mountains
are spectacular." She looked straight at Ginger as
she made a point of the last sentence.

Ginger swallowed hard. *All right, sister dear, I get
your drift.* Paige's choice of word *sunrises* rather
than *sunsets* was cruel but effective. In order to have
seen the sunrise, Paige would have spent the night at
Link's ranch. Had she made it to Link's bed? Ginger
wondered, tormenting herself with the question that

she was all too sure had an obvious answer. At the moment, there was no confusion about her feelings toward her sister. They had dissolved into anger. When Paige chose to be bitchy, she could do it with exquisite skill.

Paige inhaled deeply, then let the smoke drift from her pursed lips. She can even do that in a way that looks sensuous, Ginger thought resentfully.

Paige said, "You know, I made a mistake ten years ago, running off to Italy when Link wanted to marry me. He's twice the man of anyone I've met since then. I'm glad we're doing this film together. Perhaps it's fate bringing us together again."

Ginger found any possible reply choked in her throat. Finally, with a feeling of desperation, she looked at her wristwatch and murmured, "It's terribly late. I'm going to bed." She left the motor home and stumbled in the direction of her rented car, more blinded by tears than by the darkness.

Along with most of the members of the cast and crew, Ginger was staying at a motel in a nearby town. She spent a restless night and awoke with a sense of depression and foreboding.

They didn't need her on the set today. In fact, all the stunt work for the scenes being filmed on this location had been completed. For the remainder of this week, the production crew would be concentrating on scenes shot around a plantation mansion that had been leased for that purpose. The action would revolve around love scenes between Link and Paige.

Ginger told herself that she had no business going over there; it would be too painful to watch Paige in Link's arms. True, it was part of the make-believe lives they were living before the cameras. And certainly it was possible for actors and actresses to play passionate love scenes with detachment. But this was a different situation. Today Link and Paige would be thrown together again. Paige had made it clear enough that she was still interested in Link. And Ginger felt sure Link's torch for Paige was an eternal fire, barely smoldering at times, perhaps, but all too vulnerable to Paige's fatal beauty, which could fan it back into a raging flame.

Reason argued that she should spare herself agonizing heartbreak by staying as far away from the set as possible. She ought to be flying back to California, where the action scenes for the 1920s gangster sequence would be filmed. She had a lot of work waiting for her there, setting up the stunts with the special effects people.

But emotion won out over reason, as always seemed to be the case where Link was concerned. After a breakfast of black coffee and half a piece of toast, she drove to the mansion, where the cameras were already rolling.

She parked in an area beside other cars and truckloads of heavy equipment. Security people, who kept curious onlookers at a safe distance, nodded to Ginger and moved aside for her to pass.

Ginger did her utmost to remain as inconspicuous as possible that day, moving like a pale ghost behind lights and camera crews, keeping to shadows and hoping she wouldn't be noticed.

When she arrived, Derrick was delivering a short lecture. "The Civil War," Derrick said in a ringing voice, "was the only U.S. war in modern times to be fought on home soil. Some battles were fought only a few miles from plantations and farm homes where soldiers had friends or relatives. An officer wounded in battle might be carried to a nearby plantation home to die. In our story, we are having an intimate look into the lives and hearts of these two people, this man and woman, the cavalry officer and his sweetheart on the eve of a battle. The vastly superior enemy is camped a few miles away. Despite the stress and impending tragedy, the women in the area have put on a ball for the officers and their men in this mansion. There is music and dancing, a kind of bravado . . . a denial of impending tragedy. It is near the war's end. The men are battle weary. They carry the scars of nearly four years of war. Some have empty sleeves. Music for the quadrille is made by the tattered remnants of a military band, most of them mere boys. Still there is that dash and bravado of the cavalry officers made legendary by such Confederate heroes as Jeb Stuart. They refused to admit defeat. Now in this setting, we play out the love story. Link, you must live this part if the scene is to have meaning. You know the chances of your surviving tomorrow's battle are almost nil. But the morale of your men is defiant, and you are their leader. They respect and admire you. You carry a lot of responsibility for their lives and for the cause that has brought you to this point in your life. Paige, you have been the pampered daughter of a wealthy plantation owner. Now a whole way of life as you have known it is coming to an end. But that isn't of importance to you now. Only this man you love and the few hours left to the two of you have any meaning, any reality. In these hours before dawn, the two of you will experience the intensity of a lifetime of love.''

With a heavy heart, Ginger saw Link and Paige move to a quiet corner of the set, their heads close in personal, intimate conversation. She wished she could believe they were discussing the scene they were about to play, but her emotions told her otherwise. This was a reunion between the two of them. They were oblivious to everyone else on the set. Neither of them had noticed Ginger.

She could imagine what they were saying to each other, telling one another how good it was to be together again. And with agonizing pain, her heart imagined what they were feeling. Paige was ravishingly beautiful this morning. Link, achingly handsome. Through eyes blurred with tears, Ginger watched them and thought bitterly if ever a man and woman were designed for one another, Link and Paige were. They made a striking couple, a beautiful pair of human beings. No wonder they were such a box office attraction. The average person could see them on the screen and live out a fantasy of love between gorgeous specimens of male and female.

What kind of perverse self-torture made her keep on hanging around the set that day, Ginger asked herself? Did she have the wistful hope that something in their voices and actions would tell her they no longer felt the old chemistry between them? Or was it to prove to herself how futile it was for her to be in love with Link, now that Paige was back in his life?

When the cameras rolled and Link took Paige in his arms, she had her proof. She couldn't believe they were just acting. If they were, they would surely win an Academy Award. Their embraces were too convincing, their kisses too passionate to be faked.

Tears trickled silently down her cheeks as she stood in an obscure corner, watching the love scenes unfold. Finally she could take no more. She fled from the set, drove back to her motel room and packed her suitcases. By that afternoon, she was on an airplane bound for California.

Ginger threw herself furiously into preparations for the stunt scenes that would be filmed on the west coast. She worked long hours with the special effects people, rehearsing the stunts over and over, driving herself and the crew into a state of exhaustion. It was her way of running from the bitter heartbreak Link had once again caused her.

One day she had a surprise phone call from her cousin, Lorene Parker, in Florida. "Lorene! It's great hearing your voice! How's Aunt Judy?"

"She's fine. How's the film going?"

"Hectic. But that's normal. How's the beach-combing?"

"Pretty good. Last week I found two old Spanish coins and a ship's bell buried in the sand."

"How exciting! Gee, I wish I were down there with you." She sighed, thinking how peaceful it had been lying on the beach in the sun and going sailing before her father had turned her life upside down, before Link had come back into her life to break her heart all over again.

"Exciting?" Lorene exclaimed. "Seems pretty dull to me compared to what you're doing. And that's one reason I'm calling." She hesitated. "Ginger, I'm starting a two-week vacation. I was wondering . . . well, heck, I miss you like the dickens. You're more like my sister than my cousin. I had the notion of maybe flying out to see you—"

"Terrific!" Ginger exclaimed. "Oh, Lorene, that would be just super!" At the same time, she thought that in many ways she too felt that Lorene was her sister. There was none of the complex sibling rivalry between her and Lorene that she experienced with Paige. She felt truly at ease and comfortable with Lorene. They had always confided their innermost thoughts and secrets to one another. She had never been as relaxed with Paige as she was with Lorene. She realized how much she had missed her cousin and how happy she would be to have Lorene's sunny disposition around to help dispel the shadows that had darkened over her life.

"Sure I wouldn't be in the way . . . I mean with you so busy right now?"

"Heck no. I have an apartment here with plenty of room. And if you don't mind spending your time following me around on the set. . . ."

"Mind!" Lorene exclaimed. "Are you kidding? That sounds super exciting, getting in on the production of a real movie."

"It's not all that glamorous," Ginger confessed. "A lot of it is just plain hard work. We might even put you to work building sets!" Ginger teased.

"Great! Maybe I could learn to be a stunt girl like you. Sure would beat the dull job I have."

A sudden cold chill swept through Ginger. She swallowed hard and shook her head. "No, Lorene. I'd never let you go that route."

They chatted for a few minutes, and then Lorene gave her the flight number and arrival time of her plane.

Ginger had kept her Los Angeles apartment after her accident, even though she had gone to Florida to live with her aunt and cousin for an indefinite time. Her life had been too disorganized during her convalescence for her to cope with major decisions such as giving up her home base and disposing of or storing her belongings. Now she was glad she'd kept the apartment. She had plenty of room for a house guest.

Lorene was like a flash of sunlight coming back into Ginger's life. She arrived the next afternoon, buoyant and full of her usual cheerful platitudes. The first thing she said when she got off the plane was, "Well, here I am. A bad penny always turns up!"

They were up until four in the morning, eating pizza, drinking coffee and talking. The subjects ranged from Aunt Judy's arthritis to the progress on Derrick's film.

At one point in the conversation, Lorene asked about Paige.

"She flew in from Scotland," Ginger said. "She'd just completed a TV movie there. She looks fine, beautiful as ever. You know Paige—always glamorous."

Lorene nodded. She looked down at her coffee cup. "And I suppose you've seen Link again," she murmured, her tone of voice acknowledging that Link Rockwood was a touchy subject to broach with Ginger.

Ginger felt a tug at her throat. "Yes," she said in a strained voice. Lorene said no more, giving Ginger the opportunity to drop the matter. But Ginger found it impossible to avoid talking about Link. Her emotions had been dammed up too long. She realized she had been needing a quiet moment like this when she could confide in someone as loving and close as Lorene.

"Yes," she said, "I saw Link. In fact"—she swallowed hard—"I spent a weekend with him at his ranch in Colorado."

There was a moment's heavy silence. Lorene was

looking at her with a concerned, worried expression but kept silent.

Ginger sighed. "Lorene, I swore I was never going to have anything to do with Link Rockwood again. He's caused me nothing but sleepless nights and misery. I thought I had him entirely out of my system. I thought I hated him. But then I saw him, and he turned on that Link Rockwood charm. He's good at that, you know. I swear, I believe he can hypnotize a woman. At least he can me. That's the only reason I can think of for letting him talk me into going to Colorado with him. Once I was alone with him, I just lost all sense of reason. He acts differently toward me now from the way he used to. Ten years ago, he had a kind of big brother, protective attitude toward me. Not this time! Boy, right away he let me know I was a woman and I wasn't safe with him."

"Maybe he feels differently now," Lorene suggested. "Maybe he's found out he really cares about you."

Ginger smiled bitterly. "That's exactly the kind of lie I told myself. Then Paige flew in from Scotland. The minute the two of them were together, I could see that old chemistry boiling. Link has never gotten over Paige, Lorene. He's carrying the same old torch for her."

"How do you know? Did he tell you?"

"He didn't have to. You should have seen the love scene they played together. The film in the camera was smoking!"

Lorene frowned, her eyes filled with concern for Ginger. "I hate to see you get hurt again. I know how you feel about Link—"

"Don't feel sorry for me!" Ginger cried bitterly. "I asked for it. I don't have anybody to blame but myself. I'm a grown woman, over twenty-one. I walked into the same old trap with my eyes wide open. It's just that I never grew up where Link is concerned. I'm still running around with a teenage crush on the guy. And this time Paige has made it very clear that she considers Link her property. She realizes she made a mistake by jilting him ten years ago. I think this time she's really serious about a man, and the man is Link. So I might as well forget it!"

They talked about the situation for another hour, accomplishing nothing except to give Ginger a chance to unburden her heart. All Lorene could do was give her cousin a loving shoulder to cry on.

The next morning, Lorene drove to the set with Ginger where they were preparing to film an action scene involving a fiery car crash to be used in the 1920s gangster segment.

"I hate working with these fire scenes," Ginger said grimly. "They're very effective on the screen, but there's a real danger of a stunt person getting burned."

In the scene, two mocked-up cars built to look like 1920 vintage gangster sedans were to crash and burst into flames. A driver was to stumble out of the holocaust, ablaze from head to foot, and run several yards before collapsing.

When they arrived on the set, the special effects people had the cars ready to go. Cameras had been set up to film the sequence from several angles. The day before they had shot a chase with machine guns blazing between the two cars. Now they were set to film the crash and fire.

The stunt man who would do the fire scene was on

the set waiting. "Hi, Ginger," he greeted her cheerfully. "Great morning to burn up, hey?"

"Hi, Lefty," Ginger said in anything but a lighthearted mood. "I want you to meet my cousin, Lorene Parker. She's going to be visiting me for a couple of weeks. Lorene, this is Lefty Garcia. He's one of the best in the business."

"Coming from you, Ginger, that's a real compliment," the stunt man said with a grin.

They shot the car crash. Then the stunt men who had driven the cars got out and were replaced with dummies. Lefty Garcia began suiting up for his part in the fire scene.

Ginger explained to Lorene. "He'll put on several layers of clothes first to protect himself from the heat, then on top of that will go a special fireproof jump suit, the kind race car drivers wear, and then some outer garments. He'll wear a face mask. He'll be carrying a small oxygen tank under all that clothing with a line feeding oxygen under his face mask. Finally, we'll give him a coating of rubber cement. That will burn fast."

"Won't all that stuff show on the film?" Lorene asked curiously.

"Not from the camera angles we use. The mask is made up to look like a real face. With all that fire blazing around, the audience won't notice that all the clothing makes him kind of bulky. Some fire stunts these days are shot without the stunt man using protective garments. Then we use a gel substance right over bare skin. It protects the skin from being burned, but it has to be handled right." Then she called, "All right, Lefty, get over to the car. We're ready to shoot this."

Ginger was aware of her heart pounding, the familiar cold knot squeezing her stomach. "We have to time these things just right so we extinguish the fire before Lefty runs out of oxygen," she told Lorene.

The next few minutes were pandemonium. There were shouts from the special effects crew and the camera crews. Gasoline was lit and turned the wrecked cars into a roaring, blazing inferno. From out of the holocaust came the stunt man, Lefty Garcia, ablaze from head to foot. He staggered around the blazing scene, screaming as he writhed and lifted his arms in a chillingly realistic portrayal of a man being burned alive.

Then the fire crew was all over him with hoses to extinguish the blaze. They helped him strip away the mask and fireproof suit. Then he was grinning and joking. As far as he was concerned, it was all in a day's work.

Only then did Ginger relax. She became aware of a discomfort in her arm. She looked down and saw finger marks and realized that Lorene had been clenching her forearm during the entire scene. "I think I got wounded more than Lefty, shooting this scene," Ginger teased, rubbing her arm.

Lorene was red-faced. "I'm sorry, Ginger. It was just so darned realistic! I was sure I was seeing the poor guy being roasted alive."

Derrick flew in from the east coast. They had completed the Georgia Civil War location shots as well as the interior scenes at Asheville showing Link and Paige in the 1920s prohibition, gangster era sequence. He viewed the rushes of the stunt scenes Ginger had filmed. "Excellent! Superb!" He rubbed his hands together with delight. That evening, in an exuberant mood, he took Lorene and Ginger out to dinner at a costly Hollywood restaurant. "What a nice surprise to find you here, Lorene. How is your mother?"

"Fine. She sends her love and says she's praying for your success with this movie."

Derrick sighed, his ebullient mood dissolving into a sudden look of worry. "We need her prayers," he said soberly. "It's going to be touch and go all the way to keep to our shooting schedule and within our budget. A delay that holds up the production schedule, or any unexpected expenses could spell disaster. And I'm having problems with the screen writer, Alex Carter, who screams in agony every time I insist on a line change. And that's not to mention the author of the book, who is threatening to sue us because of the changes we made in his story."

"That all sounds normal," Ginger mused, picturing the violent clashes that were bound to occur between such volatile artists as her father and the script writer.

Then Derrick brightened. "But, everything considered, I'm pleased with what we've accomplished so far. The stunt work Ginger has coordinated is superb. And Paige and Link are both doing fine jobs. Link is turning out to have more acting ability than I'd expected."

Ginger felt her heart wrench. Link's love scenes with Paige were convincing because he didn't have to pretend she thought angrily.

"Are you learning something about how movies are made?" Derrick asked Lorene.

"I certainly am. Ginger has been showing me around the studios and giving me a crash course in film-making. I've seen how stunts are performed.

I've even found out what some of those titles mean that we see on the screen at the end of a movie. Like a 'gaffer' is the chief electrician."

"Correct. It's an old English term for *boss,* going back to the days of sailing ships," Derrick nodded. "And the old English gaffer called his right-hand man his 'best boy.' In movie credits, the best boy is the gaffer's top electrical assistant."

"Right, and the key grip is the boss of the grips, right? He's in charge of getting all the scenery in position and providing portable dressing rooms and comfort stations. The boom operator is the member of the crew who gets the boom microphone in the right spot over the actors' heads in order to pick up their voices. The dolly grip is the guy who rolls the camera around when its put on wheels. How'm I doing?" Lorene asked proudly.

"Excellent. You're starting to sound like an old stagehand. Next we'll be making you assistant director."

"That would be a heck of a lot more exciting than filling out deposit slips in my job at the bank," Lorene said wryly. "What I'd like to do is get into stunt work, like Ginger."

"Well, why not?" Derrick shrugged. "You're an active, athletic youngster. Ginger could show you the ropes—"

"Absolutely not!" Ginger exclaimed. "I love Lorene too much to see her get hurt."

"I know you're gun-shy after your dreadful injury," Derrick said sympathetically. "Still, Lorene is an adult and able to make her own decisions."

"Well, I certainly won't encourage her," Ginger said sullenly.

Then Derrick changed the subject abruptly. "Speaking of stunt work reminds me of a change in our shooting schedule. Ginger, we're going to do the big *Thunder at Dawn* action scene next week."

Ginger's eyes widened. "Next week! I thought you were going to shoot those scenes in the Mideast."

"Yes, some of them. But we've secured a nice location in a desert area not far from here. The terrain is very similar to the landscape in the Mideast. There are so many political problems dealing with governments over there, and always the danger of an outburst of violence, that it would be safer and less expensive to shoot the action sequence here. We can still fly over to film the location scenes in the streets of Jerusalem and Cairo."

Then he explained to Lorene. "We don't film a movie in the same sequence the story follows. In our scenario, the modern love story is between a young man and woman who are news correspondents stationed in the Mideast. The girl becomes involved in a political intrigue that gets her thrown into a filthy jail, accused of being a spy. She escapes, and there is a suspenseful chase scene. It takes place on a road that has been the setting of violent battles between countries in the Mideast that have been warring since Biblical times."

Ginger was listening with half an ear. She felt a surge of the old panic rush through her. This was the scene she dreaded the most. It involved a stunt girl dropping from a helicopter to a moving truck—exactly the kind of stunt she had once been so good at, though it had almost cost her her life the last time she'd done it.

The next day Ginger contacted her special effects

and stunt people, and within hours they were on their way to the desert location to join Derrick and the camera crews.

Lorene returned to Florida, her vacation over. Ginger checked into a motel a few miles from the area where the scenes would be filmed. That afternoon, she inspected the area where the dangerous stunt would be filmed. With her was the helicopter pilot, the driver of the truck and a special effects consultant. They followed a remote dirt road that wound through the hills. "Here's the spot I think we should use," the helicopter pilot said. "There's apt to be less tricky cross winds sweeping down from the hills."

They stopped the truck. Ginger got out and walked around, studying the area. It was a barren section of land. Vegetation consisted of a few scrubby trees and desert bushes. A deadly silence hung over the remote area like a threat. The heat at midday was intense.

"Who's going to do the stunt?" the pilot asked.

"Trixie Baker."

"Oh, she's good."

Ginger didn't reply. Worry rested on her shoulders like a giant lead weight. Tomorrow the stunt girl would be risking her life just to give movie audiences a thrill. And Ginger felt the pressure of her responsibility to make certain the stunt went right.

But how could she be certain? She knew the answer to that. In this business there was no certainty. Her own brush with death had demonstrated that. She wiped her damp palms on her jeans, feeling a chill in spite of the afternoon heat.

"Well," she sighed, "we'll get an early start

tomorrow. I want to run through this stunt with Trixie several times. I know she's good at high falls, but she's never done this exact kind of fall from a helicopter before."

That night she couldn't eat a bite of supper. When she passed a cigarette machine, she said, "Oh to heck with it!" and dropped some coins in the slot. She ripped open the package, lit a cigarette and inhaled deeply. Then she went to her room, where she paced the floor, chain-smoking.

The phone rang shrilly, giving her a start.

She picked up the instrument. The male voice had a stunning impact. She heard her heart pounding loudly, felt her fingers on the telephone tighten.

"Ginger," Link Rockwood said, "what's the big idea of pulling that disappearing act on me?"

"I . . . I don't know what you mean."

"You know good and well what I mean. There we were in Georgia, and all of a sudden you vanished. Next thing I heard you were back in California. Not a word to me about where you were going, not even a wave good-bye."

"You were busy," Ginger said coldly.

"We're all busy. That's no excuse."

There was a moment of uncomfortable silence. Ginger pressed a trembling finger against her throbbing temple. "Where are you calling from?"

"From my room in this motel, where do you think?"

"What . . . what are you doing here?" she asked distractedly.

"What do you mean, what am I doing here? I have the lead role in the movie you're shooting. Or did you forget?"

"I'm . . . sorry. That was stupid of me. I forgot you'll be in some of the scenes we're shooting here."

"Ginger, what's the matter with you? You sound like you're under a strain."

"That's putting it mildly," she said grimly.

There was a moment's silence, then he said, "I'm on my way to your room!"

Chapter Ten

When Link walked through the doorway of Ginger's motel room, his presence was overpowering. She took a step back from him, as if struck by an invisible force field.

In a glance, she took in his broad shoulders, strong, tanned features and his casual attire: faded blue jeans and a sport shirt with the top buttons open. She dragged her gaze away before she became hypnotized with the agony of staring at the face she both adored and hated.

His steel gray eyes were searching her relentlessly. He tried to take her in his arms, but she moved away from him. "Link, no."

The room had become charged with electric tension.

"Ginger, what is wrong?" he demanded.

She was too nervous to stand still. She picked up objects, put them down, wiped her palms on her jeans, reached for the crumpled package of cigarettes on the dresser.

"I thought you'd given up smoking," he said with a frown.

"I just took it up again."

"Ginger—"

"Link, I'm upset enough tonight. I really wish you hadn't picked right now to come barging in."

"Is that what you call it—'barging in'!" he exclaimed angrily. "After what happened between us at my ranch in Colorado, I thought I would be welcome in your room anytime."

Ginger's cheeks burned. "That was before Paige came back into your life," she said, the words wrenched from an agony deep within her.

He frowned. "Is that what's got you in this strange mood? Jealousy over your sister?"

"Partly. But 'jealousy' is not the correct interpretation. Facing facts is better. When I saw you and Paige together on the set in Georgia, I simply faced the fact you've never gotten over her—never will. I was just a handy substitute when she wasn't around."

"You seem to have it all neatly figured out to your satisfaction," he said coldly.

She shrugged, pain tearing at her throat. "I watched them film your love scene with her, Link. That wasn't just acting."

"What makes you an expert judge of such matters?"

"I've been around movie sets all my life. I think I know the difference between acting and the real thing."

"You could be wrong."

"Not in this case," she said.

Link's eyes were burning with a haunting intensity. "If you know that much about acting, you know how submerged an actor can become in a part. This role is important to me. Pulling it off is as important to me as the success of the movie is to Derrick. It's the first time I've tried to do something like this—to play a dramatic role, to portray somebody beside Link Rockwood, to actually become another person." He rubbed the back of his neck, a strange expression moving over his face. "Frankly, it's a little bit frightening. At times I'm not sure if I'm myself or the guy in the story."

"I . . . I'm not sure I understand."

"I don't know if I understand myself. It's the first time I've run into something like this. In the movie roles I've done before, I was just, as Derrick once said, a personality, a good ol' boy, lovable type that the audience recognized right off and liked. This time it's different. Y'know, Sir Laurence Olivier said in his autobiography that he thinks when he was married to Vivien Leigh, she identified so strongly with the role of Blanche Dubois in the film version of *A Streetcar Named Desire*, that she took on the same characteristics and illness in real life."

Ginger shook her head in bewilderment, not really knowing if he was sincere or feeding her some kind of elaborate line. She couldn't bring herself to trust him the way she had when she first knew him. Had the past ten years changed him so much he would say anything just to make a conquest? Paige had not come back to California with him. She'd flown on to the Mideast, where they would be filming the next location scenes. Perhaps again he was just lonely, needed a woman to share his bed tonight and thought good old Ginger would be available.

"Link, I'm not sure if I know what you're talking about . . . or if I believe you. The truth of the matter is I don't think you yourself know."

He sighed. "Ginger, all I can ask is that you be

patient with me right now. I . . . I guess I am kind of confused. I will be until we're through filming this story. All I really know right now is that I need you tonight." His voice trembled with a sudden surge of emotion, and once again he tried to hold her, but she struggled out of his arms. "Not tonight, Link. It's the wrong time and place for both of us. You have a great talent for walking into my life at the wrong time!"

"Do you mind explaining what you're talking about?"

"You know what we're doing here. Derrick has decided to shoot the big chase scene here. It looks like a stretch of Mideast desert, and he got the location at a bargain. That means we're going to do the helicopter bit tomorrow. And quite frankly, I'm just about out of my mind with worry."

Link's expression became sober. "Are you afraid the stunt isn't going to work?"

She sighed. "Link, it was exactly this kind of stunt that almost got me killed. Now I'm asking another stunt girl to do the same thing. What if something goes wrong? What if she gets hurt . . . or killed?"

Link chewed his lip thoughtfully. "Is it that tricky?"

"Yes. The timing has to be perfect. I did a lot of falls like it without a hitch. Then that one time, it went sour. . . ."

An icy chill penetrated to the depths of her being as the dark memories swept over her.

Against her protest, Link took her in his arms. This time, she couldn't struggle free; his strength held her prisoner. She was forced to look into his eyes. "Ginger, I'm sure your stunt girl knows the risks involved. She's a professional. You're the best in the business. I know you and the special effects people have done everything humanly possible to make it safe for her. But there's always some element of risk in this business. You can't carry the whole burden on your shoulders."

She suddenly felt desperately tired and lonely She felt the overpowering desire to lay her head against his broad chest, to lose herself in the protection of his strong arms. How she wished that he loved her as she loved him!

She almost fell into the trap of playing out the scene as if it were written for a love story with a happy ending. But that was fantasy, the kind of dreams movies were made of. And this was reality. And her love story did not have a happy ending.

She allowed herself another moment of the sweet comfort of his embrace, then she said firmly, "Now you must go, Link. Even if I said yes tonight, I wouldn't be any good at making love. I won't be able to think about anything else until we've finished shooting that stunt tomorrow."

Reluctantly he let his arms fall to his side, freeing her. Their eyes met and held in a long, deep look. Then he said quietly, "Good night, Ginger. I'll see you on the set in the morning."

Then he was gone, leaving her, as he always did, with fresh heartache.

Chapter Eleven

*Y*our special effects man has come up with something I think would be very effective," Derrick said. "He's designed a breakaway windshield for a car. The hero will be driving the pickup truck, pursued by terrorists in the black car. The pursuing car swerves, hits a boulder, stops dead in its tracks, and the other terrorist in the front seat beside the driver is thrown crashing through the windshield in a shower of glass and over the hood of the car. What do you think?"

Ginger nodded. "That sounds okay. You could station a camera directly in front of the spot the car stops. The man coming through the windshield would fly right at the camera. You'd get the effect in the theater of him being thrown out of the car in a shower of glass, right at the audience.

"Yes, excellent!" Derrick exclaimed.

"We can work that out later," Ginger said. "First I have to get this helicopter thing out of the way."

The sun had risen over the desert less than a half hour earlier. The sky was cloudless. They would have an entire shooting day of bright sunlight ahead of them. The chill of the desert night was rapidly being dissipated by the morning heat.

Ginger gazed around at all the paraphernalia of movie making, the camera crews, cranes, trucks, cars and helicopters and had turned the area into a sprawling, dusty parking lot. When the stunt girl, Trixie Baker, did her hair-raising fall from the helicopter to a moving truck below, several cameras would be in operation. One crew would be in the air in another helicopter. Another would be in a vehicle rolling parallel to the truck. Others would be on cranes or on the ground using telephoto lenses.

Ginger's nervousness had congealed into a single icy lump inside her. Her hands were cold. She was aware of a clammy film of perspiration bathing her body.

She saw her father stride over to the pickup truck that would appear in the chase scene. Link was standing beside the cab. They conferred briefly, then Derrick moved away. They would take some shots of Link running to the truck, getting behind the wheel and starting the engine. Then Derrick would call out "Cut!" to the camera crews, and Link would be replaced by the professional driver who would actually be driving the truck when Trixie performed the dangerous fall from the helicopter to the truck bed.

Ginger was suddenly aware of Link's gaze. She felt the impact of his stare, though they were hundreds of feet apart. The morning light cast a ruddy glow over his ruggedly handsome features in a way that wrenched at her heart. He gave her a brief wave, then turned to the business at hand. Ginger blinked a sudden fog of tears away and resolutely put aside her personal feelings. This morning was no time to allow emotions to cloud her thinking.

She turned her back on the scene that was being filmed of Link running to the truck. She walked toward the waiting helicopter. Then she spotted the stunt girl approaching from her van. Trixie was a petite redhead, close to Paige's build and height. With a black wig, she would make a good stand-in for Paige.

"Hi," Trixie called gaily.

"Good morning," Ginger said, feeling far from lighthearted. "How're you this morning, Trixie?"

"Great. I'm all set to go."

Ginger put her arm around the slim girl's shoulders as they walked together. "Trixie, I know high falls are your specialty, but this helicopter thing is going to be tricky. I want to talk you through it a few times before we actually do the stunt."

They waited until Derrick was satisfied with a take of Link sprinting to the truck. Ginger conferred with the truck driver and helicopter pilot. Then she and Trixie were in the aircraft. It lifted from the desert in a cloud of dust. They flew several hundred feet above the truck as it drove along the dirt road below.

A terrifying picture flashed through Ginger's mind. She was hurtling through the air, drenched with horror as she realized the stunt had gone wrong. She felt the impact of her body slamming against the side of the truck . . . the white-hot sheets of pain . . . then smothering darkness. . . .

It was the old memory she had relived a thousand times since her accident. Now it was as if she had come alive in a rerun of a dreadful nightmare.

She wiped her damp palms on her jeans. She drew a deep breath and somehow got her emotions under control. Over the noise of the chopper's blades and engine, Ginger called to Trixie. "Get out there like you're ready to do the jump. I want you to squeeze my hand when you think the timing is right."

The red-haired stunt girl clambered through the open door and stood on the precarious perch outside. The ground below them sped by in a blur. Ginger held Trixie's free hand tightly. The girl was looking down at the truck with an expression of intense concentration.

Ginger felt Trixie's signal: a quick squeeze of her fingers. Her heart sank with an immediate response of despair. With it came a sickening wave of fright. Trixie gave her a questioning look as she crawled back into the cab. Ginger shook her head. "Trixie, you'll have to jump away from the chopper when you start your fall. The way you were timing it, you would have missed the truck completely."

The stunt girl frowned. "Are you sure about that, Ginger? It looked good to me."

They made several more passes over the truck. The more they timed Trixie's fall, the more Ginger despaired of them doing the stunt.

Finally she signaled for the pilot to land. On the ground, Ginger reached for a cigarette with trembling fingers. Trixie had become impatient with her. "Ginger, I don't know why you want to keep going over and over this thing. You're treating me like an amateur. I know what I'm doing. I can do the fall okay if you'll just leave me alone!"

"Trixie, I know you're a pro and that you've done hundreds of falls. But this is a specialized kind of trick that you've never done before."

Trixie's eyes flashed. She pressed her lips together with an angry expression. Then she exclaimed, "Ginger, I know you used to be one of the best stunt girls in Hollywood. But I heard about your accident. You want to know what I think? I think you've lost your nerve! I think this stunt has you so spooked you're afraid for anyone to do it! I think your judgment is shot."

Ginger was smothered with a sense of frustration. Was she being too cautious? Had her phobic fear of stunt work robbed her of good judgment? She searched her mind and heart, desperately asking for the truth. All of her instincts kept flashing red warning lights. Her years of training and experience continued to warn her that Trixie did not have the kind of skill to do this kind of stunt safely, no matter how confident she sounded.

The young red-haired woman started arguing with her, but Ginger turned and walked away. The coldness in her stomach had grown into an icy knot. How could she possibly allow the stunt to be filmed when she knew with dread certainty that her decision might kill or maim the stunt girl?

Derrick approached her. "What's the holdup?"

"It's Trixie. I don't think she can do the stunt."

"What do you mean, she can't do the stunt?" Derrick demanded impatiently. "She's trained to do this sort of thing, isn't she? Why did you hire her if she can't do it?"

"She has a good reputation for doing high falls, and she's done airplane stunts," Ginger said shortly. "I thought she could handle this. But we walked through it several times. She can't get the timing right."

Derrick gave a gesture of frustration. "Do you realize what it's costing a crew of this size to sit around all day while you practice?"

"I know." Ginger sighed wearily. "But I have to be sure she's going to land on that air bag right."

"Ginger, I don't have to tell you that I have to stick to the budget on this film. If you don't think the girl can do the stunt, can you get someone else out here right away?"

Ginger shook her head with a sense of helplessness. "Leave me alone for a few minutes," she said tersely. "I'll think of something."

She turned and walked away from her father. She gazed across the desert, her eyes blurring with tears as she waged a desperate inward battle. No one else on the set knew what she was going through. She was locked in the most frightening struggle of her life. She was fighting for her sanity. How could she live with herself if she gave the signal for the cameras to roll, knowing the odds were that they would be filming a stunt girl's death? But what alternative did she have?

No one else was available. She had consulted all the stunt organizations. Trixie Baker came as close to being able to do this scene as anyone she could get.

What if she refused to let them shoot the scene? It was crucial to the story. She knew there was no way Derrick was going to cut it out of the film. He'd fire her as stunt coordinator and have Trixie do the stunt anyway before he'd sacrifice this chase scene with the fall from the helicopter.

A thought born of desperation crept into her mind, paralyzing her with fright. In the past, she had done many falls like this. They had all been perfect . . . until the one that had nearly killed her. Of all the stunt girls available, she was probably best qualified to do the fall herself. She was certainly more experienced and expert at this kind of stunt than Trixie was.

A voice in her head cried in anguish, "No! I'm not going to do it!"

Tears trickled down her cheeks. Why had she allowed herself to be put into this situation? She remembered that when her father first tried to talk her into being stunt coordinator for the film, she'd felt a sense of dread, a kind of premonition. Had some sixth sense anticipated this horrible situation? She thought she could hear Fate's hollow laughter.

Had it been her destiny to end her life in this kind of fall? She had cheated Fate that other time, so she'd been brought here for a replay. This time the script would have the ending Fate had written for her.

Was there any way out? She searched frantically for another answer. With a sense of anguish, she realized there was none. She was trapped.

She turned and walked slowly to the makeup truck and had herself fitted with a black wig. She stared at her reflection in a mirror. Her face looked like a white mask.

She drew a deep breath, swallowed hard and called to the assistant director, "We're going to do the stunt now. Get the camera crews on their toes. We'll make one pass over the truck. Then you can start them rolling."

He stared at her. "You mean you're going to—"

"I don't have time to talk about it. Tell the truck driver to start down the road when the chopper takes off."

She ran over to the helicopter. Behind her, she heard someone shout her name. It sounded like her father, but she didn't turn around. She got into the cab. "Come on," she ordered. "Let's get this thing off the ground."

He gave her a puzzled look but obeyed. As the huge blades above them whipped the air, sending up a cloud of dust, Ginger caught a glimpse of Trixie Baker on the ground below, staring up with a wide-eyed look of stunned confusion.

Not until they were actually in the air did Ginger experience the full impact of terror. She thought she was going to be ill. Her hands were white knots. Her instinct of survival screamed at her to turn back. But she told herself grimly that she had gone past the point of no return.

If she allowed Trixie to do the stunt, there was more than a fifty-fifty chance the girl would be killed or badly injured. She simply couldn't live with that on her conscience.

"Make one pass over the truck," she shouted to the pilot. "Then make your approach for the drop!"

She crawled out of the cab. The wind tore at her, blurring her vision. She watched as they sailed over the truck. She saw the air bag in the truck bed, remembering how she had checked it a dozen times this morning to make sure it was inflated properly. The cross painted in the center was her target.

The chopper pulled up and away. Then they were back over the road again, approaching the truck, which was several hundred feet below. Ginger held on with hands that had grown ice cold and slippery. Breathing was an effort. Her heartbeat was like the fluttering of an injured bird.

There was a silent countdown in her mind: three . . . two . . . one . . . NOW!

Adrenaline surged through her body. Her senses

became vibrating strings tuned to their highest pitch. She measured the distance, tensed for that split-second moment of truth. A cry tore from her lips, and she flung herself into space. Time was compressed. Conditioned reflexes took over, making her somersault in the air.

If she dove into the bag head first, it could split and she'd go right through it. But she timed her turn in the air like an expert diver. She hit the bag flat, spread-eagle. It was a perfect execution. She had landed on her target dead center! The bag held.

The truck bounced over the rutted dirt road for a few hundred yards, letting the cameras get the added footage. Then it stopped. For a moment, Ginger could only lie on her back staring up at the cloudless blue sky as indescribable relief and happiness bubbled up inside her. Then she turned over and crawled over the air bag. Suddenly her stunt crew was swarming over the truck. Eager hands lifted her to the ground. She welcomed their support. Her legs felt too weak and shaky to support her. Voices crowded in from all directions. Hands patted her. Arms hugged her.

A tremendous wave of exhilaration swept through Ginger. The weight that had burdened her for over a year evaporated. She felt freed from the slavery of unreasoning fear. The realization flooded over her that she had come face to face with all the demons from her own private hell. She had battled the demons and destroyed them. Now she knew she was capable of doing any kind of stunt work again. If she experienced fear, it would be the normal tension that went with the job, not the black, unreasoning, overpowering, paralyzing terror that had enslaved her these past months.

She was filled with a glow of triumph. She felt invincible.

She heard the assistant director call through his bullhorn, "That was a perfect wrap shot! Okay, everybody, it's a wrap!"

They had finished with the location shots a day ahead of schedule. Derrick was ecstatic. Someone suggested a party. "There's a little town a few miles from here that has a saloon and a great country and western band."

That evening, the smoky little honky-tonk called "Louise's Place" did the biggest business of its career. It was jammed with stunt people and camera crews. The country and western band turned their amplifiers to full volume. The saloon owner, Louise, a huge bosomed woman of some two hundred pounds, perspired profusely as she yelled at her bartenders and punched the cash register furiously. Harried waitresses scurried around in a desperate attempt to keep the thirsty crowd supplied with pitchers of beer. The local customers stared with awe at the invasion of Hollywood movie people.

Trixie Baker had been in a sullen mood ever since Ginger had summarily preempted her job that morning. But in the festive mood of the party, she relented somewhat. She put her arm around Ginger and admitted, "You're the best. I still think I could have done that stunt, but maybe I was wrong. Maybe I would have broken my fool neck. Anyway . . . still friends?"

"Of course," Ginger said, returning her hug. "And I'll make sure you get paid the same as if you had done the stunt. Okay?"

"Now I know we're still friends," Trixie said with a grin, the last of her resentment evaporating.

On the crowded floor, dancers were whooping it up. Ginger danced with the assistant director, the gaffer, several stunt men and half the camera crew. And then a tall, broad-shouldered figure moved between the dancers and a hand touched her arm. She looked up into a pair of steel gray eyes. Immediately a familiar weakness made her legs tremble.

"Hi, stunt lady," Link said, looking down at her with a crooked grin that melted her insides. "You're awfully popular tonight. Think you could work your hubby in for a dance?"

Ginger surrendered herself to his arms. She had no intention of arguing with him tonight about whether or not they were really married. Tonight she was in a state of intoxication, and not from the one small glass of beer she'd had. She felt deliciously happy. She was on an emotional high. Tonight she was going to enjoy being with Link and not even worry about the consequences.

"I tried to get over to talk to you after you did that crazy stunt this morning," Link said.

"What?" Ginger yelled. "The band is so loud I can't hear you."

"You're absolutely right," he shouted. "Come with me."

He grabbed her hand and led her outside to his convertible in the parking lot. Above them the black sky sparkled with diamonds. The clear desert night air was cool and dry.

Link opened the car door for her and then went around to the other side and slid in beside her. He rested an arm on the back of the car seat, twisted around to look at her, gazing at her face intently, giving her a look of total concentration as if nothing else in the world was of any importance. Then he said, "What I was trying to tell you on the dance floor was that I tried to get close enough to talk to you this morning, but your stunt crew kidnapped you and ran off with you before I could get to you. I couldn't decide if I wanted to spank you for taking a chance like that or tell you how proud I was of you."

"Maybe you could have done both." She grinned.

"I felt like it. Ginger, honey, I know how terrified you've been of stunt work since you took that bad fall. Whatever possessed you to do that stunt yourself?"

She shrugged. "What it came down to was that I didn't have a choice. I could see that Trixie couldn't do it. She just couldn't get the timing right. She would have killed herself trying. The stunt had to be filmed. Somehow I got myself psyched up enough to do it. Don't ask me how."

He shook his head with a sober expression. "One day soon, people will sit in a movie theater to see this film and eat popcorn and never realize for a minute that stunt people risked their lives to give them a couple of hours of entertainment."

"Well, that's our business, isn't it?" Ginger shrugged. "People risk their lives when they build bridges for us to drive over or drill for oil to make our cars run . . . or a hundred other things. Our business happens to be weaving the fabric of dreams."

"I suppose that's true . . ."

"Anyway, Link, I'm glad I did it. This thing has been hanging over my head like a black cloud ever since I had the accident. It was something I had to lick. Y'know, when a stunt person is learning to ride a horse, if a horse throws him, they make him get right back on and ride some more, or he'll be afraid of horses from then on. I guess doing the helicopter fall was the horse I had to get back on and ride again. I don't say I'll never get scared again when I have to do a stunt, but it won't be as bad. It won't be sheer panic. I really feel good inside about what happened today. I'm more at peace with myself."

"And just a little proud of yourself?'

"Yes, that too," she admitted.

"Well, you have every right to be. That was some accomplishment." Then he turned the key, starting the engine.

"Just where do you think you're going?" she demanded.

" 'We,' " he corrected. "Where are *we* going?"

"Exactly!"

"Well, I thought we might go for a little ride. The desert is beautiful in the moonlight."

"What moonlight?"

"It hasn't come up yet. But it will . . . soon. A full moon. You can't beat that."

"Link, I have absolutely no business riding around in the desert with you watching a full moon come up."

"Oh? Why not?"

"Because," she admitted, her cheeks flushed, "you're catching me in a weak moment. I feel in a reckless mood tonight because of what happened today. And that is not a safe mood for me to be in when I'm alone with you."

Link grinned.

Ginger sighed, realizing her protests were wasted breath. Link was not going to turn back. And she wasn't at all sure she wanted him to.

Dumb me, she thought. *I'm asking for it. Heartbreak, here I come again*. Then she smiled wryly, wondering if that was the name of a country and western tune. "If it isn't, it ought to be," she said aloud.

"What?"

"Nothing. Just talking to myself." She gazed at his strong profile, which was visible in the glow from the dash lights. As always, the sight of him brought a sweet aching to her throat. Would she ever get this man out of her system? she wondered half angrily.

Then she said, "I guess you'll be flying to the Mideast now that we're finished here."

"Yes. We'll be there on location for several weeks. Are you coming?"

"No. Everything there will be handled by set crews and special effects people. The script doesn't call for any stunt work until you're on location in Spain. They don't need me before then."

"Well, come along with me anyway," he urged.

She sighed. "I wish I could, Link. But I have too much to do here: some more stunts to work out with special effects people, plus a lot of detail work. Derrick should have called me his assistant producer instead of stunt coordinator. He even has me flying to New York for a conference with some distributors."

"Looks like I won't be seeing you again until we've finished all the foreign location shots."

Ginger bit her lip. She was silent for a moment, then said grimly, "You won't be lonely. Paige will be there with you the whole time."

He looked at her sharply. "Are you going to start that again?"

She shook her head. "No. As a matter of fact, for tonight, I won't even think about Paige. Which proves I'm not in my right mind."

Link started to say something but then shrugged and turned his attention to his driving. He had turned onto the lonely dirt road where the filming had taken place that morning. Ginger wondered if he had chosen this spot because it had a special meaning for her. She was still keyed up, on an emotional high . . . and extremely vulnerable.

Ginger relaxed against the plush upholstery and drank in the vision of a full moon rising over a distant mountain range. It bathed the desert vegetation, boulders and ravines with silver. It was a dangerous setting to be in alone with Link, but the mood she was in tonight disregarded any thought of tomorrow. She felt in tune with the story Derrick was filming. Perhaps it was true that under some circumstances a man and woman could compress a lifetime of love into a single night.

Link drove for a while longer, then pulled into a secluded gulley and parked. In this spot, they sat facing the rising moon. Link's arm slipped around Ginger's waist and gently pulled her close to him. His kiss was tender and deep. Tonight she did not resist him. He opened the buttons of her blouse and slipped his hand under her bra, cupping her breast. Achingly, she thought, *Yes . . . it's all right.*

His kisses trailed down her throat, becoming more passionate. But then she whispered, "Wait just a minute, Link."

She reached for her purse, searched an inner compartment, then held up a small object. "I don't guess you remember what this is."

With a puzzled expression, Link stared at the split washer she was holding.

"Mexico. Our wedding night—"

"Of course!" He laughed. "I do remember! That

taxi driver, Ramón, found a washer in his toolbox. It was the closest thing we could locate to use for a wedding ring. Do you mean to tell me you kept it all these years?"

"I was on the verge of throwing it away a dozen times," she admitted. "I really can't explain why I kept it."

"You must not have hated me as much as you thought you did."

She shrugged. "Maybe I wanted to keep it around to remind myself what a dumb little fool I'd been! But tonight I'm not going to make any attempt to analyze the situation. I'm just going to be a fool again!"

She slipped the washer on her ring finger and held it up in the moonlight. "There! You see? Now I'm Mrs. Link Rockwood. At least for tonight."

They kissed. She surrendered to him with total abandon, eager in her growing passion.

From the back seat, Link took a blanket and spread it on the soft sand. Then she was naked in his arms, both giving and demanding in the tidal wave of emotion that swept her to heights of delicious ecstasy and left her exhausted and fulfilled.

She felt warm and secure, nestling her head in the hollow of his shoulder. But then a lonely tear trickled down her cheek as she thought that this might be the last time they would be together. Tomorrow he was flying to the Mideast, where Paige was waiting for him.

With a heavy heart, she remembered what Link had said the night before in her motel room about identifying with the hero in *Thunder at Dawn*. What would happen in the coming weeks when Link became submerged in the love story in romantic foreign settings with Paige? Would he become the "guy in the story," in love with his story heroine?

They would be acting out a moving love story. Time and again, Paige would be in his arms on movie sets. They would be thrown together in the inevitable partying that went along with a movie production. How could Link keep from falling in love all over again with the glamorous old flame who had once broken his heart?

Ginger shivered in the chill of the desert night air. She snuggled closer to the man she loved, already feeling lost and alone

Chapter Twelve

The story in the celebrity gossip column confirmed Ginger's fears: "Link Rockwood, on location in the Mideast in the starring role of the film *Thunder at Dawn*, directed by Derrick Lombard, is playing more than a make-believe love story with his leading lady, Paige Lombard. Fans may recall that an earlier engagement between the two stars went sour. But reliable sources tell us that now the romance is back on the track and just like in the movie; there will be a happy ending. Their wedding date is set for the week that shooting on the current production is complete. . . ."

Heartbreak where Link was concerned was not new to Ginger, but after the nights she had shared with Link in Colorado and in the desert, this final blow was almost more than she could bear. Her emotions ranged from shock to a terrible sense of loss. She felt herself burning with anger at Link and Paige, then cold with a helpless feeling of depression. Now she knew beyond doubt that she had meant nothing to Link. Whatever hope she might have had quietly died.

The weeks had been hectic since Ginger said

good-bye to Link after the desert location. She had rushed around the country on endless production details. She coordinated more stunt sequences filmed in California. Part of her time was spent in the labs where positive prints were being made from the negatives that came from the camera. Color balance in the prints was critical. It was like fine tuning the picture color of a TV set. The timers, the men who controlled the color balance, had to make artistic decisions about the delicate tone. A slight shift of color could change the mood of a scene. Derrick was tied up with directing the location scenes in Jerusalem, and he didn't trust anyone except Ginger to keep an eye on vital production details.

One of those details was working with the composer who would create the all-important musical score for the film. He had to wait until the filmed segments were edited and assembled in completed form so his compositions could be timed to the second to fit the changing scenes and moods of the story. But because of his tight budget and time schedule, Derrick didn't want any delays. Ginger had the composer read the story and view scenes as they were completed so he could begin to create themes and melodies that would fit the story.

During those hectic weeks, she didn't hear from Link. She knew he was working long hours. Derrick was driving everyone ragged to keep to his shooting schedule. Ginger had seen portions of scenes shipped to the labs from the production location. In most of the scenes, Link and Paige were together. It was agony for Ginger to stand by helplessly and see the man she loved in the arms of her beautiful sister.

When the stories about Link and Paige began breaking in the gossip columns, they only confirmed what her heart had dreaded all along. Suddenly it seemed every talk show she saw on TV, every fan magazine she picked up was filled with the torrid romance between Link Rockwood and Paige Lombard.

From the stories and pictures, it appeared that the two lovers were jet hopping all over Europe when they weren't on the set. They were seen together sight-seeing in Greece, having dinner in Paris and shopping in Rome.

"I guess I wasn't surprised," she told her cousin, Lorene Parker, sadly. "Deep down, I've known all along it was going to turn out this way. But I've always been a darn fool where Link was concerned. I guess I still wanted to believe in fairy stories, that somehow Link was going to be my prince who would break the spell of the beautiful dark witch and come riding back to me on his shining steed."

Ginger had taken a week off before flying to Spain, where she was to coordinate the final stunt scenes of the film. She was spending the week in Florida with her aunt and cousin. She and Lorene were in Lorene's little boat, sailing across a peaceful lagoon. There was just enough breeze to drift the boat along.

Ginger felt herself dangerously close to tears. The subject of Link and Paige had been too painful for her to discuss. Now when she found herself talking about the situation, a flood of pent-up emotions choked her.

"I don't know if it's any of my business," Lorene said sympathetically, "but it seems to me Link is something of a dirty rat not to at least break the news to you himself."

Ginger sighed. "Oh, he probably wanted to wait

until he could tell me in person. You know, Link isn't much for writing letters. He knows I'll be joining the production company in Spain. Probably he was planning to tell me then, but the gossip magazines and scandal sheets broke the story first. He should have known you can't keep a secret from those people. They have radar where romance between celebrities is concerned."

"I . . . I don't know what to say, Ginger," Lorene murmured tearfully. "Link has been nothing but bad news for you. He's broken your heart so many times . . ."

"You might call me a few choice names, like 'stupid'." Ginger sighed. "Lorene, I don't have anyone to blame but myself. That first time, in Mexico, I was little more than a child. But now I'm a grown woman, and still I walked right into the same old booby trap. I didn't do it blindly. I could see what was coming. I told myself that Link was still carrying that old torch for Paige. He didn't lie to me; I'll have to give him credit for that. He didn't say anything about being in love with me. I guess in a way he tried to warn me. He told me he had become so involved with his role in this movie that at times he couldn't separate his own ego from that of the hero. Under those circumstances, what else could I expect except that he and Paige would get back together again?'

She was silent for a moment, blinking back tears. Then, swallowing hard, she admitted, "Still, it hurts just the same. But at least it's gotten Link out of my system at last. I don't even hate him anymore. I just don't want to have anything to do with him!"

She groped in a pocket and took out the split washer that she had carried with her for ten years.

"My wedding ring," she said wryly. She looked at it for a moment through a haze of tears, then tossed it into the lagoon. She watched sadly as it made a tiny splash and disappeared forever.

Lorene pointed out, "You told me Link claimed that Mexican marriage was legal. How can he marry Paige? Won't that be bigamy?"

Ginger shrugged. "I don't know if he was telling me the truth. More than likely it was just a line. If there was any legality to it, I'm sure his lawyers wouldn't have any trouble getting it annulled. Mexican marriages aren't readily acknowledged in the U.S. In my heart, I guess I thought we were married. But not anymore."

They had reached the tiny island across the lagoon. Lorene beached her craft. They stepped out on the white sand. The tropical sunshine felt warm on Ginger's back.

"This is where I found those two old Spanish doubloons," Lorene said.

"Why didn't you bring your metal detector along today? Maybe you could find some more."

"Oh, I can go treasure hunting anytime. I'd rather spend today visiting with you."

They picked out a strip of clean white beach and stretched out for a sun bath.

"What will you be doing in Spain?" Lorene asked.

"We're going to do the big 1930s Spanish Civil War scenes. Lots of stunt work will be involved. At that point the story revolves around a struggle between General Francisco Franco's fascist forces and Spain's Republican government over a bridge in a small village. There were actually some three thousand American volunteers in a unit called the Abraham Lincoln Brigade fighting on the side of the

Republican government against Franco's Nazi-backed fascists. Some of those young men were killed in Spain. In this episode in the story, the hero is one of those American volunteers and has fallen in love with a Spanish girl. The action revolves around their love affair in the last hours before they die in the bombardment of the village. That battle scene is going to take a lot of work. We'll be setting explosives all over the place, blowing up houses and the bridge. It's going to cost a pile of money, but you know Derrick. He has to do everything in a big way. Nothing miniaturized. He wants authenticity. He wouldn't settle for anything less than a location in Spain and a set with real houses and a real bridge. He's hired hundreds of extras in addition to dozens of my stunt people. It's going to be up to me to see that one of those amateurs doesn't get his fool head blown off."

"Oh, Ginger, that's going to be rough on you."

"Yes, but not the way it once was. In fact, I'm going to be doing some of the stunts myself."

Lorene's eyes widened. "You will?"

Ginger had been on her back, staring up at the sky. Now she rolled over, her wide, tawny eyes gazing at her cousin. "Lorene, I haven't had a chance to tell you this, but I did the helicopter drop for the Mideast chase scene."

Lorene sat up, her face registering stunned amazement. "Ginger, you didn't!"

"It's true. There we were, all set to do the stunt, and the girl I hired, Trixie Baker, couldn't do it. She was willing enough. In fact, she was furious with me for not letting her try. But, Lorene, I could see she couldn't pull it off. It was either do it myself or have her life on my conscience. So somehow I screwed up my nerve and did the drop. I felt great afterward. No more phobia about stunt work. I licked it, Lorene!"

Her cousin gave her an impetuous hug. "I'm so glad, Ginger! Now you really have recovered completely."

"Yes, I have. Y'know, at first I was furious with my father for talking me into being stunt coordinator on this film of his. But now I'm grateful. Because of the job on this film, I'm back to normal. When we're through with this production, I can go right on with my career in stunt work."

"How about teaching me to do stunt work?" Lorene begged. "Honestly, Ginger, I'm so bored with my job here!"

"Lorene, if you're serious about wanting to get into the motion picture industry, I can help you get a job. But I wish you'd think about something less dangerous than stunt work. As smart as you are, there are dozens of interesting possibilities. You could get a job as a set decorator, in the wardrobe departments or in a film lab—"

"Anything beside filling out deposit slips and trying to get my accounts to balance!" Lorene sighed. Then she asked, "How soon will you be through filming *Thunder at Dawn?*"

"This stuff we're doing in Spain will wrap it up. Then there'll be weeks of film editing and splicing. The recording mixers will have to work with the sound track. A lot of the sound that's recorded when we're actually filming on location isn't good enough for today's high quality sound demands. When the shooting is over, the actors have to spend more time in the dubbing studio, repeating their lines, trying to get their words to synchronize with their lip move-

ments on the screen. The composer has to fit his
music to the scenes, and then an orchestra has to be
recorded. Derrick has to complete his deal with a
distributor. The big studios have their own indepen-
dently produced film. Derrick thought he pulled
enough weight with the studios to get one of them to
take on distribution, but he didn't have any luck
there. So he has to go to an independent distributor,
and that can sometimes be a tricky business. I'm not
worried, though. Derrick knows his way around the
film industry too well."

Ginger's cousin sat up and dusted the sand from
her shapely legs. "Listen, I'm going to remind you of
your promise. As soon as you've finished in Spain
and get back to Los Angeles, you're going to find me
camped on your doorstep!"

At the end of the week, Ginger was on an airliner
on her way to Spain, steeling herself for the agony of
coming face to face with Link and Paige.

When Ginger arrived in Spain, Derrick was at the
airport to meet her. He greeted her profusely, with a
hug that lifted her off the ground. He was obviously
in one of his exuberant moods. After they secured
her luggage, he led the way to a rented car. "The set
is a couple of hours drive from here," he explained
as they headed out of the airport. "The special
effects people have been working on the place for a
week, planting explosive charges everywhere." He
chuckled. "Looks like you're planning to blow the
set sky high."

Ginger shrugged. "You want a realistic battle
scene. Have all my stunt people arrived?"

Derrick nodded. "They've been coming in by
plane for the past two days. It's a rural section.

Accommodations are pretty sketchy. But we managed to find a hotel in a town a few kilometers from the set."

"That's where we're headed now?"

"To the set. Yes. I've given orders for the special effects people and your stunt crew to be there when we arrive. I want to spend today going over this scene with you and your people. This is one of those things that has to be shot right the first time. There's no chance for retakes after we've blown up half the town."

"You're not wasting any time."

"Can't afford to, Ginger. You know that. We've had the usual frustrating delays and problems. It's been touch and go. But if we can get this last big action scene shot tomorrow, we'll just get in under the wire, budgetwise."

"Tomorrow?" she exclaimed. "I'd like to have more time to work with my stunt crew. These battle scenes with all the explosive charges can be tricky."

"Sorry, love. We simply haven't got the time. Have to wrap this thing up now. We're scraping the bottom of the money barrel."

"This is going to wrap it up, then?"

"Yes. All the scenes involving Link and Paige have been shot."

Hearing their names aloud sent a knife slash of pain through her heart. Ginger looked away, at the rugged Spanish countryside, hiding the sudden rush of tears.

Derrick, busy driving, appeared not to notice her sudden silence. He went on, chatting happily. "I had an enthusiastic phone call last night from the distributor I contacted, Max Kliener. He's looked at runs of some of the scenes we've completed. He's convinced *Thunder at Dawn* is going to be a box office smash. He's lined up a national movie house chain to premiere the film simultaneously all over the country. The publicity we've gotten over Paige and Link has been extraordinary. The fans are panting to see them together in this film. My publicity people have us scheduled for the major late night talk shows. Oh, and you'll be interested in this: We've been approached by that TV prime time network show built around hair-raising human feats. They want to do a segment on that incredible jump you did from the helicopter. How does that strike you?"

"Fine," Ginger murmured, her heart too heavy to respond to Derrick's triumphant mood.

He took a hand off the steering wheel to pat her arm. "Can't begin to tell you how proud I am of you, Ginger. You really showed the stuff you're made of when you conquered your fear and did that jump."

Under other circumstances, Ginger would have glowed at her father's praise. But her heart could feel nothing but sadness today. They were nearing the end of the production. Shooting the movie had brought Link back into her life . . . and then had taken him away forever.

They topped a rise. Below them, stark and white in the bright sunlight of Spain, was the village that had been built for this movie. When they drove into the streets, Ginger felt as if they had entered a time warp. It was 1938. In the streets and cafes were the soldiers of the Republican forces in their uniforms and berets, bravely awaiting the moment when General Franco's forces would sweep down on the village.

Derrick stopped at a building used as a wardrobe department. There Ginger changed into comfortable jeans, shirt and boots. Then she joined Derrick, the special effects specialist, Nick Davidson, and her stunt crew. They walked around the set as Davidson explained where and how the explosives had been set. As he talked, Ginger remembered an old movie lot joke about how to tell if a special effects man was any good: If he was over thirty-five and still had all his fingers, he probably knew what he was doing. She took comfort from the fact that Davidson still had all his fingers.

"That building is going sky high," he said, pointing to one of the structures. "We have squibbs planted all along this street to give the effect of a machine gun raking it."

"Ginger," Derrick said, "I want a shot of one of your people tumbling from the roof of a building as he gets shot."

Ginger nodded. "Joe?" she asked one of her people.

"Sure. Piece of cake. Where do you want me to get shot?"

"How about that roof over there?" Derrick asked.

"That's good," Davidson agreed.

"We'll hide an air bag behind all those crates for you to land on," Ginger said. "I think you should be holding a rifle. When you get hit, throw up your arms, letting the rifle fall, then come tumbling off the roof."

"No sweat," said the stunt man. "I've done lots of war scenes, Ginger. I get killed real good."

"Don't ham it up too much. I want this to look realistic."

They arrived at the end of the street.

"Now here," Derrick said, "is where the main action takes place. In the story, the hero and heroine have been in that cafe having their last drink together. The fascists come swarming down from the hills to the north. At the same time, the village is strafed by Nazi planes. The hero and heroine run out of the cafe. At that point, the stunt girl has taken her place."

"I'm going to do that bit myself," Ginger said.

"Excellent!" Derrick exclaimed. "You'll be standing in for Paige, then. And one of your stunt men will be Link's stand-in. He'll take your hand, and the two of you will run for the bridge there at the end of the street."

"We have the bridge set to blow," the special effects man said.

"Yes," Derrick continued. "The bit of it is that the two of you start across the bridge. When you reach a spot we have marked, you go over the side into the river below. At that exact moment, they blow the bridge. The way we'll handle it with camera angles, it will look as if the explosion threw you off the bridge. The screen will show a village under bombardment from artillary as well as being strafed by low-flying aircraft. The planes will also include dive bombers. It will look as if a diving plane made a hit dead center on the bridge with one of its bombs."

"What do we do then?"

"Well, you're in the river, so be sure you use a stunt man with you who is a good swimmer. The river has a pretty strong current. It will carry you downstream a ways; then you get out on the east bank. You run up that bank to the barn there." Derrick pointed at a wooden structure on the other side of the bank and some distance downstream. "The significance of that, you see, is that in our story, the heroine and hero spent the night before together in each other's arms in the hayloft of that very barn. The sequel is going to end when a plane dives at the barn. Then we blow the barn apart. We don't need it anymore, since we've already shot the inside scene with Link and Paige in the hayloft."

Ginger grimaced as she imagined the steamy love scene that must have taken place between Link and Paige in the hayloft. Then she said, "Kindly wait until we get out the back way before you blow the barn up!"

"Oh, don't worry," the special effects expert assured her. "But get out as soon as you can. We want to synchronize the explosion of the barn with the height of the battle."

"Okay, I've got it squared away in my mind," Ginger said. "Now I want to spend the rest of today setting up my stunt people for the battle effects. I want a diagram of where you have all the explosives set, Nick."

"Sure."

"I'd like to do a bit with a shell landing in a group of soldiers, throwing them sky high."

"No problem. We can work that out with your people. Show me where you want to do the gag."

Ginger worked with the stunt and special effects people until the sun set that day. Then Derrick drove her to the hotel in the nearby town. She shared a light supper in a cafe with her father, then she went up to her room, washed the dust and grime of the set off in a quick shower and fell into bed, exhausted. But sleep would not come. She had lacked the courage to ask where Link and Paige were staying. She knew they were finished with their scenes, so they had probably left the area. No doubt they were spending tonight in some romantic Spanish city far from here.

Dawn came in blood red streaks across a cloudless sky. It was barely light when Derrick knocked at her door. "Rise and shine," he called. "Big day ahead of us!"

They gulped a hasty breakfast, then they were on the road, Derrick driving impatiently.

On the set, Derrick spent some time that morning with his camera crews, making certain all the angles he wanted were going to be covered. Ginger went over the stunts with her group for a final time.

The men were in their uniforms. Ginger spent the next hour in the makeup tent. A black wig and the right makeup transformed her into a likeness of her sister. It was a wig she had specially designed for stunt work, with a clear plastic band under her chin to keep it on her head when she dove into the water. Filmed at a distance, in the dust and confusion of the simulated battle, the fact that she was a stand-in for Paige would never be noticed by a movie audience.

She felt a mounting tension, a quickening of her pulse as she left the tent and started down the street. The assistant director was calling for the stunt people and extras to take their places. The streets were filled with men in uniform running in all directions. She glanced up at the hills north of town and saw a whole army waiting to attack the village. From the sky above came the drone of airplanes.

There was an electric charge in the air, as if a real battle were about to begin. Ginger felt her own measure of suspense, knowing how much money her father had sunk into this scene. She was acutely aware of the importance of having it go right. When today's filming ended, the set would be in shambles. There would be no second chance. It would take weeks to rebuild the set, and there was no more money in the budget for that.

Ginger hurried to the cafe. Inside, she looked around impatiently for the stunt man who would be doubling for Link. He was supposed to be in the cafe with her when the action began. She was alone in the room.

She started for the front door when she heard a sound behind her. She spun around angrily, on the point of chewing out the stunt man for being late.

The words froze on her lips.

Link Rockwood came in through the back entrance, his handsome face displaying one of his casual grins. "Hi, Ginger, honey."

Her senses reeled. She opened her mouth but couldn't produce a sound. Finally she spluttered, "What are you doing here?"

"I think we have a movie to shoot, don't we?"

Then she realized he was wearing makeup and was dressed in the uniform and beret of a soldier of the Republican forces.

"Link—"

But her next words were drowned in a violent eruption of sound outside. Rifle fire mingled with the shouts and cries of men. An explosion shook the building. There were the staccato reports of a machine gun.

"Come on!" Link shouted in her ear. "The war's begun!"

He grabbed her arm, hustled her through the doorway. Outside, in the street, pandemonium reigned. Smoke and dust filled the air. Men were running in all directions. Splinters flew from buildings and window panes crashed. A few yards away, a soldier screamed and sprawled in the dirt. There was a howl of a mortar shell and a huge eruption of fire and dirt, sending a company of men flying through the air. From above came the whining roar of a diving plane and the rattle of machine gun fire. On a building top, a soldier dropped his rifle and toppled over the edge, falling head over heels.

Instinctively, Ginger remembered to crouch so the difference between her height and Paige's would not be noticed by the audience. The makeup people had smeared her face with streaks of dirt and blood. Link's face, too, was made up that way.

Ginger looked around frantically, then back at Link. "Link Rockwood," Ginger swore through her teeth. "What possessed you to do a crazy thing like this? Where is the stunt man who is supposed to be doing this scene with me?"

"Oh, I gave him something else to do."

Crouched in the street amidst the dust, smoke and sound of battle, Ginger knew there was no way their words would be picked up by the sound equipment. She said, "Derrick is going to kill you for this."

"No he won't. I'm all through with my scenes. They don't need me for the movie anymore. Derrick doesn't care if I break my neck now."

"Then I'll kill you!" she yelled. "I need a real stunt man, not some actor clown playing a game. You're going to ruin this whole scene!"

"No I'm not. All I have to do is run to the bridge with you and dive into the water. Anybody can do that."

"Well, I just hope you know how to swim!" she cried. "Come on!"

She knew there was nothing to be gained by

further recrimination. And there was no stopping the action. Like it or not, she had to play out the scene with Link.

She grabbed his hand. "Watch out for the squibbs," she shouted. "There's a whole row of them planted between here and the bridge. We're supposed to be running zig-zag to dodge bullets."

They started running to the bridge. Suddenly dirt was exploding and flying around their feet. Ginger ran in a half crouch, dodging right and left.

They reached the bridge. "Up ahead!" she yelled, almost out of breath. "When we reach that red cross painted in the middle of the bridge, we go over the side!"

From above, she heard the engine of a diving airplane. She paused for a moment, looked up. The sight of the dive bomber coming straight at them, guns blazing, was terrifying, even though she knew it was firing blanks. She thought about the people back when this war actually took place, when real bullets were whistling through the air, when the scream of wounded men was real and the blood splattering the streets and sidewalks wasn't fake. A cold shudder coursed through her.

Still holding Link's hand, she ran again. They were at the marker on the bridge. "Now!" she yelled, and went over the side. In the split second before she struck the cold water, she heard a thunderous explosion above her. It was the bridge being blown up. Then she plunged into the river, the force of her drop sending her almost to the bottom. She came up spluttering and gasping. All around her, she heard broken pieces of the wooden bridge splashing into the water. Instinctively she checked her wig. The plastic strap had held: the wig was still in place.

The current began sweeping her downstream. She struggled to keep her head above water. Suddenly she felt a strong arm around her. In a blur, she caught sight of Link's face close to hers. She realized the streak of blood on his forehead was real.

"Hang on," he shouted. "We're almost to the bank."

Her foot scraped gravel. Then they sprawled on the bank, both of them out of breath.

"C'mon!" she gasped out. "Have to make it to the barn!"

She struggled to her feet and stumbled up the hill, panting. Her throat ached. Her lungs felt as if they were on fire.

In the barn, she collapsed to her knees. Link, close behind, rested for a moment, his weight supported by a wall. Then he scooped her up and carried her into the loft, where they both sprawled dripping wet in the hay.

"Boy," he said, his big chest rising and falling, "you stunt people play rough."

Ginger closed her eyes, too weak for the moment to move. Not until she got her breath back and her thudding heart regained a semblance of a normal beat did she open her eyes. "Well, you got what was coming to you! What do you know about stunt work, Link Rockwood? You could have gotten killed! Or gotten me killed! Not that you care!"

She got a better look at him. He looked devilishly handsome and sexy in his wet uniform, his curly hair stuck to his forehead in damp ringlets. Her voice softened somewhat. "You really did get hurt. There's blood on your forehead."

"It's nothing," he said, wiping a sleeve across his

brow. "A piece of the bridge clunked me on the head as I surfaced."

"Serves you right," she muttered. "Why did you do it, Link? Will you tell me that? You swore to me you weren't going to pull one of these grandstand stunts of yours again."

"Oh, but that was back when we were first starting the picture, when I would have thrown a monkey wrench in the production if I'd gotten myself hurt. I told you—Derrick has shot all my important scenes. He couldn't care less if I broke my neck now."

"You still haven't told me why you did this crazy thing!"

She was on her back in the hay. Link was resting on an elbow, looking down at her. A gentle smile crossed his lips. He touched her forehead and ran his fingers down her cheeks, sending a shiver through her entire body. "Well," he drawled, "I just thought I'd like to play one scene in this film with my wife."

Bitter tears rushed to Ginger's eyes. "You don't know when to stop hurting me, do you? Paige is your wife, or will be now that *Thunder at Dawn* is completed."

He raised an eyebrow. "Is that so? Who told you?"

"Who told me?" she exploded. "Just every fan magazine and talk show in the country, that's all!"

"As long as you've been in the film industry! You mean you actually believe those scandal rags?"

"Well . . . s-sure," she stammered. "They had pictures of you and Paige together all over Europe."

"That was Derrick's bright idea. Link shrugged. "He's after all the publicity he can get. I went along with him because I wanted to do all I could to help him make it big with this film. It started out with just Paige and me being seen together. Then some scandal rag got the idea we were having a romance. Derrick's kept me so snowed under with his heavy filming schedule, I really didn't know what was going on in the outside world. I didn't know how they were building this thing up between Paige and me until we got a break in the schedule a week or two ago and I read some of the magazines and newspapers. It was Derrick who hinted to the press that Paige and I were going to get married as soon as we finished work on the film. The media bought it and Derrick was delighted."

Ginger stared at Link, desperately searching his eyes for the truth as a tiny glow of hope and joy began to come alive inside her like the flickering of a small flame. "If you're telling me the truth," she began, "I'm going to commit patricide. Isn't that what you call it when you kill your own father?"

Link chuckled. "Don't be too hard on him, Ginger. I was sore at first, too. Then I just laughed it off. It's so typical of Derrick. He'll do anything to accomplish what he wants. And what the heck? If all's fair in love and war, maybe it is in the entertainment business too, especially when you're fighting for your life the way Derrick has been with this film. But he's got it made now. He's going to have a big hit with this picture. It will establish him as one of the top directors in the industry. From now on he'll be able to write his own ticket. He's starting a whole new career. Be glad for him, Ginger. They don't come along like him very often. I wish I had the talent that he's got in just one little finger."

Ginger felt her heart begin to pound as hard as

when she'd run up the hill from the river. "But . . . if what you're saying is true, and if you care anything about me at all, why didn't you tell me before this?"

"Well, for one thing, as I said, Derrick has kept us on such a heavy shooting schedule that I really didn't know how far the media had gone with this gossip until a week or two ago. I'm not much for writing important feelings in a letter. I knew you'd be here soon, so I decided to do it this way."

Tears trickled down Ginger's cheeks. "Link, please don't tell me these things if they're not true."

Gently he kissed away the tears. "I'm not lying to you, baby. When I left you the last time, I told you playing the role in this film had me pretty confused. I had to identify with the hero completely, or I couldn't play the part right. It's true playing those love scenes with Paige got some old feeling stirred up. Maybe it's a good thing that happened. It gave me the chance to take those old feelings and look at them real hard, and when I did, I knew that I'd never really loved Paige. I was just a country boy when I first saw her. She represented all the glamor and excitement a man could dream about. But now I know that was nothing but infatuation. In my way, I was as naive as you were, Ginger, honey. But you were smarter than I. You knew all along we belonged together, you and I. And it took losing you to make me see the truth. That morning in Mexico after we got married, I woke up and saw you so young and pretty and desirable curled up beside me. Lord, how I wanted you then. But my conscience wouldn't let me because I thought I'd be taking advantage of a sweet, young kid. I didn't know it then, but I wasn't looking at a kid. I was looking at a woman, at my wife. Now I know, and I want to make up for lost time . . . if you'll let me, Ginger."

She gazed at him through hot tears, wanting to believe him, yet not daring to.

"Do you still have your wedding ring—the split washer?" he asked.

"No. I threw it away."

He smiled. "That's okay. Guess what. I found a jewelry maker in a little town near here. He's a real artist. Look." From under his shirt, Link drew a small leather pouch tied around his neck with a string. He opened the pouch and took out a small, shining object and held it up for her to see. It was a wedding ring in the shape of a split washer but made of solid gold.

Ginger felt stunned as Link took her left hand and slipped the uniquely designed ring on her finger. "How about that," he said softly. "A perfect fit. Just like it belongs there. And when we get back to the States we can have a real American wedding if you want."

Slowly, as if afraid she'd awaken from a dream, her arms slipped around his neck. Their wet bodies were molded together.

Outside the battle was raging furiously. She fantasized that they were the lovers in *Thunder at Dawn* and that in this moment they were experiencing the intensity of the love of an entire lifetime. His lips came down on hers and his arms were tight around hers. Flames raged through her body in wild response to his kiss.

Then suddenly realization struck her. She pushed him away. "Link," she screamed, "we've got to get out of here! They're going to blow up this building!"

They scrambled out of the loft and ran out of the barn through a back door. Even after they were a safe distance away from the building, they continued running. Ginger held Link's hand tightly as they ran. She knew that as long as they lived, she was never going to let go of him again.

January Special Editions
Available Now

Thunder At Dawn by Patti Beckman

As a stuntwoman, Ginger Lombard lived with
danger, but nothing had prepared her for the
greatest danger of all: falling in love again
with her ex-husband Link Rockwood.

Reach Out To Cherish by Dixie Browning

Jed Dancy wanted to settle down, but he
had no idea A. R. Kenner was the right
woman—because he assumed that A.R. was a
man. But the moment Aurelia Rose walked into
his life, he knew just how wrong he was!

Make-Believe Magic by April Thorne

If only Jill could pretend that the ill-starred
affair with Greg Shepard had never happened.
Now, only risking another heartbreak with
Greg could save her. It wasn't a challenge
she welcomed, but one she had to take.

**January Special Editions
Available Now**

From The Beginning by Kathryn Belmont

Somewhere in Cal's past there was a secret,
a secret that had left him both vulnerable and
completely armoured against love. But Santina
was determined to break through his armour
and reach him with her love.

For Love Or Money by Elaine Camp

Wylde Tremaine had been the love of
Bethany's youth. Now business brought them
together again, and the lush tropical
setting in which they met made it very
hard not to mix business with pleasure!

Rainy Day Dreams by Margaret Ripy

He was Jordan Trent, gentleman farmer.
She was Alexis Summers, novelist and New Yorker,
down in Mississippi on business. Such a meeting
of opposites was against all the rules—
but rules are made to be broken.

Silhouette Special Edition

Coming Next Month

Summer Course In Love
by Carole Halston

For Rebecca Blakely writing about the past
was no longer enough once thriller author
Ryan Prescott walked into her life. Together
they discovered that what they shared was
too powerful to be put into words.

Dance Of Dreams by Nora Roberts

Ruth Bannion had never met anyone like
Russian emigre choreographer Nickolai Davidov.
Nickolai's background had left him reserved,
even wary—but Ruth was determined to wipe
away his fear and replace it with her love.

The Coral Sea by Jane Converse

Bryan Stewart made his living diving beneath
the sea. The underwater world held no terrors
for him but Laurel Rand, who had fallen
deeply in love with him, was altogether
another story.

Silhouette Special Edition

Coming Next Month

A Twist Of Fate by Lisa Jackson

When Kane Webster bought the Seattle bank
where Erin O'Toole worked he bought trouble.
One embezzler had already been uncovered and
there was certain to be an accomplice—and
all the evidence seemed to point to Erin!

Beloved Gambler by Ruth Langan

Lane had left Ross Matthews in her
quest to become a success. Her dream come
true, she now faced Ross again, and this
time, she'd never find the strength
to leave.

Lia's Daughter by Diana Dixon

Lia's daughter, but her own woman—that
was Kaly Rossiter. She sought to hide her
connection to her famous mother, but Mick
Demarkis wanted the truth—and her
love forever.

Silhouette Special Edition

£1.10 each

91 ☐ LOVE'S GENTLE
CHAINS
Sondra Stanford

92 ☐ ALL'S FAIR
Lucy Hamilton

93 ☐ LOVE FEUD
Anne Lacey

94 ☐ CRY MERCY,
CRY LOVE
Monica Barrie

95 ☐ A MATTER
OF TRUST
Emily Doyle

96 ☐ AUTUMN
AWAKENING
Mary Lynn Baxter

97 ☐ WAY OF THE
WILLOW
Linda Shaw

98 ☐ TOUCH OF
GREATNESS
Ann Hurley

99 ☐ QUEST FOR
PARADISE
Diana Dixon

100 ☐ REFLECTIONS
Nora Roberts

101 ☐ GOLDEN IMPULSE
Fran Bergen

102 ☐ DREAMS LOST,
DREAMS FOUND
Pamela Wallace

103 ☐ WILD IS
THE HEART
Abra Taylor

104 ☐ MY LOVING
ENEMY
Pat Wallace

105 ☐ FAIR EXCHANGE
Tracy Sinclair

106 ☐ NEVER TOO
LATE
Nancy John

107 ☐ FLOWER OF
THE ORIENT
Erin Ross

108 ☐ NO OTHER
LOVE
Jeanne Stephens

109 ☐ THUNDER AT
DAWN
Patti Beckman

110 ☐ REACH OUT
TO CHERISH
Dixie Browning

111 ☐ MAKE-BELIEVE
MAGIC
April Thorne

112 ☐ FROM THE
BEGINNING
Kathryn Belmont

113 ☐ FOR LOVE
OR MONEY
Elaine Camp

114 ☐ RAINY DAY
DREAMS
Margaret Ripy

All these books are available at your local bookshop or newsagent, or can be ordered direct from the publisher. Just tick the titles you want and fill in the form below.

Prices and availability subject to change without notice.

SILHOUETTE BOOKS, P.O. Box 11, Falmouth, Cornwall.

Please send cheque or postal order, and allow the following for postage and packing:

U.K. – 45p for one book, plus 20p for the second book, and 14p for each additional book ordered up to a £1.63 maximum.

B.F.P.O. and EIRE – 45p for the first book, plus 20p for the second book, and 14p per copy for the next 7 books, 8p per book thereafter.

OTHER OVERSEAS CUSTOMERS – 75p for the first book, plus 21p per copy for each additional book.

Name ....

Address ....

....